EVERYTHING
BUT THE TRUTH

More in the Young, Loaded, and Fabulous series:

Pretty on the Outside

EVERYTHING
BUT THE TRUTH

Young, Loaded, and Fabulous

KATE KINGSLEY

Simon Pulse
New York   London   Toronto   Sydney

SIMON PULSE
An imprint of Simon & Schuster Children's Publishing Division
1230 Avenue of the Americas, New York, NY 10020
First Simon Pulse paperback edition September 2010
Copyright © 2009 by Brubaker & Ford, Ltd.
Originally published in Great Britain in 2009
by the HEADLINE PUBLISHING GROUP as *Secrets and Liars*.
Published by arrangement with the Headline Publishing Group.
All rights reserved, including the right of reproduction
in whole or in part in any form.
SIMON PULSE and colophon are registered trademarks
of Simon & Schuster, Inc.
For information about special discounts for bulk purchases,
please contact Simon & Schuster Special Sales at 1-866-506-1949
or business@simonandschuster.com.
The Simon & Schuster Speakers Bureau can bring authors
to your live event. For more information or to book an event contact
the Simon & Schuster Speakers Bureau at 1-866-248-3049 or visit
our website at www.simonspeakers.com.
Designed by Cara E. Petrus
The text of this book was set in New Baskerville.
Manufactured in the United States of America
2 4 6 8 10 9 7 5 3 1
Library of Congress Control Number 2010921794
ISBN 978-1-4169-9400-8
ISBN 978-1-4424-0950-7 (eBook)

CHAPTER ONE

The Rochester family's rain-streaked Bentley looked utterly out of place as it pulled up on a grimy East London street, and so did the angular face glaring out of its backseat window.

"This is *it*?" Alice Rochester sniffed. She was scrutinizing the cracked concrete facade of Formica, Dalston's hippest new music venue. "Could this place be any less glamorous? What the hell were they thinking?"

"Babe. Chill." Natalya Abbott, Alice's best boarding-school friend, twirled a strand of white-blond hair round her fingers. Slumming it on the frontier of civilization once in a while was fine by Tally: She'd grown up most of her life in Russia, and compared to Moscow, London was tame. "It's the boys' first-ever gig. What were you expecting—the Royal Opera House?"

"Well, I wasn't expecting a royal dump." Alice squinted harder into the street. The only streetlamp actually working kept sputtering on and off, but that didn't hide the knot of arty-looking East Londoners huddled next to a Dumpster. They were smoking cloves, of course. *So* alternative. Whatever. Alice started to size up one of the girls in the group, who was wearing metallic leggings with crumpled red ankle boots, and an oversize brooch pinned above her left boob. But just then, a bark of laughter ricocheted down the street and her eyes darted to its source. A long-haired boy, smirking at the Bentley, was nudging his mate and pointing at the car's capped chauffeur.

Flushing pink, Alice shrank back from the window.

"Er, Marshy." She leaned toward the front seat. "Be a darling and drop us off in that alley round the corner. Would you? Please?"

"Tell me another one," the driver snorted. "In this area? You'll get mugged just crossing the road. Have you gone mad?"

"*No.*" Alice recoiled defensively. "I just feel like stretching my legs a little. Exercise is important. God." She stroked her cream leather armrest. "Anyway, it feels a bit rude blocking the street like this. I wouldn't want to obstruct people's view of all those run-down warehouses."

Tally giggled.

"Very considerate of you," Marshy remarked, leaning back and folding his arms. "But you're getting out *here.* Not in some dodgy alleyway."

"Ugh. Fine." Snatching her Miu Miu handbag, Alice poked one kitten heel, then the other, onto the cobblestones and shivered slightly. Tally caught the movement.

"No need to be nervous, babe," she soothed. "I'm sure it'll all be fine with him tonight. After all, he invited you."

Alice recoiled. "I'm not nervous. Why would you think that? Don't I look calm?"

Rolling her eyes, Tally surveyed their surroundings. The antique diamond ring her grandfather had given her last summer in Moscow flashed with each blink of the defective streetlamp. "I've been dying to come out to Dalston for months," she said, changing the subject. When Alice got into one of her moods, there was nothing else to do. "I'm so unbelievably bored of all our usual clubs. Mayfair. The King's Road. Blah, blah, blah. Same crowd, same champagne, weekend after weekend."

"Tals!" Alice cut in. "For fuck's sake, watch out!"

"What? Shit!" Tally shrieked. "Help!" She'd slammed her purple Luella ruffle skirt in the Bentley's door and was being tugged backward. "Marshy, stop, please, you'll rip my new outfit! Stoooppp!"

Tottering alongside the car in her four-inch heels, she pounded at the window, her white-blond hair whipping her face. The brakes screeched.

Alice glanced up and down the street. Thank god the smokers had disappeared inside. This was typical Tally, causing some crisis at the last minute. At St. Cecilia's, the exclusive girls' boarding school where the two of them ruled the junior class, Tally was constantly in chaos. She showed up late for lessons, spilled caffe lattes all over her homework, and only made her bed if Alice forced her. Lately, she'd come up with a disaster of a whole new magnitude—falling hopelessly, embarrassingly in love with their hot new English teacher.

But that was a different story altogether. And Alice had more important things to think about right now. Such as her own love life.

Nervously, she scanned her reflection in the club's frosted-glass door, checking that her olive skin still sparkled with gold shimmer, that her deep-set, catlike eyes were still outlined in dramatic black, and that the shorts of her green silk jump-suit still just skimmed the curve of her butt cheeks. Perfect. There was room for improvement in the lips, though: the more kissable they looked, the better. She slicked on more scarlet Chanel lipstick and pouted seductively. But her eyes remained uncertain. Would he go for it? Would this be her lucky night?

"Nooo!" wailed Tally's anguished voice.

Alice jumped.

"It's ruined! Ali, don't just stand there, help!"

She waddled over like a bedraggled peacock, strips of lace trailing behind her.

"Complete disaster," she moaned. "Look."

"For fuck's sake!" Alice gawked at the sheer pink thong that was the only thing covering Tally's butt. In fact, "covering" was an overstatement. "You can't go inside like that. Your entire ass is exposed."

"Seriously?" Tally's expression glinted with mischief. "Marshy must be mortified," she whispered. "Which panties am I wearing, the Agent Provocateurs? The La Perlas?"

Alice raised her eyebrows. "Oh, hang on a sec, I'll just check the label, shall I?" She dragged Tally to one side. "Back against the wall."

"Girls." Marshy's muffled voice sounded from the car's trunk, where he was rifling through some sort of rag pile. "Tally, dear, have a look at this. I've found something to cover your, ahem . . ."—he frowned severely—". . . bottom."

Tally snorted with giggles and reached for the rumpled garment. "Ewww!" she squealed, dropping it as a shower of dirt poured out. "No, no, no. What the hell is that?"

"Only Hugo's rugby uniform!" Marshy retrieved the bundle from the gutter and held up a pair of shorts, streaked with grass stains and matted together with dried mud. "A bit of muck never hurt anyone," he declared bracingly. "It's better than looking like a stripper."

"Not," Tally muttered. Looking like a stripper most definitely had the edge over wearing Alice's fourteen-year-old brother's dirty shorts into a club. "I mean, thanks and everything, Marshy, I know you're only trying to help, but those aren't coming anywhere near me. I'd prefer to rip off all my clothes and go in naked."

"Bad idea, bad idea." Alice shook her head rapidly. She knew Tally too well to dismiss those words as an empty threat.

Something beeped inside Marshy's navy blue chauffeur jacket.

"That's your father, Alice. I've got to go collect him from the von Holstadts' cocktail party. Right, girls, er . . ." Marshy cast a glance at Tally, who'd folded her arms stubbornly across her chest, as if someone might try to thrust the rugby shorts on her at any second. "Have fun. Go straight inside, and call me when you're ready for a lift home. You'll never find a cab round here."

Alice watched, shoulders slumped, as the car door slammed and the Bentley rolled off through the rain.

"Now what are we gonna do?" She glared at the Dumpster. What a mess. Tristan's band went on in five minutes and she was stuck out here with a half-naked exhibitionist. This was not how she'd pictured the evening.

Tally wasn't listening. Instead, she was staring at the pavement under her purple patent leather stilettos—and something sharp and delicate was winking back—a large black-and-white brooch in the shape of a rose. The same one Alice had seen on the girl with the red boots.

"Brilliant!" Tally beamed. "How lucky is that? Pin it to my skirt, Al. It'll hide my thong."

"What . . . ?" Alice stared. "We can't just take something off the street—it belongs to that girl. We should give it back."

Tally twisted the brooch to and fro. "The black and white'll really stand out against my skirt," she gushed. "And I can wear it pinned to my winter coat as well. How chic!"

"Tally!" Alice snapped. "Get a grip. That thing's high-quality vintage—it was probably her grandmother's or something. Anyway, it's not *yours*."

"It is now." Tally's jaw was set. "It's just like I always say about men: finders keepers. Babe." She elbowed Alice in the ribs. "Lighten up."

Alice clenched her jaw. Lighten up. What the hell was that supposed to mean? She knew how to have fun—and she knew it better than anyone else in her clique. Just because she was careful not to get into trouble for it did *not* make her a goody-goody. She set her jaw.

But there was no time to be pissed off. Suddenly, inside Formica, the music fell away and the crowd cheered. Shadows milled behind the glass doors.

Shit. They must be gearing up for Tristan's set now. He was on next. She had to get in there.

"Fine." Alice held out her palm. "Give it."

"Wicked!" Tally beamed. "I knew you'd come round."

"Whatever." Taking a deep breath, Alice stuck the brooch into the skirt's splintered lace. Then she swung open the door.

CHAPTER TWO

*D*arling!" squealed Sonia Khan as Alice's tall, thoroughbred figure appeared in the view-finder of her £10,000 digital camcorder. Sonia had been filming the crowd, waiting for her friends to arrive, and now her tiny ski-jump nose—recently redesigned and sculpted by the Khans' celebrated plastic surgeon—crinkled in delight. She'd seen Alice just a few hours earlier at school, but that didn't count. When their crowd was out partying, the social clock got automatically reset.

"Where *were* you?" Sonia demanded petulantly. "I've been fighting for the past half hour to save our spots." She gestured at the ocean of club-goers that was tossing and heaving her like a dinghy on the waves.

Alice shrugged and inspected their surroundings. Formica's interior more than made up for its lame facade. A cavernous ex-coffee warehouse, the place had been recently refurbished to look like a party house for hippies with trust funds. The main room had lofty ceilings, giant skylights, and concrete floors spread with woven rugs. Off to the sides, comfy lounging areas were furnished with restored vintage couches and coffee tables. Candles flickered on every surface. Tangled fairy lights and a spidery antique chandelier illuminated a low stage at the back. And, true to the venue's name, a long Formica bar dominated the section of the room nearest the entrance. The place was clearly beneath police radar too—a few people were daring to smoke indoors, and Tally could definitely smell weed.

In answer to Sonia's question, Tally twirled and shook her butt. "Wardrobe malfunction."

"Oh my god," Sonia tittered, covering her small, heart-shaped mouth with her hand. "I would not go out like that if I were you."

"Well you're *not* me. Thank god."

"Whatever. Hold my drink, I've got to interview Alice for my music-video-documentary-special." Sonia thrust out her cocktail, which was pale green and stuffed to the brim with some kind of vegetable.

"Umm, what the hell is that?" Alice pointed. "A ritual Indian concoction? Did you bring it especially from home? Mom's favorite recipe?"

"No, it's a cucumber gimlet." Sonia was training her lens on Alice's face, ignoring her friend's barb, as always. "House speciality. Have that one, Ali. I'll buy another. I don't mind."

"Well I *do*. Keep that thing away from me."

Sonia peered harder through the lens, trying to hide her

9

hurt expression. Doing favors for Alice Rochester was one of her most cherished hobbies. In fact, it was her only hobby—besides shooting artistic documentaries, and anyway, that was more of a *career*. Back when Sonia and Alice had both joined St. Cecilia's at age eleven (three years before Tally had been shipped over from Russia), Sonia used to follow her idol round, lugging her satchel to lessons and buying things for her from the cafeteria and agreeing with everything she said. The reason Sonia had done those things wasn't that Alice was the cleverest, or the funniest, or even the most stunning girl at school. It was that Alice was the coolest. And years later, now that they were sixteen, she still was. There was something about her that made everyone crave her approval. Whenever she entered a room, people shut up and listened.

"Right." Sonia put on her professional director's voice. "*Action!* Hello, I'm here with Alice Rochester. Tell me, Alice, how do you feel about the debut performance of the Paper Bandits? After all, you've known the boys longer than any of us."

"Well, Sonia." Alice batted her eyelids at the camera. "I'm very proud of my boys and I'd like to wish the entire band the absolute best of luck. All my love, Paper Bandits!" She blew a kiss.

"Ooh, Ali, do that again so I can zoom in! It'll be my closing shot."

Tally rolled her eyes. "I hate to butt in, Sone, but aren't documentaries meant to be, like, un-posed?" She took a sip of Sonia's gimlet and made a face.

"For your information, there's a difference between *posed*

and *refined.*" Sonia glared. "Not that you'd know." She swung her camera round to face the stage. "Oh. My. God."

Through her lens, Seb Ogilvy had appeared. He was tuning his bass guitar, his skinny jeans and skinny white cord jacket clinging to his lanky frame. "Fuck. Fuck." Sonia was practically drooling. "He is So. Incredibly. Hot."

"I see you've gotten over your crush, then." Alice snorted.

"Shut up! He might hear. Have you ever seen anyone more gorgeous?"

"Um, yeah—like, every other guy in this room. Come on, it's *Seb*. How can you fancy him?"

"Al, keep it down," Tally hissed. "He's less than a meter away from us." She shook her head. "I cannot *believe* the boys are in a band. I mean, what if they turn out to be famous?"

"We'll be their groupies."

"I'll be Seb's groupie anyway," Sonia sighed.

"If you can run fast enough." Tally smirked.

Sonia ignored her. "Hey, Ali, where's Mimah, by the way? She's about to miss everything."

It was true. Jemimah Calthorpe de Vyle-Hanswicke, their other best friend and the fourth member of their crew, hadn't shown up all evening.

Alice shrugged. "She's not coming. Said she had to go to dinner or something."

"Dinner? With who? Everybody's *here*."

"I know. She was being totally cagey."

The lights dimmed.

Seb leapt into place. Tom Randall-Stubbs materialized and perched at the drum kit.

Tally pinched Alice's arm. "Doesn't Rando look professional? *Rando!*" she squealed. Tom Randall-Stubbs jerked up his head, caught sight of Tally, turned bright pink, and dropped his drumsticks.

But Alice didn't notice. She was staring straight ahead, holding her breath.

Where was the one person she'd come to see?

A split second later, her heart went wild. There he was: Tristan Murray-Middleton. His arms were strong and suntanned from captaining the Hasted House junior-class rugby team. His face looked nervous yet determined beneath his unruly hair. Tristan looked smoldering at the worst of times, but now that he was onstage Alice didn't have a hope in hell. She traced one of her white peep-toes over the scuffed floor, suddenly back in the Easter holidays last year, when T had first decided to start a band. He'd hauled his guitar to her house one night and the two of them had stayed up till the sunrise, drinking red wine and making up ridiculous song lyrics and falling over each other with laughter, the way they used to do when Tristan had been nothing more than her oldest, closest friend in the world.

Alice sighed. Things were different now. They'd been different for over a month, ever since the beginning of term— ever since the night that Tristan had kissed her in secret in the fields between their two schools. The two of them had smoked a joint together and rolled in the grass for ages, breathing in the smell of pot and earth and each other. Alice had fallen for him, harder than she ever had for anyone. But things had quickly gone wrong—and now she was dying to get him back.

Tristan cradled his guitar in his hands.

"Hello, everybody." He spoke tentatively into the microphone. "Thanks for coming. We're the Paper Bandits."

"Woohoo!" someone cheered. Tristan chuckled.

"I'd like to sing a song." He flushed nervously. "Actually, I mean, I'd like to sing a few."

The audience laughed.

"Cute!" Tally mouthed to Alice.

Sonia was staring at Seb, her mouth hanging open.

"It's called"—Tristan cleared his throat—"'If This Is Love.'"

Alice stiffened almost imperceptibly between her friends. That title! *She* was the only girl T had ever been in love with— she knew it. He must have written this song for her.

Tristan struck a chord on his guitar and Alice waited, hardly breathing.

"Your kisses thawed
My hibernation.
Your love's beyond
Imagination."

As the lyrics filled the room, a smile broke over Alice's face. Yes. It was true—*beyond imagination.* No one could love

Tristan like she did. She'd known him her whole life. They shared everything—all their secrets. All their ambitions. All their insecurities. Everything.

> *"But you take so much*
> *I don't want to give.*
> *Why can't you just*
> *Live and let live?"*

Wait a second. . . . That wasn't right. Alice's eyes narrowed as the drums kicked in for the chorus. Tristan rocked his head to the beat.

> *"If this is love*
> *I'll do without it.*
> *If this is love*
> *I think I'll pass.*
> *I don't want love*
> *No doubt about it.*
> *Thought love was slow*
> *But you're moving too fast.*

> *No, I don't want love.*
> *I'll do without it.*
> *Your love's iron.*
> *Mine breaks like glass."*

The room spun. Alice reached out to steady herself, but there was nothing to hold. *"You take so much I don't want to give?" "If this is love, I think I'll pass?"* What the hell were those lyrics supposed to mean? Was this how T felt about her?

"Need some air," Alice muttered to Sonia, swinging on her heel.

There was only one thing to do: Get drunk and forget about everything. But before she could even start, things went downhill. Toward the back of the crowd, Alice's gaze was arrested by a familiar figure. A few meters away, a girl was gyrating to the music, hips undulating, blond hair shining under the spotlights. Alice stared.

What the fuck did Dylan Taylor think she was doing here? That American bitch had a talent for cropping up in inconvenient places. Dylan had burst into Tristan's life over the summer holidays, seducing him while he'd been visiting his uncle in New York. Then she'd followed him back to London, barged into Alice's year at St. Cecilia's, and insisted on flaunting her balloon-size boobs to anyone who'd look. Thank goodness Tristan had dumped her. Fine, he'd subsequently dumped Alice, too, but that wasn't the point. The point was, what would it take to make Dylan go away for good?

A swarm of girls was blocking the last few meters to the bar, and Alice began to shove her way through.

"This band is bloody *hot,*" a leggy redhead was squawking in a ridiculous faux-cockney accent.

15

"Oy, hands off," ordered her mate—a snaggletoothed blonde. "The lead singer's mine. Ten quid says I can seduce him before midnight. I swear he just winked at me from the stage."

"You lucky bitch, Lulu. Did he really?"

"Yeah. He wanted me. Badly. Ouch!" Lulu yelped, rubbing her rib cage as Alice's elbow landed a particularly good blow.

Just then a hand seized Alice's shoulder.

"Excuse me!" demanded a posh male voice. "You there! Where do you think you're going? Haven't you ever heard of a queue?"

"Haven't *you* ever heard of a loser?" Alice wheeled round. Oh shit. The boy she'd just insulted was film-star hot. His deep green eyes flashed from under his cropped brown hair. Sexy stubble softened his manly jaw.

"I didn't mean—," she mumbled.

"Shhh," the boy pressed a finger to his lips. "What's your poison? My treat."

Alice gaped at him. Then she melted into a smile. This might turn out to be her lucky night after all.

CHAPTER THREE

*A*pplause drowned out the final notes of the Paper Bandits' first set and Tristan Murray-Middleton slapped his hand over his guitar strings, glowing in triumph. He'd been freaking out for days about this gig—dreading his debut performance in front of a crowd, shrinking from the moment when his heartfelt music would be judged by the masses—but now that he'd recovered his nerves there was no doubt about it: Being a musician was his calling. Singing for his fans was the best drug in the world.

T scanned the audience as he jumped offstage for the ten-minute break. Where had she gone? He was sure he'd seen Alice Rochester near the front, four or five songs ago. In fact, there were her best friends Tally Abbott and Sonia Khan, who was sipping a creepy-looking green drink. Maybe Alice was at the bar. A chorus of laughter burst from that direction, and Tristan turned to see Seb and Rando being fed tequila shots by a cluster of admiring fans. Admiring *girl* fans. T grinned, all thoughts of Alice fleeing his head. He should have started a band years ago, he thought, leaping over a tangle of wires and skidding over the concrete floor to join the fun. Then someone tugged at his sleeve.

"Hey!"

"Hey. D-Dylan?" Tristan stammered, doing a double take. "Uhhh, hey. How's things?" He winced inwardly. *What the hell are you doing here?* would have been a more apt question. The last time T had seen his ex-girlfriend, she'd been topless and humiliated onstage at a disastrous St. Cecilia's fashion show. The time before that, she'd furiously flung a box of condoms at him in the middle of a party. And the time before that, he'd snogged her in secret in the pub even though he'd been going out with Alice. So yeah, to put it mildly, the two of them had hardly been on the simplest of terms since Dylan moved to London last month.

"I'm great, thanks. Congrats." Dylan was tilting her head to one side, an inscrutable glimmer in her eyes. The sign for the unisex bathrooms glowed luridly above her head. "You guys aren't bad. I had no idea you could write love songs. The lyrics were kind of, I don't know, touching."

"Cheers." Tristan smiled back despite his doubts. His manners were too polished for him to do anything else, and plus, flattery was flattery—even from a suspicious source. "I've been working on them for months."

"I could tell."

Tristan traced Dylan's movement as she ran her hand through her honey-blond hair. It was shorter than it had been in August—less beach-tousled than when he'd first glimpsed her at his uncle's yacht club in the Hamptons. She'd caught his eye that night all the way across the moonlit deck, her thin dress rippling in the wind, her irises sea-blue in the candlelight, her shoulders bare and golden from days of sailing.

"Anyway . . ." Tristan exhaled through his nose to snuff the image from his mind. "I'm off for a drink."

"Oh. Yeah. Good idea."

Tristan's eyes followed Dylan's down to her own empty glass. Was that her idea of a subtle hint? Shoving his hands in his pockets, he peeked again at the babe-packed bar. "Ummm. Do you want me to buy you a drink?"

"Wow." Dylan beamed. "Aren't you sweet? I'd really love that, but—" she checked the time on her phone and sighed dramatically. "Oh dear, no. I really have to find Jasper."

"Jasper?" Tristan cleared his throat. He hadn't meant to sound so surprised. "What for?"

"He's the one who invited me tonight. Me and Jas, we're here together." Dylan smiled innocently. "Didn't you know? Anyway, better go. Bye!" Rippling her fingers, she plunged into the crowd.

Tristan stared at Dylan's receding figure, his eyebrows knotted together. Of course he didn't bloody know. Jasper hadn't bloody told him. And neither had Rando, who was probably in on the secret, considering he was Jasper's cousin.

T shook his head. Typical of his old friend to play dirty. Handsome, charming, cocky Jasper von Holstadt had been getting his way with women pretty much since the moment he was born, and he clearly expected to continue getting it—even if it meant trampling the feelings of everyone he knew. Tristan slouched against the concrete wall. He probably had no right to care about Dylan—he'd dumped her a month ago. But it was more complicated than that. For starters, there was that secret kiss . . .

"Oy, T!"

Behind Tristan, Seb Ogilvy was balancing four Stellas in his long, spidery hands. "Is there a reason you're lurking back here instead of getting sloshed?"

Tristan extracted one of the pints and half-downed it without answering.

"Oh, sure mate, take it. Um, by the way, are you okay?"

"Yeah, fine." Tristan was silent for a second. Then, "What the hell's up with Jasper making moves on Dylan tonight?" he exploded.

"Oh, shit." Seb pursed his lips. "Yeah. I didn't think he'd go through with that."

"Go through with *what?*"

"His big plan. Come on, you must have heard Jas go on about how hot Dylan is."

Tristan shrugged.

"And . . . well . . ." Seb's face was uncertain. "He's decided now's the perfect time to get her in the sack."

"Excuse me?"

"Yeah, you know, since she's got no friends at St. C's. He's convinced she'll see him as her savior for paying any attention to her at all. Tonight's step one of the campaign."

"Sneaky bastard!" Tristan strained in the direction Dylan had disappeared. "I should have known. Dylan's not the kind of girl you can treat like that. Quick, someone needs to warn her!"

"'Someone needs to warn her'?" Seb laughed. "What is this, an episode of *24*? And who's meant to warn her—you? Dylan would only accuse you of being jealous." He squinted at his friend. "And she wouldn't be right—would she?"

"Don't be an idiot," T said, gulping his drink and glancing past Seb. He grinned. "Uh-oh, better watch out. Here comes your biggest fan."

"No! Bollocks!" Turning white, Seb tried to make a dash for it but sent all three beers sloshing toward his jacket instead.

"Take one of these," he grunted.

"Already got one," T said, holding up his pint mockingly. "Chill, dude. Sonia's hot."

Seb pursed his lips. He knew Sonia was hot. That wasn't the issue. The issue was . . . Well, it wasn't about Sonia. It was about him. And it was too big to even think about right now. "Come on, T, help me out," he pleaded. "Pretend we're having a private chat."

"Awww, too late!"

"Sebby!" Sonia cried. Her glossy black hair fanned out as

she launched herself toward Seb, and her dark cheek brushed his pale one. She inhaled deeply. He smelled of cigarettes, and of a sort of boozy aftershave. Or maybe it was just booze. Whatever. Sonia had better things to think about than Seb's drinking habits. She was sure he'd been on the verge of kissing her at a party a few weeks ago, and she was determined to make it happen for real soon.

"You guys were amazing!" she gushed. "Sebby, I never knew you were so *musical*. The way you handled those guitar strings—such skillful fingers." She gave him what she hoped was a smoldering stare.

"Er, thanks, Sone." Seb swallowed, his thin face reddening to the roots of his haystack hair.

"You don't have to thank me. I mean it, Sebby." Sonia hoisted her camcorder onto her shoulder. "Now, come on, let's do our interview, before you have to go back on. I'm dying to know what inspires your songs."

"Well, actually . . ." Seb shifted uncomfortably. He wasn't one to revel in the limelight. "T writes the music. And the lyrics. He's the one you should be talking to."

"But I want to talk to *you*."

"Oy, quiet. Look," Tristan cut in, tapping Sonia's arm and pointing to a corner by the bar. "Who's that jerk bothering Alice?"

Seb retreated in relief, gazing at his three pints and wishing he had a free hand to down at least one.

Sonia followed Tristan's stare toward the front of the club.

Alice was perched on a stool, leaning very close to a tall, suave stranger who appeared to be ordering drinks.

"No idea," she announced. "And I wouldn't say he's bothering her either." Her black eyes were pinned closely on T. "Why do you care?"

"I don't." Tristan shrugged. But it was a lie.

CHAPTER FOUR

*D*eplorable wine list they've got here," drawled Alice's companion, shaking his head as he handed her a bucket-size glass of pinot grigio. "Don't know what the owners think they're playing at. I mean, honestly, this place is far enough in the middle of nowhere without having substandard drinks. Right?"

"Huh? I mean, um, thanks," Alice stuttered, taking her wine. The deep red polish on her fingernails gleamed against the glass. Even though it had been at least two minutes since this mysterious boy had first spoken to her, she still couldn't get over his hotness. Just now, she'd noticed how his lips turned up gently at the corners when he spoke, like he was enjoying some kind of fascinating hot person's joke. When he glanced back to the bartender for his change, Alice subtly dropped her gaze to the triangle of perfectly tanned chest at the top of his ice-blue shirt.

"So." Her companion smiled, raising his glass. "Cheers!" He

took a sip of his whiskey on the rocks, then the next second banged it down. "My *god*, how rude of me—I'm Boy, by the way. Boy Stanley-Soames."

"Oh—Alice Rochester." Alice shook his hand, her whole body tingling under the light of Boy's green eyes. It was almost enough to make her forget that T was about to come back onstage, singing his heart out about their failed love. Almost.

Anyway, Boy had bought her a drink, which meant one point to her, zero to Tally and Sonia in their favorite going-out game. Alice would have to remember to gloat to them later. Maybe she could even take a sneaky picture of Boy on her iPhone and swing an extra point for the fact that he was so gorgeous. Maybe she could even make sure Tristan saw the picture by mistake . . .

"Hang on!" Boy suddenly said, sounding eager. "Alice Rochester? Now, there's a last name I recognize. Any relation to Richard?"

"Well, yes actually: Richard Rochester's my father."

Predictably, Boy seemed impressed. "Your father?" He leaned forward. "That's an insane coincidence. I happen to be working at a trading firm at the moment, and of course Rochester & Rochester is *the* most prestigious. It's practically the only place that's surviving in this economic swamp. Your dad's a clever man. I aim to land a job somewhere like that in a few years."

Working at a trading firm? Alice shifted on her stool, wondering exactly how old this Boy Stanley-Soames character was.

"Oh, right. So when did you finish uni, then?" she asked.

Boy gave a self-deprecating chuckle. "Haven't even started. I'm on my gap year, doing work experience. Spent the summer kicking round Asia and then came to London to train up."

"For what?"

"My degree. I start studying economics at Bristol next September and I'm planning to get higher marks than all those other jerks in the course."

"Um, okay, good luck with that." Alice giggled, relaxing a little. Gap year—two years above her—that was fine. Her older brother, Dominic, had introduced her to plenty of people who were already at college and she always fitted in perfectly with them. Dom was at Edinburgh studying land economy, and of course hung out with a superglamorous crowd. Alice ran a hand through her hair. Come to think of it, maybe it was about time she started setting her sights on older men. Guys her age were just so immature—Daddy was always saying that. Mostly in reference to Tristan, if she was honest. Alice cringed at the thought of how her father disapproved of T, who he'd known practically from birth. Daddy was constantly lecturing T about doing irresponsible things, like neglecting to prepare for his future career as an Oxford-educated politician, or growing his hair too long. Or wasting his time starting a band.

Alice took a gulp of wine. Not that she should even be thinking about T right now. Seriously, she was being bought drinks by a rich, suave, sophisticated model look-alike—how hard could it be to chill the hell out and enjoy it? Smiling, she leaned a tanned, slender arm on the bar.

"Exploring Asia must have been cool. I absolutely *adore* Chinese food. Did you have the best time ever?"

"No," Boy scoffed, swirling his whiskey. "I wasn't all that impressed. I mean, I grew up in Singapore, so I've traveled a lot—Thailand, Vietnam, Laos, Cambodia." He stifled a yawn. "Not bad beaches in Thailand, but once you've seen one, you've seen them all, and those dreadful backpackers have really brought the tone down, of course. But enough about me." Boy fixed his eyes on Alice. "What brings *you* to Formica?"

"What if that's a secret?" Alice said flirtatiously, trailing her fingertips round the edge of her coaster.

This seemed to have quite an effect on Boy, who grinned like a wolf and leaned in so close that his breath warmed her cheek. "Oh, really? In that case, I suppose I'd have to . . . coax it out of you."

Alice giggled idiotically, her pulse hurtling like an express train. "Actually," she babbled breathlessly, "a bunch of us came up from school tonight just to see the gig. All of us girls go to St. Cecilia's, and the guys in the band are at Hasted House, just down the—"

Shit. Alice shut her mouth. What was she doing ranting on about school when Boy must have assumed she was at least on her gap year like him? In the mirror behind the bar she caught sight of her reflection, framed by jagged lines of bottles. For fuck's sake, she could definitely pass for eighteen—she'd done it a million times before. Why on earth had she had to go and blow her cover?

Meanwhile, Boy was nodding pleasantly. "St. Cecilia's? I've heard loads about that old place. My mum was a student there—decades ago, of course. Wow, looks like you and I have got a lot in common."

"Maybe we do." Alice gave a sly smile. "Or maybe you're just flattering yourself."

"Ohhh, really?" Boy laughed. "And that's coming from the girl who tried to push in front of me in the queue 'by accident.' Come on, you didn't think I fell for that trick, did you? I know you were only trying to get close to me." He clinked her glass.

Alice was gazing into his eyes when suddenly, on the bar, someone's Blackberry lit up, vibrating to "Poker Face" by Lady Gaga. She grimaced. It was unbelievably tacky when people had songs as their ringtones, especially songs by slutty boy-candy like that. And especially when they ruined the moment. She reached out to shove the phone away.

"'Scuse me a sec," said Boy, his hand beating her there. "Hey," he answered the call.

Oops.

His voice was so low that Alice had to strain to hear.

"Did you get back okay?" he said, obviously speaking to someone he knew well. There had been no caller ID, but the number had looked long. Maybe European.

"Just a bar," Boy said into the phone. "Nothing. No one. Of course." He slid his hand over the mouthpiece. "Would you mind giving me a minute?" he asked Alice.

"Oh, sure. Whatever," she said, watching Boy jump off his stool and stride away, doing her best not to look awkward and friendless even though sitting alone in clubs was possibly the lamest activity in the world. Why couldn't Boy have had his little chat right here? Alice traced her fingers over the Formica bar, pretending to be utterly absorbed in its mottled pattern, as if somebody as self-possessed as her didn't need company, anyway.

And then, from across the room, a voice soared into her ears. It was Tristan's voice, singing. Alice started—she hadn't even noticed the band come back onstage. Her gaze locked on to T as he rocked his head to the drums, his dark caramel hair bent low over the microphone, his eyes soft with a trusting, vulnerable look, like he had a special secret to confide to each and every member of the audience. A current of longing tugged at Alice's heart.

Then someone's hand brushed her shoulder. "Sorry for the interruption," Boy was saying, straddling his stool, drawing it closer to hers than before. Alice sighed. Of course T wasn't even looking this way. If only he wasn't so involved in his bloody music. What good would it do talking to other guys if he didn't even notice?

"Another round," Boy told the bartender, giving Alice a conspiratorial smile. "By the way, I've just realized, if your father's Richard Rochester, that must mean you're a cousin of Caroline Frisk."

Alice twirled her new glass of wine. She was used to people knowing random facts about her family. After all, they were constantly in *Tatler* and the *Evening Standard,* and the society pages of *Hello!* "Yeah. Coco and I are quite close. We always have been, even though she's nine years older than me."

"Sweet. So are you going to her big engagement bash in Rome?"

Alice nodded, trying not to let her face betray her at the mention of Rome. Just a few weeks ago, she'd been so excited about her gang's half-term trip there. Everyone who was anyone was going to Coco's party; it was all set to be the event of the year. But now, thanks to Tristan, her daydreams were in shreds. Alice had had a special night for them all planned out: T was going to sneak into her suite at the fabulously trendy Hotel de Russie (after their parents were safely asleep), run her a deep, hot bubble bath surrounded by scented candles, and massage her all over with lavender oil. Then, under the hotel's soft, high-thread-count sheets, they were going to make love. For the first time. In fact, it was going to be the first time Alice had ever had sex with anyone. She'd been waiting for someone special before she gave it up—and who was more special than her oldest friend?

"Hey." Boy nudged her. "Earth to Alice. Am I boring you?"

"No! Of course not."

"Then why aren't you answering my question?"

"Question?"

Boy rolled his gorgeous green eyes. "About Lorenzo. Do you know him?"

Alice smirked. Lorenzo da Fonseca, Coco's fiancé, was a hot up-and-coming Italian film star. "Why should you care? Has *someone* got a little crush?"

"Oh, yeah, totally. I'm *so* jealous he's marrying your cousin. *Not.*" Boy sipped his whiskey. "Just curious."

"Sure, whatever." Alice grinned. "Yeah, I've met him a few times. Once at a big family lunch a few months ago with all the parents. Oooh actually . . ."—her eyes gleamed—"I found out some pretty juicy gossip about the da Fonseca family. It's all terribly scandalous and filthy." She zipped her lips in mock secrecy. "I *really* shouldn't tell you."

"Oh, go on, you're dying to tell me. You're bursting. Spill it."

"Well . . . okay! Renzo has a stepmother."

"Ummm, so? That's nothing revolutionary."

"Wait till I've finished. She's called Adrianna. And guess how old she is."

Boy shrugged. "Haven't a clue. Anyway, I don't ca—"

"Twenty-three. *Twenty-three!* And Coco's twenty-five, which means her mother-in-law's totally gonna be younger than her! And at that lunch, Adrianna didn't bother even *pretending* to love Lorenzo's father—she slurped up the champagne, boasted to us all how much money he's got, and then went off and bought like thirty thousand pounds' worth of designer clothes. And guess what else?" Alice sneered. "Adrianna doesn't ever stay in Rome for more than a few days—she's always jetting round Europe chasing after younger men. How tacky is *that*?"

Boy looked suitably appalled. He drained the rest of his whiskey and slammed the glass on the table. "Bloody Italians," he scoffed, sounding choked, probably from the alcohol burning his throat.

Alice hardly had time to agree before Boy interrupted.

"Listen . . ." There was an undecided look on his face. "I was wondering . . . See, I have vague plans to be in Rome the weekend of Coco's party."

"Uh-huh." Alice flicked her hair, trying to look nonchalant. No way—was Boy about to ask her on a *date*? Wait till everyone heard about this!

If they ever heard about it. A threat was looming, right over Boy's shoulder.

"Hi, kids!" Tally chirped.

Alice pursed her lips. Of course Tally had to come over right now, at the crucial moment. As soon as she showed her face, men became blubbering idiots incapable of focusing on anything else—it was worse than the World Cup final. Tally was breathtakingly beautiful, of course, but Alice knew there was more to it than that. She knew that boys loved how scatter-brained and vulnerable Tally was: They somehow found it flattering, as if her helplessness was a reflection of their own finesse. And naturally, the fact that Tally was half-Russian, with the lingering flavor of a Moscow accent, didn't hinder the effect.

"Go away," Alice mouthed.

"What?" Tally widened her eyes. She wiggled her butt, and the giant rose pin on it wagged like a puppy's tail. Alice snorted, covering her mouth with her hand.

"What's so funny?" Boy asked, clearly a couple of steps behind.

Fantastic. "Boy," Alice sighed, "this is my friend Tally."

"Lovely to meet you!" Tally burst out.

"Pleasure," Boy drawled, turning slowly round with his hand outstretched.

"Pleasure," Alice repeated loathingly under her breath, waiting for Boy's face to turn all soppy and doe-eyed.

Then she realized Boy wasn't even looking at Tally any more. He was looking at *her.* Hastily, she resuscitated her smile.

"Listen, I'd better run," Boy said, sweeping his gray jacket off the bar. "But I was gonna say—how about we go out sometime soon? Just the two of us?"

Tally just had time to give a ridiculous thumbs-up over Boy's shoulder before she was swallowed by the crowd.

"Oh," Alice breathed. "Cool. Sure, why not?"

"It'd seem an awful waste not to see each other again, after all." Boy scribbled something on a corner of napkin and slipped it into her hand. "Here. Take my number."

Alice hesitated. Wasn't *he* supposed to ask for *her* number?

"I would phone you," Boy interrupted, "but I don't want to be one of those jerks who bothers you if you're not interested. I mean, I obviously want to see *you* again, so just call me if you feel the same way."

"I'm sure you're not a jerk." Alice smiled. She'd obviously been right about older men—Boy was so gentlemanly, letting her make the first move.

"Oh, and one more thing," he added, turning his back on the room so that the two of them were hidden in their very own corner.

Alice looked up into his sea-green eyes. They were questioning yet determined. He leaned in close.

"You're just so kissable," he murmured. "I have to, I can't resist." Suddenly, he pressed his lips to hers, parting her mouth with his soft, tantalizing tongue. As he kissed her, he stroked her neck with his fingertips. She moved in closer, for more. His hand trailed downward, brushing the silk of her jumpsuit, toying with its top button. Then he slipped it around the curve of her breast. Alice drew a sharp breath, half of indignation, half of desire. Boy chuckled, his lips still on hers. Her whole body was tingling when he finally straightened up.

"Call me," he whispered.

The next instant, he'd dissolved into the crowd.

Alice stared after him, her cheeks on fire. Had that really just happened? Had she imagined it? It seemed like a dream. But there was the scrap of napkin where he'd scrawled his number, real and solid in her fist.

CHAPTER FIVE

Tuck In Café, ten minutes, read the text message on Tally's sleek black Prada phone. Surreptitiously, to escape the chipmunky eyes of Mr. Bianco, the History of Art teacher, she slipped the phone back into the pocket of her gray wool school skirt, pushed her textbooks into her vintage leather satchel, and tapped her pen against her palm with mounting impatience.

Twenty ticks of the second hand later, as soon as the bell rang for break, all ten girls in the class sprang up like race-horses out of the starting gate.

"OMG, could that have been any more boring?" groaned Bella Scott, catching up with Tally next to the overhead projector.

"Doubtful. I practically fell asleep."

"You *did* fall asleep! Your mouth was hanging way open." Bella lolled back her head and grunted out a snore in imitation. "Lucky the lights were out for the slide show."

"Luck has nothing to do with it." Tally giggled. "That's exactly why I chose History of Art in the first place. How else am I supposed to catch up on shut-eye, when Ali and I stay up every night drinking?"

Bella looked at her enviously. It was common knowledge that Tally Abbott and Alice Rochester had the most fun of anyone in school, which was why the rest of the junior class were always angling for invitations to sneak into their shared dorm room after lights-out.

"Well, you never look tired. How late did you—"

"Cool, see you later!" Tally cut in, abruptly turning down a narrow path that led past the sunken garden and leaving Bella to stare after her, mid-sentence. It wasn't that Tally didn't like Bella Scott; she did, and she also liked being invited to the annual Christmas party thrown by Bella's father, Lucian Scott, the world-famous film director. It was just that their crew's morning gossip sessions over coffee and croissants were strictly members-only. And once you let in a nonmember, you never knew *what* riffraff might try to join.

The path Tally strolled was silent except for the twittering of tiny sparrows, the rustling of rust-colored leaves, and the crunching of Tally's crimson wedges. The grass on either side of her flicked lazily in the early October breeze, while the watered-down sunlight nosed through the clouds and warmed the back of her yellow school blouse.

Through gaps in the hedge, Tally caught flashes of blossoms in the sunken garden—a burst of color planted with seasonal flowers every term by the award-winning St. Cecilia's gardeners. She peeled off her gray wool cardigan and let it trail from her fingertips. It was refreshing, for once, to avoid the break-time stampede and snatch a few minutes of solitude. Tally may have been one of the most popular and admired girls at St. C's, but she was used to being alone. During the holidays (well, whenever she wasn't chilling at Alice's place or sunbathing in France or sailing round Italy or skiing in Switzerland), she lived practically alone in the Fulham house her dad owned with his bitchy new wife. The pair of them were too wrapped up in each other and their coke-fueled city friends to even pretend to look after her. In fact, Tally had taken care of herself for as long as she could remember—her mother, who lived all the way in Moscow, wasn't the maternal type at the best of times.

Tally bit her lip. Not that she really gave a shit. She loved her independence. It was great having no bossy adults to meddle in her business . . .

"Natalya!" came a man's call through the shrubbery.

Tally stopped short, gripping her satchel. Even after almost half a term of knowing that voice, it still knocked her breathless.

A man had appeared on the path in front of her. He was athletic-looking, with dark, wavy hair and a jaw-droppingly gorgeous face that made it hard to believe he taught advanced-level English. Tally should have known Mr. Logan would be out here: He was obsessed with holding classes in the sunken garden when the weather was good. He had his students act out scenes from Shakespeare around the fountain while he made corrections and shouted out stage directions. "About time someone breathed some life into these musty old pages," he was fond of repeating, with that sexy dimpled smile of his. "The Bard must be applauding in his grave."

"This is a nice surprise, Natalya," Mr. Logan said, the dimples making an appearance now. Even though he knew very well that she preferred Tally, he insisted on calling her Natalya—he enjoyed savoring all three syllables of the name. "How was your weekend? You went to London, didn't you?"

"Yeah, it was fun."

"Suppose you made all kinds of mischief." Mr. Logan raised his eyebrows suggestively, and Tally blushed.

"No more than usual."

"Sorry to hear it. Mind if I walk with you?"

"Of course not, I'd love you to!" Tally reddened even more at her outburst, and nonchalantly tossed her cardigan over one shoulder. "I'm on my way to the Tuck In for my morning coffee fix. I'm a total zombie without it."

"Really? You look *very* alive to me." Mr. Logan took in the flush suffusing Tally's porcelain skin. He gazed at her sea-gray eyes, her tangled hair, her petite shoulders, and down at her short, pleated skirt with its fraying hem. "By the way, when are you coming for your first tutorial?"

Tally's heart skipped. Those were the exact words she'd been waiting to hear. Just over a week ago, Mr. Logan had offered to tutor her after-hours in his private study in the old part of school—but he hadn't mentioned the plan since. Not that Tally should have been worried: Mr. Logan had never yet let her down. Quite the opposite: He called on her in lessons more than he called on anyone else; he took her aside to remark on what a gifted student she was; he'd even, once, read poetry to her—*love* poetry—aloud in the library. Tally had later stolen the book to keep under her pillow, and those special pages were now smudged and dog-eared with caresses. Fine, Tally admitted it—she was in deep. But Mr. Logan was worth it. He was the most sensitive, passionate, sexy man she'd ever met.

"I have a slot this evening," Mr. Logan said. "How does that sound?"

"Oh, tonight! Umm, sure." Tally was certain her heart was hammering loudly enough for him to hear. "Good. Yeah. Cool."

"Let's say six thirty, then. Go to dinner early and pop round afterward. It'll be the first meeting of our secret literary society."

Tally giggled. Then, reluctantly, she trailed off. Their sheltered path had ended all too soon and they'd emerged into the open school. At their feet, a gently undulating lawn spread into the distance, its grass shorn as short as a carpet. Thick, gnarled oak trees provided generous pools of shade, while in the pale, sunlit islands between them, girls were tucking into iced buns and flapjacks and chocolate bars for break. Here and there, the grass was latticed with unpaved paths, the main one of which led down from a cascade of sweeping, redbrick steps at the back of the school's main Quad. Far away, at the opposite end of the green carpet, nestled several boarding houses, each in its own neat garden. Everywhere, students were scurrying back and forth in twos and threes, shrieking with laughter, sending each other texts across the school, and trying desperately to finish last-minute homework.

This was the Great Lawn, the social hub of St. Cecilia's—and it was where Tally had to leave Mr. Logan, or people would talk.

"Here's my stop," she remarked, inclining her head to the left.

Mr. Logan turned. Just off the grass lay the cafeteria and the shiny, glass-enclosed Tuck In Café, where Alice Rochester, Jemimah Calthorpe de Vyle-Hanswicke, and Sonia Khan were all sitting at a table right up against the panes, sipping from identical jumbo cardboard cups.

Jemimah was already looking in his and Tally's direction. As he watched, she nudged Alice Rochester, a smirk on her naturally rather smug face.

Mr. Logan gave Tally a hasty nod and swung on his heel.

"Six thirty," he called over his shoulder. "Don't be late. And"—he winked—"don't forget your books."

CHAPTER SIX

*A*li, come ooon," pleaded Sonia on the other side of the Tuck In's glass, drumming her perfectly manicured nails on their crew's stainless steel table. "You still haven't told us anything about that hottie you were flirting with Saturday night. I can't believe you're keeping all the gossip to yourself. It's, like, selfish."

"Yeah, well, maybe there *is* no gossip. Ever think of that?" Alice opened her jaw wide and stuffed in an extra-large mouthful of her croissant (if the dry, turd-shaped things they sold in here could possibly deserve that name) so she wouldn't have to answer any more questions. Sonia was as clingy as a wad of chewing gum. And she was nosy. In fact, *Nose* should be Sonia's nickname, especially because, since her nose job over the summer, she'd been completely obsessed with her new and "improved" face.

Alice pried open the top of her latte and blew at the

steam. Tally was the only one who knew she'd snogged Boy at Formica, and she wanted to keep it that way, at least till she'd decided on her next move.

"Where's Tally?" Mimah asked, as if reading Alice's mind.

"Paying for her coffee." Alice jerked her head toward the cash register, then sneaked a look at the lawn. Mr. Logan was still out there, schmoozing with their housemistress, Miss Sharkreve, and the headmistress, Mrs. Traphorn. Alice despised that man. She'd despised him from the moment he'd strutted into their classroom a few weeks ago, on the first day of term, and made fun of her in front of their entire English class. And now she despised him even more for stalking Tally round the grounds, trying to chat her up. It was disgusting, the way he'd looked at Tals just now on the Great Lawn—not to mention the way he drooled all over her in class. In fact, it was worse than disgusting: It was sick.

Alice eyed her food again, with no appetite. The thing was, she was genuinely worried about Tally. You only had to look at the girl's parents—a slutty mum who hosted a fashion talk show in Moscow, and a totally neglectful cokehead dad—to guess that she might be a bit messed up. For example, it was so obvious that Tally saw Mr. Logan as some sort of perverted father figure. A few weeks ago, Alice had hinted as much— she'd *only* been trying to be understanding—and had almost derailed their friendship in the process.

"Hey there, teacher's pet," cackled Mimah Calthorpe de Vyle-Hanswicke in her famously husky voice, as Tally flopped into their table's only empty chair. The small beauty mark under Mimah's left eye always gave her an extra-saucy air at moments like this. "What took you so long? Getting in some *private* tutoring?" She nudged Sonia, who laughed, and Alice, who pursed her lips and said nothing.

Tally poured four packets of sugar into her mocha cappuccino with extra chocolate and smiled mysteriously. She was keeping her lips sealed about her tutorials with Mr. Logan. Even with her closest mates. And even though she couldn't think about anything else. What would it be like tonight? What would happen when she was all alone in the English teacher's wood-paneled study, cradling a glass of red wine, listening to him read aloud from intellectual books? Maybe she'd finally get to see the butterfly tattoo on his chest that he'd told her about a few weeks back.

"Ali!" Sonia's high-pitched voice jerked Tally back to the table. Between her fingernails, Sonia was waving a rectangle of silver card inscribed with elegant calligraphy. "What on *earth* are you wearing to Coco's party in Rome? I've got absolutely nothing except those two dresses I bought last week, and they're both absolutely hideous."

"You sure it's the dresses that are hideous?" Tally grinned.

"Shut up."

Alice laughed. "No clue what I'm wearing yet. I'll probably go shopping beforehand in Harvey Nics or something, as usual." She glanced questioningly at Tally, who nodded.

"*Hey* . . ." Sonia's eyes were darting back and forth between her two friends, like a dog hoping for table scraps. "Can I come?"

Alice stuck her last corner of croissant in her mouth and chewed it deliberately before answering. "I guess so."

"It's *shopping*," Tally added. "Not a private event."

Sonia ignored this comment; her eyes were glued to Alice. "Thanks, babe. OMG, I cannot wait for half term! Rome is so cool and the Hotel de Russie is such a hot hangout." She sighed wistfully. "When I get engaged, I want to have my party in the hottest place ever. You girls can throw it for me, since you'll be my maids of honor. I'll design flattering dresses so you won't look too much like giant fruit pastels next to me in my gown."

Tally almost choked on her coffee. "I need the bathroom," she gasped, suppressing laughter as she scraped back her chair.

"Well, no one will have to worry about being a bridesmaid at my wedding," Mimah cut in, her eyes mocking underneath her blunt, black fringe. She turned her habitual Red Bull can upside down and drained the last drop. "I wouldn't have them if you paid me. It's much cooler to have page girls and page boys."

"*Cooler?*" Sonia sneered. "What on earth do you mean?"

"I mean that anyone who has any taste should avoid the whole bridesmaid thing. It's so much more sophisticated to have your little cousins and nieces and nephews and stuff carrying flowers and scattering rose petals. That way, there's no hassle about making people wear hideous meringues."

"Absolutely," Alice declared. "Mummy told me that's what Coco's planning, and it's definitely what I'm going to do when I get married."

Glowering, Sonia sipped her cappuccino, so incensed that she forgot to stir the foam away first. A pointy white peak of it clung to her nose. It was annoying how Mimah could do no wrong in their clique at the moment; she'd been totally out of favor over the entire spring term and summer holidays, and Sonia, for one, had rather enjoyed it. Not because she was a bitch or anything, but because Mimah had been acting like a moody bitch for months—ever since her dad, a respected judge whom she'd idolized, had been busted with a prostitute and had his face plastered all over the tabloids. Mimah had started doing cringeworthy things, like snapping at people all the time and randomly bursting into tears. Disgusting things too, like *paying* Seb Ogilvy a thousand quid to sleep with her. Well, no one knew if that was really true, but Sonia wouldn't be surprised—Mimah had fancied Seb for years. Which was another reason why her absence from the group had been a bonus: It had given Sonia a chance to stake her own claim.

Anyway, now Mimah was back in. Just over a week ago, she'd done Alice an unexpected favor, humiliating Dylan Taylor during a racy school fashion show, in front of the whole school. Sonia wished she'd come up with that first. Especially since she was the one who was stuck sharing a room with Dylan. It wasn't fair.

"You lot. Listen," Tally said urgently, reappearing at the

table with a newspaper clutched to her chest. "Has anyone seen the papers today?" She threw a glance at Mimah.

"No." Mimah checked the time on her Cartier Tank. "Why?"

"It's just . . ." Tally sighed and laid the newspaper in the center of the table. "That's why."

Stamped across the tabloid's front page was a blaring headline: BREACH OF JUSTICE! Next to it was a huge picture of Mimah's father exiting a restaurant—and by his side, with her black bangs hanging straight over her dark, piercing eyes, was Mimah herself.

"Shit!" Sonia squealed.

Underneath came the article:

On Saturday night, disgraced ex-judge Jeremiah Calthorpe de Vyle-Hanswicke was spotted dining at the elegant Candela restaurant in London, accompanied by his sixteen-year-old daughter, Jemimah. Calthorpe de Vyle-Hanswicke, swilling a bottle of wine, appeared tanned and carefree just six months after being caught in the act with a prostitute less than half his age. Since last spring, the sex-crazed ex-judge has been residing in Benidorm, sunning himself and enjoying the local "talent."

A silence descended over the table.

"Did—did you know they'd taken that photo, Mime?" Alice ventured at last, shooting her friend a worried look. But instead of the horrified expression she'd expected, she saw something else: Mimah looked livid. Furious.

46

"No," Mimah fumed. "Daddy swore he'd got the paparazzi under control—that's how he persuaded me to have dinner with him in the first place. *Fuck* him. I told him I'd had enough of being in the papers." She was breathing through her nose like an angry bull. "He's a dirty liar and I'll never speak to him again. I'll—shit!" Mimah's face was suddenly horrified. "What on earth is Charlie gonna do when she sees this?"

Charlotte Calthorpe de Vyle-Hanswicke, Mimah's fourteen-year-old sister, was in ninth grade at St. C's, and had not been dealing well with Daddy's humiliation. In the past six months, she'd gone from being chatty and popular to morose and, rumor had it, totally out of control.

Riiing!

Alice leaped to her feet. "French! Can't be late. Oh my god, where's my bag? Look, Mime, try to cheer up. Let's talk at lunch, okay?"

Mimah shrugged and crumpled the paper in her fist. "Sure."

"Feel better, Mime," Tally said, spilling coffee down her blouse as she was swept up in the exiting herd.

Once on the Great Lawn, Tally turned her footsteps toward Tudor House, home to the junior class. Luckily all she had now was a free period, the perfect opportunity to try out different shoe-and-jewelry combos for tonight. Tally hugged herself. Who cared if there was already a shitload of work on her plate? This was far more important. She had to find a way of keeping Mr. Logan titillated while she had her school uniform on. How else was she going to seduce him into taking it off?

CHAPTER SEVEN

*F*inished!" crowed Seb Ogilvy, gesturing at the Classics essay on his computer screen as if it were the grand prize in *Deal or No Deal*. "And it's a work of fucking genius, if I may say so myself."

He jumped up, flung a blue-and-maroon Hasted House scarf round his neck, and did a drumroll on his desk. "Come on, T. Time for my reward."

Tristan glanced up from the economics essay he was sweating over, one eyebrow raised in suspicion. "I take it by 'reward,' you mean 'drink'?"

Seb grinned. "Well, if you wanted to be crass about it. Go on, go on, go ooon! You know you want to."

He fixed his eyes imploringly on T across their bedroom, which was perched at the top of one of Hasted House's gray stone towers. Below the boys' thick, vaulted windows, the courtyard was muffled in darkness, punctured only by lamps marking the entrances to buildings. Founded three hundred years ago, the school resembled a mini version of an Oxford or Cambridge college—most likely as a hint to its students that Oxbridge was where they were expected to end up. Not that Tristan or Seb seemed to have read that particular memo, judging from the state of their room. The place looked like a rat's nest on crack. T's rugby uniform was strewn across the floor. Huge drifts of Seb's papers, scrawled in his tiny, blotched script, were piled around the carpet, mixed with bags of chips, crumbs, half-eaten chocolate bars, muddy shoes, and Rizla rolling papers. Football posters, already dog-eared even though it was only a month into term, were tacked crookedly to the walls, along with posters of Seb's favorite vintage films, *Breathless* and *Blow-up*, which he'd finally got Tristan into as well. A poster of Radiohead, T's most idolized band, hung above his bed. It was intended to give him musical inspiration while he slept.

"Shit, Seb, I think a drink's out of the question . . ." T frowned at his economics textbook. "I'm meant to hand in these equations tomorrow. Briggsy'll throw a fit if they're late. Have you done yours?"

"Yeah. Piece of piss."

"For fuck's sake, you think everything's a piece of piss. I can't get my head round this shit." T lolled his head back with a sigh. He was only taking economics because of his father's lifelong obsession that he go to Oxford and become an important politician, which he had absolutely zero intention of fulfilling. Personally, he wanted to drop the subject and study music instead. He hadn't exactly had the courage to do so yet. But he was sure he would. Soon.

"Forget about it, mate," Seb urged. "Just copy mine."

"I can't. Briggsy'll be suspicious if I get everything right."

"So slip in a couple of fuck-ups. He'll never—"

"Evening, gentlemen." Their door had swung open, and Tom Randall-Stubbs was poking his dark-haired mug into the room.

"All right, Rando." Seb waved him in. "I was just trying to persuade T to come have a drink at the Oakes. But he's suddenly turned into a massive geek."

"T, mate, what are you thinking? Don't be lame. Everyone's already there. Whoooa. Wow." Halfway over the carpet, Rando had stopped, his foot suspended mid-step. Lying beneath it was a photo of Tally, Alice, and Tristan. Tally had one eye closed and was beckoning to the camera, her creamy skin made translucent by the flash. "Shit," he sighed, swiping up the picture and cradling it in his palm. "Tals is amazing, isn't she?"

Behind his back, Tristan and Seb exchanged grins.

"Oh, hang on!" Rando snapped his fingers. "I've been meaning to ask—have you heard from Alice since the gig Saturday night?"

Tristan jerked to attention, as if someone had shoved a poker down his polo shirt. "No. Why?"

"It's just, did you see that guy chatting her up? I could be wrong, but he looked a lot like Boy Stanley-Soames." Rando's lip curled into a sneer.

"Who?" Tristan snapped.

"Oh. You haven't heard about him, then?"

"Am I meant to have?" Tristan snatched his pencil and started doodling jagged lines across his notebook, pressing the tip down hard.

"Well, let's just put it this way: He was pretty famous around my old school." Rando had only just joined Hasted House at the beginning of term. He flashed a grin, made cheeky by his small, pointy teeth. "Boy was two years above me. Had a bit of a reputation with the ladies, if you know what I mean. Last I heard, he'd got a twenty-five-year-old cocktail waitress pregnant in Singapore. That's where his family lives. Apparently he really screwed her over."

The tip of Tristan's pencil lead snapped off.

"'Course, it sounds like a bullshit rumor to me. But there's no smoke without fire, right?"

Tristan's palms had gone clammy. He had to do something. There was no fucking *way* he could let Alice get involved with a bastard like this Boy Spanner-Spoons or whatever his bloody name was. As he thought of Alice, Tristan felt a surge of protectiveness. True, last time he'd suggested warning a girl about imminent danger, Seb had laughed in his face—but the feeling he was having now was ten times worse than it had been when Dylan was at stake.

"Right." He jumped up. "I've changed my mind, I'm coming for a drink. Let's go."

"Hang on." Seb was staring at him. "Didn't you hear what Rando just said about Alice's bloke?"

"Hmm? Oh, yeah, course I did. Whatever. She can take care of herself." Tristan gave a laugh that sounded like a truck backfiring. "Come on, then, ready?"

Seb shrugged and five minutes later, the boys were crossing the dark grounds in the direction of the woods, Tristan striding ahead. Way out here, hidden in the shadows of three giant trees, stood the Oakes—the senior class club in its own private building that only the best-connected Hasted House students were invited to join. Back when the Oakes had been founded, at the same time as the school itself, it had been an intellectual society whose members staged debates, held readings, declaimed about politics, and drank whiskey. These days, they pretty much just drank whiskey. True, two or three total nerds still organized chess matches and discussion groups, but only losers with no life went to those. The real reason to go to the Oakes was that it was the safest place to drink for miles around. That wasn't because the Hasted House teachers were in the dark about what went on inside its walls: It was because they'd never dare bust the place. Some of the school's richest patrons were old Oakesians, and there was no way they'd stand to see it shut down.

"Well, look who's finally here!" a voice bellowed as Seb, Tristan, and Rando sauntered in. George Demetrios, sprawled on a brown leather couch next to Jasper von Holstadt, was waving his drink at them. A bottle of Jameson rested on a lamplit table by his side.

"Sink your teeth into this," he slurred, filling three more

glasses with whiskey. Tristan accepted his tumbler without a word, sinking into a tattered leather chair. He seemed fixated on the pool game in full swing nearby.

"Cheers." Seb clinked glasses with the others and took a long sip, his face relaxing as he ran a hand through his blond, haystack hair. "Oy, Jas." He nodded at the iPhone in Jasper's hand. "What are you staring at that thing for?"

"Ha!" boomed George Demetrios. "You may very well ask."

"Yeah, thanks, I just did." Seb turned back to Jasper. "So?"

"So!" George Demetrios butted in again. "The answer to your inquiry is top-secret." He put on a fake whisper. "Let's just say it has to do with a certain *American* girl. We'll call her Dylan Tay—"

"Shut it," Jasper ordered, casting a glance in Tristan's direction. "I'll handle this."

But it was too late. Tristan had already flicked his eyes away from the pool table and was staring at Jasper. "What's going on *now*?"

Jasper heaved what was clearly supposed to be an appeasing sigh. "The thing is . . ." He raised his eyebrows, looking slightly bored, the way he did whenever he had to ask for something he felt he was already entitled to. "I've been meaning to bring this up for days. Look, you know I think Dylan's really hot. You wouldn't mind if I asked her out, would you? Not like Formica. I mean on a proper date."

George slapped his leg. "Yeah. A proper date between her thighs!"

For a second, Tristan felt a twist of rage, as it looked like Jasper might snicker. But Jas managed to keep his long, aristocratic face straight. "So, what do you think, T? No hard feelings?"

"Hard feelings?" Tristan scuffed the rug with his foot. Suddenly, all he wanted was to be back in his room, writing songs about the cold, dead winter of romance. He set his jaw. "Of course not, Jas—chill. Dylan's ancient news. There are bigger fish in the sea."

Jasper nodded. Then his satisfied expression tightened into a smirk. "Bigger fish? I beg to differ, mate. That rack of hers, you know . . ." He broke off suggestively.

"I most certainly do!" George Demetrios pounded the table with his fist. "Dylan must be dynamite in bed. Tell us, T, how many times did you two shag in one night?"

Seb rolled his eyes.

Tristan took a large gulp of whiskey. The truth was, the answer was *none*. He and Dylan had never managed to sleep together during the whole month they were dating in the Hamptons. She'd kept holding out till his very last night there—and then, when she'd finally decided she was ready, he'd totally fucked everything up. Stupid condoms. He shut his eyes. It was too embarrassing to even *think* about. Tristan straightened up.

"I've told you before," he said, tapping a finger to his nose, "ask me no questions and I'll tell you no lies." He nodded at Jasper. "What are you waiting for, then? Text her. Ask her out."

Jasper and George Demetrios exchanged looks and exploded into guffaws.

"Er, that's the funny thing, mate!" Jasper slapped the sofa, making its brown leather resound unpleasantly. "I already did."

George hooted with laughter, throwing his arm round T's shoulders. "Mate! It's a good thing you said it was okay!"

Tristan swirled his drink, forcing his mouth into a smile.

Suddenly, Jasper's phone vibrated and everyone looked at the table as he shot out a hand to pick it up. A sharklike grin widened his mouth.

"Excellent," he said, stroking his index finger over the screen. "Here's her answer now."

CHAPTER EIGHT

*H*alf an hour earlier, Dylan had been sprawled across the gray regulation carpet in the bedroom she shared with Sonia Khan, her long blond hair trailing down her back. They were on the second floor of Tudor House, the ivy-covered redbrick building where the junior class boarded, and Dylan was surrounded by stacks of colored paper, from which she was crafting an entire menagerie of origami animals.

Sonia, hunched over her MacBook, gave a sigh that sounded like a broken heating pipe. Trust Dylan to sit there rustling and ripping for hours on end while *she* was trying to do her chemistry homework—in other words, *real* work. Sonia probably deserved a reward for putting up with such a nightmare roommate. Shoving back her chair, she stalked across the room to fetch one of the bottles of San Pellegrino she kept lined up on their very own shelf. She'd read somewhere that half the time you thought you were hungry, you were actually just thirsty—so whenever Sonia felt like a snack, she guzzled down an entire bottle of water. It was terribly purifying.

As she passed Dylan's messy little horde on the floor, Sonia's expression became even more furious. "Oops!" Her cashmere-clad foot crunched down on an intricate hedgehog that she'd seen Dylan laboring over for ages.

"What the—?" Dylan's eyes widened. "You did that on purpose!"

"Oh my god, no way!" Sonia gaped in exaggerated shock. "Was that your *art*? I didn't realize—I thought you'd just knocked over the rubbish bin."

Dylan snatched up the crushed paper. "Oh, really? Why would you think that? Do you see empty diet-pill packets everywhere?"

"No." Sonia looked nonplussed. "What does that have to do with anything?"

"Because you pop those pills so fast, the trash is always full of your empties. If I'd knocked it over, they'd be all over the room."

"That is so out of order! Just—just because I make an effort with my appearance," Sonia snapped, tossing her shiny black hair. Her cheeks were burning. It was none of Dylan's business if she wanted to stay skinny by picking at salads and guzzling laxatives. Alice and Tally already ridiculed her for it, and that was enough.

Forgetting all about her sparkling water, Sonia swept back

to her side of the bedroom. Dylan stared after her, still balancing the crushed hedgehog on her palm, and biting her lower lip. The wall above Sonia's desk was decorated with row after orderly row of photos, mostly showing Sonia, Alice, Tally, and Mimah, accompanied by their Hasted House crew—Tristan Murray-Middleton, George Demetrios, Jasper von Holstadt, Seb Ogilvy, and the newest addition, Tom Randall-Stubbs. Examining the pictures was like taking a tour of Europe's most exclusive destinations. In one, the boys were swimming naked in the pool of Mimah's villa near Seville, their bare butts glimmering in the moonlight; in another, the entire gang were tucking into a huge, boozy Italian lunch under the grapevines at the Rochesters' house in Positano; in yet another, Tally and Alice, clad in tiny bikinis, were climbing over rocks to reach the sea below the Demetrios family's olive groves in Corfu.

Dylan's eyes continued round the room. Sonia's bed was adorned with a purple silk duvet cover that she'd clearly brought back from India. Her bedside table and armchair were both draped in embroidered throws. And instead of her regulation school lamp, Sonia was using a stylish wooden one from home, which cast a golden glow over her woven wool rug.

In contrast, Dylan's bed, furniture, and wall looked positively prisonlike. As soon as she'd moved in, Sonia had made it clear that Dylan was to keep away from her things—and, since Dylan had never been to boarding school before now, she hadn't thought to bring anything to make her area more homey.

Not that she *had* much of a home, now that her mother had messed everything up. A few months ago, Dylan's mom had fallen in love with a slimy Englishman named Victor Dalgleish, who had greasy sideburns and hosted a terrible quiz show called *MindQuest*, watched only by bored house-wives with nothing to do at three o'clock on weekday after-noons. Not exactly star material. But that hadn't stopped Dylan's mother from dumping Dylan's father and chasing Victor all the way across the Atlantic to London. Which was why Dylan had ended up at horrible St. Cecilia's in the first place—she'd become a casualty of her mom's sex life. What a joke. Dylan threaded an origami crane onto a string. At least her mobile for Miss Baskin's art class was looking decent. Maybe she'd use the leftovers to brighten up her half of the room.

Beep beep. Beep beep.

Absently, Dylan picked up her vibrating phone, expecting to see a text from her fourteen-year-old sister. Lauren had somehow managed to avoid St. Cecilia's and went to a day school in London instead.

"Oh my god!" Dylan cried, almost dropping her phone in shock.

"What?" demanded Sonia before she could stop herself.

Dylan narrowed her eyes. "Nothing," she snapped, and read the message again:

Ur totally irresistible. U looked ravishing Sat night.
Can't get u out of my head. Drinks this week? JvH

JvH . . . JvH . . . Wait, could this be Jasper von Holstadt? It had to be! Who else had such silly initials? But how had he got her number?

Dylan racked her memory. That was it! Saturday night at Formica—she'd asked him to watch her phone. Suddenly she felt drunk, even though she hadn't touched a drop of the booze stashed in her desk drawer. Jasper must really be into her. How unbelievably flattering, considering his charm and his good looks and his to-die-for cool. Not to mention his place at the epicenter of the very best social scene. Dylan sneaked another look at Sonia's picture gallery, just as two loud, casual knocks sounded on the door.

"Come in!" Sonia said immediately. Maybe it was Alice. She sat up straight and smoothed her school sweater.

A tall, striking girl appeared, her hair razor-chopped and her eyes smoky with makeup.

"Oh." Sonia slouched back down. Farah Assadi. Pretentious bitch. Trust Dylan to be friends with *her.*

"Hey, Dill." Farah's voice was low and grainy and she didn't even look at Sonia. "Cool mobile you're making. God, I wish I was as talented as you."

"Don't be ridiculous, I'm terrible at art." Dylan had learned the hard way that in England, you were never supposed to accept compliments. Otherwise people thought you were up your own ass. "*You're* the one who's amazing at art. You're, like, the best in our class."

"No way. *You* are."

A loud snort came from Sonia's side of the room.

"Can I help you?" Farah asked. "Did you say something?"

"Oh, no," Sonia smirked. "Of course not. I wouldn't want to interrupt your lesbian love affair. But actually, do you two think you could stop drooling all over each other for one second? I'm trying to work."

Farah rolled her eyes. "Whatever. Dill, can I have a word?" She jerked her head toward the corridor. "Emilia and I wanted your opinion on some new eyeshadow we've bought."

"Sure," Dylan said, scattering paper scraps and origami shapes as she rose. Farah Assadi and Emilia Charles were the only two girls in Tudor House who treated her like a normal person and not a social outcast. She always leaped at invitations from them.

As the door clicked shut, Sonia's glossy lips curled into a frown. As if anyone would want Dylan's advice on what makeup to wear. Farah and Emilia should have asked *her* instead: Everyone knew she had impeccable taste. She started to turn back to her chemistry homework, but as she did so, something caught her eye. Dylan's phone, half-buried under a pile of stupid "artwork." Perfect! What kind of idiot left personal evidence like that lying around? *Now* she'd see what all the fuss had been about.

Tiptoeing over, Sonia pinched the silver rectangle between her fingertips. A text was still open on the screen. Her eyes darted over the words.

"Oh my god, fuck!" she gasped. Carefully replacing the phone to avoid suspicion, she trampled over what was left of Dylan's menagerie and threw herself out the door.

Wait till Alice heard about this.

CHAPTER NINE

"And so, in conclusion, we can deduce that King Henry VIII would stop at nothing to fulfill the desires that gnawed at his jealous, passionate, and love-torn heart."

Feverishly, Alice typed the last sentence of her history essay, read it over, and let out a mournful sigh. Then she punched delete until the whole thing disappeared. What was wrong with her this week? All she could think about was love, love, love and heartbreak, heartbreak, heartbreak and boys, boys, boys. It was getting ridiculous. How was she ever going to get into Oxford if she couldn't concentrate on her homework? The problem was, homework was getting more boring by the second.

Sliding open her desk drawer a crack, Alice peeked inside. Yes, it was still there—the folded scrap of napkin that Boy had thrust into her hand on Saturday night. Not that she'd worked up the guts to dial the number yet. If only Boy had just taken hers instead—it was way too much pressure having to get in touch with him. Besides, making the first move might mean she was expected to be over Tristan. And she wasn't. Not by a long shot.

As she thought of T, Alice's fingers tightened over her mouse. She jerked the cursor to the bottom of her screen and brought up his Facebook page from where she'd minimized it a minute and a half ago. Nothing had changed. His profile picture was still him waterskiing on a family holiday in Thailand last Easter, his chest taut and tanned as he cut through the cobalt sea. Those stale old comments on his wall were still the same too. Fantastic. How the hell was Alice supposed to keep tabs on him if he refused to update his status or post new photos or even make a new bloody friend? Maybe he'd posted a new Twitter message. She grabbed her iPhone. Nothing from TristanMM—only a stupid update from SoniaSweetie: "Chemistry homework suckzzz. Waiting for Hollywood to call :-)"

Alice hurled away her phone and shut her eyes. Okay. Deep breath. She was becoming an official stalker. The only good thing was that no one else was here to witness it—Tally had run off to the library just after dinner looking strangely excited—so her reputation was safe.

"Hi, babe!"

Alice lunged for her mouse as the door banged open.

"Ohmygod, ohmy*god*," cried Sonia, hurtling in, wearing gray St. Cecilia's track pants and a manically overexcited expression on her face. "You are never going to believe . . . Ow!"

She staggered as Alice's yellow-and-gray school diary whacked her shins, knocked off the desk by Alice's mad dash.

"For fuck's sake!" Alice swiped it from the floor. "Can't you ever knock?"

"*Knock?*" Sonia's mouth dropped open. "Why would I knock? It's not like you're, like, naked." Her eyes narrowed as she craned to get a glimpse of Alice's MacBook. "What were you looking at, anyway?"

"*Nothing.* Nosy." Putting on a studious face, Alice pretended to read her history essay. "Well? Did you want something?"

Looking uncertain, Sonia backed into Alice and Tally's entertaining nook, a large alcove in the wall that they'd furnished with school-regulation armchairs, a sheepskin rug, shaded fairy lights, and a trunk doubling as a coffee table. Her eyes fell on an edition of this week's *Grazia* and their manic gleam reignited. Gossip. She had gossip.

"Honestly, Ali, just wait till you hear this! Guess what's happening with Dylan? Guess! Guess who asked her out?"

Dylan. Alice's stomach clenched. Even though Dylan and Tristan were totally over (and had been since the beginning of term), she still couldn't get the bitch out of her head. And no, it wasn't because Dylan was a blond, busty bimbo—Alice was perfectly fine with her own angular, sophisticated style, thank you very much. At least she could wear tube tops without looking like she was playing hide-the-watermelon. It was because she knew, she just knew, that Dylan and T had *done it.* You could tell that Dylan wasn't a virgin just from the way she walked. Or maybe it was from that over-confident look in her eyes. Whatever. The point was, the girl was a slut. And thinking about it drove Alice fucking mad.

She sneered. "Someone asked Dylan on a *date?* Who, the handyman? Or, hang on, I bet it was Freddie Frye. He's desperate enough: No one who knows him will go near him." She cackled, keeping one eye on Sonia, hoping she was right.

"Wrong! Guess again."

"I don't fucking know. Who?"

"Guess!"

"Sone, spit it out. The suspense is boring me to death."

"Fine. You'll never believe it: Jasper!"

"Jasper von Holstadt?" Alice sat bolt upright.

"Yes, actual Jasper! He sent her the soppiest text I've ever read."

"But I thought that whole thing was a joke! Jas thinks Dylan's a slut. And a waste of space. Doesn't he?" Alice's voice squeaked a little on the last few words.

"Don't know. Maybe Jasper likes sluts. I reckon he genuinely fancies her." Sonia giggled. "His text said he thought she was ravishing."

"Ravishing? She's the least ravishing thing I've ever seen. She's about as ravishing as a turd. Why can't Dylan stay the hell away from me and my friends?"

"Well, yeah, I mean, I agree with you, Ali," said Sonia, struggling to keep a frown on her face. She adored giving Alice important news. "But what are you gonna do about it?

It's not like you can get rid of her. I mean, this is, like, a free country. Isnit?"

Arching her back, Alice ran her hand over her long, dark ponytail and twisted the end, tighter and tighter, round her fingers.

"I fucking well *can* get rid of her," she said. "Just let me think of a way."

CHAPTER TEN

lack! Clack! Clack! Tally's new knee-high Prada boots echoed like gunshots up the stairs to Mr. Logan's study. The sound shuddered through the empty corridors and landings, round the twisting wooden staircase, and off the cracked, loose-fitting windowpanes. This ancient part of school, up in the eaves of the main Quad, was hardly ever used. The rooms were small and cramped; the floors tilted and creaked; and when it rained, the damp soaked through the crumbling brick walls, chilling any unfortunate occupants to the bone.

As Tally reached Mr. Logan's corridor, she slowed to catch her breath. Her heart was jumping. She gave her outfit one last check. Yes, the boots (brown and supple with pointy toes, a small, delicate heel, and a zip running up the back) definitely looked hot—she'd been saving them for just this kind of occasion. To complement the effect, Tally had dug out her shortest school skirt from the pile of clothes at the bottom of her wardrobe, found her snuggest school shirt, and accessorized with gold earrings, a gold necklace, a gold chain bracelet, and bright red lipstick. Simple. Classic. Sexy. During the day all this jewelry would never be allowed, not in a million years, but now it was night and it was dark and no one would ever notice. Except, she hoped, *him.*

Tally knocked on the old-fashioned study door, criss-crossed with two beams, looming right in front of her.

"Enter."

She pushed. The room was almost exactly as Tally remembered it from almost two weeks ago, the only other time she'd set foot inside. There was Mr. Logan, kicked back in his cushy office chair, whose stuffing had finally managed to burst free from its seams. There was his desk, its green reading lamp casting a glow onto his bookshelves, which were set into the oak-paneled wall and crammed with intellectual and distinguished-looking tomes. There was his Fulham FC scarf flung across the hissing radiator; his bottle of John Varvatos cologne.

But this time, Tally noticed, Mr. Logan had added a little something to the scene: two wine glasses and a bottle of Shiraz were laid out on the shabby coffee table. Two school armchairs (cushions plumped) had been angled toward each other nearby. Strains of soft jazz—a melody Tally had heard before but whose name she didn't know—were playing in the background.

Something about the setup made Tally's tummy flutter. Her

eyes darted from the coffee table to Mr. Logan. The teacher hadn't even looked up yet. She could still bolt, if she wanted to. She could always come up with some excuse . . .

"Natalya!"

Too late.

"Is it half past six already? Come on in. I'm just finishing something up. Have a seat and get out your books; we'll start in a moment."

Tally's stomach calmed as she heard Mr. Logan's cheerful, businesslike tone. For god's sake, she was such a fool to have been nervous. It wasn't like this was a *date*; it was just a friendly tutorial to encourage a promising student. And Mr. Logan probably drank wine and listened to jazz all by himself every night. Right?

"Right. Ready." Shutting his clunky old PC laptop, the teacher hauled himself from his seat and stretched his arms above his head. His triceps strained against his green cotton sweater and its hem skimmed above his belt to expose a flash of bare torso. "That feels good. Sorry to keep you waiting, Natalya, I was just finalizing the plans for Dublin. Can you believe we're going in two and a half weeks?"

"No way! It's so soon, I can't wait." Tally clapped her hands to show how much she meant it. The literary trip to Dublin that Mr. Logan was leading was going to be the highlight of her term. Ever since she'd first signed up for it, she'd been envisioning the romantic weekend they'd spend in the city, curtained in mist, hurrying from pub to pub and monument to monument, bundled in cozy scarves. Who cared if other students were going to be there too? They were just extras. Tally's dreams starred her and Mr. Logan alone.

He smiled. "Nice enthusiasm. I've just booked us all rooms at my favorite little B&B, right next to the river so you can practically see the boats sailing by. You girls will love it, Miss Baskin and I are sure."

"Miss Baskin?" Tally pouted petulantly. What did the stupid art teacher have to do with anything? Surely Mr. Logan hadn't invited her along too? Surely there wasn't something . . . between them? "Since when is *she* coming?"

Mr. Logan chuckled. "She's always been part of the plan. You don't think St. Cecilia's would let me chaperone you all by myself, do you? There'd be far too much room for scandal."

Tally caught her breath. Scandal. Yes. Exactly!

"Besides, Miss Baskin will be an asset—she knows lots about Irish art. Well, I know a little too, naturally. My mother's Irish. I've mentioned that, right?"

"No," Tally said. Mr. Logan had never mentioned family before. "Where's she from?"

"Cork. Which means you and I have something in common."

"Ummm, okay. Except my mum's *not* from Cork."

"Yes, but she *is* from Moscow. Which means we're both half from somewhere else. We're both strangers in a strange land."

"I'm not a stranger," said Tally, offended. "I've got loads of friends."

"Of course you do. You're a popular girl. That's not what I

meant. I meant there's something *other* about you. Something special—poetic—that makes you stand out. In my opinion, all great people, all people who achieve exceptional things, are different like that."

Tally breathed deeply. Some kinds of flattery she was used to—bored to death of, in fact. Drunk boys at parties telling her she was hot. Desperate mates like George Demetrios feeling her up when he thought she was too pissed to notice. But this was something else entirely. Mr. Logan was so kind, so sincere, so authoritative. As he settled into the next chair, her eyes roved over his face, trying to take in as much as they could without betraying her obsession. She lingered over his longish, unkempt hair, his soft mouth, the small cleft in his chin.

"Wine?" He was holding up the bottle.

"God, yeah." Tally stuck out her glass, still lost in her reverie. Then she blinked. "I didn't—I'm not a wino or anything . . ."

"Oh, I know what you are." Mr. Logan grinned. "I know what you boarding school girls get up to." Deftly, he untwirled the seal over the cork. "Not that I blame you, being locked up in this place all the time. Never getting out. Never getting to see your boyfriend."

Boyfriend? "What? I don't have a boyfriend."

"Please." Mr. Logan was concentrating on pouring. "I don't believe it. A beautiful, clever girl like you? I'm sure you have them queuing up."

"Why?" Tally retorted. "Have you got a girlfriend?"

Mr. Logan chuckled and wagged his finger. "Ah, young lady, now that's a bit personal, isn't it?"

Tally bit her lip. This wasn't how the conversation was supposed to go. She contemplated her wine, wishing she was as good as Alice in these situations. Alice had this way of controlling herself, of hiding how she really felt. But Tally had always been terrible at that.

"Sorry," she said. "I didn't mean to be rude. But I thought since you asked me . . ."

"No need to apologize. Let's just say I'm keeping my options open. Sometimes, love crops up in the most unexpected places. Don't you think?" Mr. Logan picked up his copy of *The Portrait of a Lady* and cleared his throat. "Ahem. I'm getting carried away. What do you think this novel's about?"

"Oh. Ummm . . . Well . . ." Her heart pounding, Tally turned over her book, hoping the back cover might offer some clue. The truth was, she hadn't even cracked the thing open. They weren't due to start it in class till after half term.

"No, no, no." Mr. Logan slid the volume from her fingers. "That's not the way we do things now. At advanced level, we think for ourselves. Let me help." He took a sip of wine. "This book is about a beautiful, adventurous, inexperienced girl from a foreign country who has no one to guide her." He looked at Tally, and his eyes seemed to flash.

The blood rushed to Tally's cheeks—but when she tried to meet his gaze again, he'd turned away.

"The heroine follows her heart and her destiny across

Europe. Eventually, she becomes a woman, manipulated by the older, cleverer, and craftier people around her. Tell me,"—Mr. Logan's eyes were on hers again—"what do you think of that?"

"I think . . ." Tally rubbed her hands over her skirt, disoriented. "I think . . . I think you should stop right there before you ruin the ending," she finished flirtatiously.

"Oh, but books are about more than just their endings," Mr. Logan said, his eyes still intent on hers. "The best part is usually how you *get* to the end. Exactly like certain . . . other things in life."

Tally felt her heartbeat quicken. Was Mr. Logan talking about what she thought he was talking about? All she could see was that passionate fire reignite in his eyes—and then it died down just as quickly as before.

Tally blinked. Maybe she was imagining things. Maybe she was just seeing what she wanted to see. But how was she ever supposed to find out?

Her fingers trembling, she turned to the first page of the book.

CHAPTER ELEVEN

Hurry up, they'll drench us!" Alice yelped as a car roared past along the road to Hasted, its wheels skimming a giant puddle. She leaped onto the muddy grass embankment, clamped one hand over her houndstooth-patterned pageboy cap, and ducked through a wire fence into the field beyond. Tally skidded in her wake.

It was Saturday, and it was drizzling. A low cloud bank clogged the sky. Fat raindrops beat fallen leaves into the grass. Normally on an afternoon like this, Alice and Tally would have been snuggled in their entertaining nook, watching DVDs on one of their laptops or (if they were feeling guilty) getting a head start on the weekend's home-work. Alice might even have been forcing herself to practice the flute, one of her most reviled activities ever. She'd been taking lessons since she was eleven, and her parents were insisting that she keep at it until she graduated—despite the fact that she was about as musical as a stone.

Today, however, the thought of staying at school had been unbearable. Half term was still three whole weeks away, and time seemed to be sagging like someone's old mattress. Short of slogging up to London on the train, there was only one thing for it—to wrap up in jackets and scarves, take advantage of the junior class privilege of being allowed out on weekends, and brave the mile-and-a-half walk into town. Hasted was a few thousand degrees short of thrilling, but at least it had a Top Shop. And two or three acceptable boutiques. Oh, and Estelle's Café, where the antique armchairs and decadent hot chocolate with marshmallows could almost make you forget about lessons and homework and exams altogether.

"Shiiit!" Tally squealed as a gust of rain lashed the field and rattled through the trees. She scurried under the canopy of an oak. "The weather's out to get us. Let's stop here and have a cig, Al. It can't carry on like this for long."

"It better fucking not," groaned Alice, shivering inside her leather jacket. She pulled two cigarettes from her Prada pouch bag, handed one to Tally, lit one for herself, and took a thoughtful drag, frowning up at the oak's rust-red crown. All week, ever since Monday, when Sonia had come bursting into her room, Alice's mind had been spinning and spinning back to the same old topic like a hyperactive homing pigeon. She couldn't deal with it anymore.

"Hey, Tals."

"Yeah?"

"Well . . ." Alice took another drag of her cigarette. Things always seemed more philosophical if you said them while you were smoking. "Do you think you can tell just by looking at someone how . . . experienced they are?"

"Experienced? What, you mean with sex?"

"Dunno," Alice shrugged, in a tone implying that if Tally wanted to talk about sex, Alice wasn't one to stop her. "I guess."

"Of course you can!" Tally burst out. Ever since she'd lost her virginity to a hot Frenchman last year, she'd considered herself a bit of an expert on this topic. "People who've had sex get a certain look in their eye. It's like, the *eye of knowledge*. They've been let into one of the secrets of life, because you have no idea what it feels like till you've done it." She giggled. "Why?"

Alice tapped the ash off her cigarette. "No reason. Just curious."

Tally scrutinized her friend. Typical Alice, being all closed about how she felt. Not that you could blame the girl—anyone who met her mum or dad would think she was an open book in comparison.

Suddenly, Tally clamped her hand over her mouth. "Oh my god, babe. I didn't mean *you* by the way—people would never be able to tell *you're* a virgin. You're, like, cool."

"Excuse me? Of course I'm cool! What's wrong with being a virgin? Just because I want to wait till I'm ready doesn't mean I'm a loser."

"Of course, no way," Tally jumped in hurriedly. "I just meant that you know loads of boys, that's all. You're not like those retards who still care about pony club and have no social life. You went out with Tristan, and he's, like, the hottest guy at Hasted House."

Alice flinched at the sound of Tristan's name.

"Babe, are you all right?"

"Fine." Stamping out her cigarette, Alice shoved her hands in her pockets and set off at a ridiculously fast pace. Tally trotted to catch up, her brown boots squelching in the mud, her yellow Pucci scarf (the one she'd stolen from her mother) flowing out behind her.

"Shit, babe, are you still sad about T?"

Alice wiped a speck of rain from her cheek and said nothing.

"Awww, hon, why didn't you say anything? Right. We've got to sort this out. If you want to get over him, there's only one thing to do."

Alice stopped and faced Tally full on. "But I don't want to get over him, that's the thing. I want to get him *back*."

"Oh." Tally's forehead furrowed, but only for a second. "Well, in that case there's still only one thing to do. The exact *same* thing, in fact." She slipped her arm through Alice's. "Text Boy."

"Boy? That's useless. Don't you mean Tristan?"

"No way! Come on, Al, you're being way dense. First of all, if you see Boy and snog him again, it'll give you such a confidence boost. And confidence is attractive. Any magazine'll tell you that. Second of all, it'll make T jealous. It's a classic move—he'll totally realize how much he wants you."

"Hmmm." Alice nodded slowly. That did seem obvious—why on earth hadn't she thought of it herself?

"And there's more." Tally smiled slyly. "Maybe with Boy, you'll finally feel ready to give it up. I bet he knows *exactly* what he's doing in bed. I mean, he's practically nineteen."

"Tals, shut up!" Alice giggled. "Okay, we're doing it. Help me draft a text." She slipped her iPhone from its special pouch in her bag—it was so helpful when everything had its proper place—and started typing.

"Give us a look." Tally strained to see the screen. "What've you got so far?"

"Hey, Boy," Alice read in a sultry voice. *"Cool to meet you Sat night. Hope you had a nice time—"*

"No, no, no! That sounds, like, totally insecure. Of course he had a nice time—he snogged you, didn't he? Make it flirty!"

"Okay. *Hey, Boy, it's Alice. Cool to meet you Sat night* . . . Ummm . . . *I'd love to go out sometime, if you feel like distracting me from school."*

"Oooh, I like it, I like it!" Tally bounced up and down. "But wait, put this." She snatched the phone and added . . . *;-)* after the last words, then pressed send.

"Oh my god!" Alice shrieked. "I can't believe you just did that. The wink sounds totally suggestive. He's gonna think I'm well up for it!"

"Well, you are, aren't you?" Tally cackled. "Sex fiend."

"Look who's bloody well talking!"

Still laughing, the girls passed through the stile at the end of the field and emerged onto the last sliver of road into

Hasted. The rain was letting up, and a fresher breeze was blowing dry the tendrils of Alice's hair. They rounded the side of a pub and swung into an alley just off the main street.

"Boy and Alice, sitting in a tree," Tally sang mockingly. Her words ricocheted off the sandstone buildings rising from the old, uneven pavement.

"Quiet!" Alice rammed into her, cracking up all over again.

Then suddenly, the grin on her face froze. A familiar figure was crossing the road at the end of the alleyway, his hair sticking out in all directions, his striped scarf wound at least ten times round his neck. Alice stumbled as she tried to drag Tally backward into the shadows.

But it was too late: He'd seen her.

CHAPTER TWELVE

*G*et a move on, T," prodded Jasper von Holstadt, an impatient look fretting his lean, handsome face. Tristan had stopped short in the middle of the road and was peering down an alleyway like a stray dog. "I thought we were going to the pub."

"Yeah, I'm fucking thirsty," announced Seb, drawing up next to them. His fingers wandered toward the miniature whiskey flask that he kept in his back pocket and carried with him everywhere. It had been a sixteenth-birthday present from his father and was monogrammed with his initials, *SWPO.* Sebastian Winston Patrick Ogilvy. "What are you staring at, anyway?" Seb squinted into the shadowy passage, his blond hair tumbling into his eyes. "Oh, hang on a sec. Is that . . . ?"

"Oy, Alice!" Jasper interrupted. "Tally! All right. Come out here!"

"Hey, boys!" Tally waved, seizing Alice's hand and pulling her toward the open street.

"Stop," Alice hissed, tugging free. "There's no way I'm going out there. I look like a drowned rat."

"Gosh." Tally raised her eyebrows. "What a good point. You're so right, you should definitely stay here. I mean, if you want T back, the last thing you should do is actually *talk* to him."

Alice rolled her eyes. "Okay, I get it. You win. But *wait*." Nervously, she straightened her cap. "Makeup check! How's my mascara? It's run all over my face, hasn't it? Oh no, it has, give me your mirror!"

"Babe. Chill. Take a deep breath." Tally demonstrated. "You're looking hot. Absolutely top-notch. Come on." She tugged Alice toward the brightness of the street, where Jasper sauntered forward to kiss them hello.

"Girls! Good to see you," he exclaimed. "Bloody relief, too. I was just getting bored of this lot."

"Not as bored as we are of you," Tristan shot back. "Hi, Tals. Umm, hey." He turned to Alice, attempting to catch her eye. "How are you?"

Not that he needed to ask. It was pretty obvious how Alice was. Her eyes sparkled in the brisk air. Her angular cheeks shone pink from the rain and from the walk across the fields. A few droplets of moisture glistened on her olive skin. Alice's hair was gathered up under her cap, its luster hidden except for a few loose strands drifting around her face. She reminded

Tristan of a character out of Shakespeare—one of those heroines who run away to the woods disguised as a boy, but still look just as radiant underneath. He shoved his hands in his pockets.

"Hello, you," Alice smiled.

Tristan glowed with pleasure—he hadn't heard her voice this friendly in ages. He moved forward to kiss her cheek.

"I just love this new trench coat you're wearing," Alice trilled.

T stopped short. He wasn't wearing a trench. He didn't even own one. He followed the movement of Alice's hand, and saw her stroke Seb's lapel. Jealousy and embarrassment twisted inside him. Alice hadn't been saying hello to him at all. She hadn't even acknowledged his presence.

"Where are you boys off to, then?" came Alice's voice again, sounding very far away. "Hang on, let me guess: the pub."

"Touché." Jasper grinned. "Someone knows us too well. Can't blame us, though. What else is there to do in this ghastly weather but drink?"

"Absolutely fuck-all," Seb said, kicking his foot in the direction of the Four Horsemen, their crew's favorite afternoon boozing spot. "Want to come along?"

Tally started to nod. "Def—"

"No!" Alice cut in. "I mean, we'd love to, of course, but I'm afraid we can't. Tals and I have the most amazing afternoon planned. *So* indulgent." She gave a conspiratorial giggle and winked at Tally, her long eyelashes fluttering against her cheeks.

Tally stared at her.

"Babe!" Alice prodded. "Isn't that right?"

"Oh! Oh, yeah. Totally." Suddenly, Tally started nodding vigorously. "Indulgent, yeah. Can't wait. We're doing the coolest stuff."

"Really? Like what?" T knew his voice had fallen like a rock among the others' airy banter, but he didn't care. Alice hadn't looked at him once, and he was determined to get some kind of response.

She giggled again, apparently still deaf to him. "Stop looking at us like that, Jasper," she ordered. "You can't come. No boys allowed."

"I seeee. Is that so?" With a mock grimace, Jasper clamped his arm round Alice's shoulders. "I'm going to have to keep you prisoner, then."

She squealed playfully. "Let me go!"

"Tell me all your secrets first." He pulled her pageboy cap low over her eyes and marched her off down the pavement, trailed by Tally and Seb.

Alice could feel Tristan's eyes on her back. She drew a little closer to Jasper, swinging her narrow hips against his, timing her footsteps to his rhythm. This was ideal—and not only because of T: It was the perfect chance to take care of some other business too. She poked Jas in the ribs.

"You naughty boy. I know all about your little game."

"Huh?"

"Oh yes, I've been hearing things about you. Dylan's been giving me some pretty juicy gossip."

"Has she?" Jasper's voice was surprised. "Since when are you two friends?"

"Since always!" Alice sounded offended that he could even ask such a thing. "Oh my god, Dill and I are really close. She's absolutely awesome."

"What, even though you both went out with the same guy? I thought women, like, hated that shit."

"Only some women." Alice shrugged. This was annoying: *She* was meant to be the one asking the questions. Boys were so dense. "Anyway. Dill told me you two might be going on a date."

"Might be?" Jasper released her shoulders. "What's this about 'might'? We definitely are. Next Tuesday night. She's going to sneak out and meet me. I'm thinking of taking her to the Palms."

"The *Palms*?" Alice recoiled at the name of Hasted's swankiest bar. "Gosh. Okay . . ."

"What? What's wrong with that?"

"Oh, nothing, nothing. It's just . . . well, the Palms is a bit *refined*. That's not exactly Dylan's style, is it?"

"Isn't it?" Jasper raised his eyebrows.

"Don't get me wrong, I'm sure she wouldn't hate you or anything if you took her there. But if I were you, I'd show some proper thought. I'd take her somewhere a bit more . . . you know, down and dirty." Alice winked.

"What on earth are you getting at?"

Alice let out a peal of silvery laughter. She was sure T could hear it. "You mean you really don't know? I'm talking about you acting macho, silly! Dylan's totally into that stuff."

"She is?"

"Of course! She can't stand the whole cheesy, fake gentleman thing—she likes guys to be superforward. About sex and stuff, I mean. She'll play games and pretend she doesn't, but that's the whole fun of it." Alice dropped her voice. "According to her, that's why things didn't work out with Tristan." She was practically whispering now. "She told me he was too . . . tame."

Jasper's eyes had lit up like those of a hunter preparing to trap its prey. "So . . . good old Dylan." He stroked his designer stubble. "She's a secret sex kitten, is she?"

"Exactly. You just have to coax it out."

"That I can do. Damn, thanks, Al. I owe you one."

Alice was about to agree that yes, he most certainly did, when suddenly her phone pinged. She whipped it out.

"No way, it's from him! Look!" As she spun round to show the phone to Tally, Alice glimpsed Tristan, only a few steps behind.

Perfect. The timing of Boy's reply couldn't have been sweeter if she'd planned it.

"Shiiit!" Tally broke away from Seb. "What does it say?"

"Read, read!"

"Next Saturday! Fuck, Ali, he's gonna drive up and collect you from school? I'll bet he takes you to London. Ooh, maybe you'll go to that supercool Japanese place that just opened in Mayfair!"

"Can you imagine? This is So. Exciting." Alice squeezed Tally's arm.

Tristan was staring at her from behind; she could sense it.

"Who's that message from?" his voice suddenly broke in.

Alice turned slowly and, for the first time that afternoon, forced herself to meet T's eyes. They looked sullen—and maybe, possibly, a tad anxious, too?

"Oh, no one." With an effort, she kept her voice casual. "Just this guy I met at the gig on Saturday night. Funny, I hardly saw you there at all; I hope you had fun. Anyway, his name is Boy."

T tried to open his mouth. This was his cue: If he was going to deliver his warning, it should be now.

But no words came. What was going on? Maybe he was too proud. Maybe he'd realized how fucking petty anything he tried to say would sound.

Tristan scuffed his right sneaker against the pavement. The fact was, in the sixteen years he'd been friends with Alice, he'd seen her in pretty much every situation under the sun: dancing at dawn, her fist clutching a bottle of champagne; snoring in bed, her fingers curling round an old soft toy; shivering on a rock ledge, her teeth chattering with fear before she plunged into the sea.

In other words, anything there was to know about Alice Rochester, Tristan had thought he already knew. How bizarre then, that no one had ever seemed as mysterious, as unfathomable, as she did now.

CHAPTER THIRTEEN

*S*weetie, you were magnificent!" Tally crowed,
skipping down the pavement. She and Alice
had ditched the boys at the Four Horsemen and
were headed toward Estelle's Café for some much needed
debriefing. "You handled T like he was your dog or something.
Soon you'll have him eating out of your hand!"

"Well, I don't know about *that*." Alice straightened the
collar of her leather bomber jacket so that it stuck straight up
and grazed her cheekbones. She didn't agree out loud—only
tacky, insecure people paid themselves compliments—but it
was obvious she'd played everything just right. "Seriously, Tals,
it was your advice that did it," she offered magnanimously. "If
it wasn't for you, I might still be cowering down that alleyway."

"True, true. Clever me, in that case." Tally tossed her hair
theatrically. "Oooh, hang on—let's go in there!" She gestured
across the narrow street.

"Where?" The only thing Alice could see was a sign for a

rickety hardware store called Handy Andy's. "What, do you need a new power drill or something? A new screwdriver for your collection?"

"No, duh. I'm talking about the bookshop. There." Tally pointed. Next to Handy Andy's—so small and dingy that it wasn't even worth noticing—was a shopfront piled with ratty books.

"Yeah, right!" Alice cracked up. "Good one! Since when do *you* give a shit about bookshops?"

Tally froze, looking offended. "Excuse me, what are you implying? That I'm stupid or something? I'm not illiterate— I like to read just as much as anyone else." She turned and stalked across the road.

Alice gaped after her.

"Tals! Wait!" she called, breaking into a jog. "That's not what I meant."

"Oh, yeah? What did you mean?"

"Just . . . just that I'm really happy you've found a new interest. I didn't know about it, that's all."

Tally glared for a second before her expression softened. Alice was always making snap judgments about people and saying harsh things without realizing their effect—that was simply something you had to accept as her friend. But still, her reaction had stung. Tally frowned, pushing a stray tendril of hair behind her ear. If even Alice, her best mate, made fun of her for trying to be intellectual, then what must everyone else think? Did all their friends see her as just another dumb, party-girl blonde? In fact, was there only one person in the world who knew she had more to offer than that?

"Whatever." Tally shook her head. "Forget about it. Let's go in."

She gave the shop door a shove. A tiny bell tinkled as she passed the threshold, and a musty smell filled her nostrils. It was the smell of paper crumbling after decades of damp, of leather and glue bindings flaking and evaporating into the air. Tally wiped her feet on the worn brown mat. Dust coated the windows, smothering the daylight. Wooden bookcases, dozens of them, jutted out and stretched to the ceiling—but instead of being crowded with literature, their shelves held only small clusters of books separated by random gaps. *Like mouths with teeth missing*, Tally thought. It was weird how neglected the shop looked. It seemed like no one had bought or sold anything here in years.

"Welcome."

Tally jumped at the disembodied voice. She squinted round. In the shadows at the back of the shop, she finally managed to discern a tiny, gray-haired woman sitting at a desk, her pen poised above a newspaper crossword as if she'd been interrupted mid-clue.

"Come in," the woman said. "Are you searching for anything special?"

"Oh, no." Tally shook her head. "Just browsing, thanks. You've got a lovely shop here."

"That's very kind, my dear. Browse away, browse away. That's what rainy Saturdays are for."

Alice, attempting to warm her hands on the stone-cold radiator, gave a small snort. What a moronic conversation. This was the opposite of a lovely shop, and moping around it was certainly not what rainy Saturdays were for. Rainy Saturdays were for shopping. Or for going to the cinema. Or for getting manicures. Or, more to the point, for drinking mugs of hot chocolate at Estelle's. With a look of annoyance, she watched Tally disappear into a side room and heard her start sliding things off the shelves. This was ridiculous. Personally, Alice had no intention of venturing any farther into this creepy den.

"Hey, Tals?" she called.

"In here!"

Behind the wall, Tally trailed her eyes along a row of ancient, leather-bound books. It was the most bizarre collection she'd ever seen—every volume seemed chock-full of useless, outdated information. *Insects of East Anglia*. Great. What a thrilling read. *A Dictionary of Wild Berries. The Dog-Walker's Companion. How to Polish Silver.*

Tally ran her fingers over their spines. Mr. Logan would love this place: It was just the kind of Hasted nook he'd discover and spend hours exploring. She shut her eyes, imagining him touching these very same books, taking them down and caressing their worn-out pages. Just wait till she mentioned it to him at their next tutorial: He'd be so impressed she'd found it all by herself. Maybe, soon, they could even come here together.

Suddenly, the title of a large, ornate volume jumped out at Tally. *Dublin Secrets*, said the swirly, old-fashioned letters. She reached up for the book and flipped through, skimming the author's chapter-by-chapter descriptions of his favorite spots in the city. He kept going off on rants, reminiscing and telling anecdotes and dropping in literary quotations. He'd adorned page after page with black-and-white photos of foggy streets and misty bridges—places that would be just perfect for a stolen, forbidden kiss. Tally's fingers tightened over the book. Turning to the front cover, she found the price scribbled in pencil on the inside: £18. How much was in her wallet? Damn. Thanks to the boys, she'd completely forgotten to get cash out earlier on—

"Tally!" Alice snapped, clattering through the doorway. "What's happening? Let's go."

"Go? Already?" Tally pouted. "But this place is amazing! It's like our own private lair."

"Our own private shit hole, you mean. Come on, this isn't even a real bookshop—I swear it's that freaky old lady's house."

"But look what I found." Tally held out *Dublin Secrets*. "Have a read, it's so cool."

"You've got to be joking. I'm not touching that smelly pile of mold. Put it back, let's get out of here." Alice swept away through the opening, hoping to hear Tally's footsteps following her. But all she heard was a light rustling of material. At least ten seconds went by.

What the hell was taking so long?

"Hurry *up*, Tals! I'm hungry."

"Me too. Yeah, yeah. Coming."

At long last, Tally emerged. She shot Alice a smile and pulled her jacket tightly round her chest. "Let's go."

They reached the door, and Tally shot out her hand to turn the knob. She'd got halfway over the threshold when—

"Young lady!" a voice rang out from the back. "Stop right there."

Tally stiffened.

Alice rolled her eyes. "For fuck's sake, just keep going. Of course she doesn't want us to leave—we were, like, her only customers in a hundred years."

But the woman was glaring holes into Tally over the top of her spectacles. Deliberately, she rose. "I trust you were planning to pay for that book hidden in your jacket," she enunciated.

A snicker escaped from Alice. "What the fuck?" she whispered in Tally's ear. "I told you this place was a freak show. Tell the old bat she can't go round accusing innocent people. Tell her we'll lodge a complaint about her!"

Tally said nothing. It was only then that Alice noticed the stark pallor of her face—and the fact that she was actually drifting in the direction of the desk.

"Hello? Tals, you okay? What's going on? Just set her straight and let's split."

"That's right, girl," the woman nodded as Tally continued to approach. "Just put it right here in front of me and you can go. I won't make a fuss."

"How *dare* you talk to her like that?"Alice began. "Do you know who we—"

And then she stopped. Openmouthed, she watched as Tally unzipped her jacket and slid out a book—the same book she'd tried to show Alice in the side room five minutes before.

"Here," Tally mumbled, laying it down on the desk. "I'm really sorry. I . . . I forgot I was holding it. Um, yeah, mistake." She turned bright red.

The old woman's lips were now as thin as a piece of string.

"Leave!" she suddenly screeched. "Get out of my shop."

"B-but I—"

"And never set foot in here again!"

"—didn't mean—" Tally tried to speak, but the rest of the syllables stuck in her throat. She turned on her heel and bolted past the looming bookshelves, past the dirty windows, into the street.

Alice emerged a split second later.

"Wow." Tally gave a sheepish grin. "Didn't mean for that to happen. Oops."

"Oops?" Alice was gawking at her. "*Oops?* You just fucking stole something! You're not, like, poor. What the hell were you thinking?"

"Babe, chill!" Tally widened her eyes. "I only wanted that book, I just didn't have any cash. I didn't think she'd miss it. God, how embarrassing that she saw!"

"Embarrassing?" Alice spat. "Don't you mean, like, totally shameful? Stealing's immoral, you know. You can't just *take* things."

"Come on, Al, get off your high horse. You and I stole chocolate bars from Waitrose that time, remember?"

"That was three years ago! And it was Waitrose! I wouldn't steal from some poor old granny's secondhand shop that she probably slaves her heart out for."

Tally frowned and started gnawing on her thumbnail. "Shit, Al, it's not that bad. You're making me sound like a monster."

"Stupid book. What did you even want it for?" Alice sniffed.

"Well . . . for . . ."—Tally blushed—"Mr. Logan. As a present. His mum's Irish, you know. He loves old leather-bound books, they're all over his office."

"How do you know what's all over his office?" Alice asked suspiciously. Tally had never mentioned seeing the place.

"Oh . . ." Tally scuffed the ground. She'd purposely kept her tutorials a secret from Alice—all signs pointed to the fact that her friend wouldn't approve, and besides, there were so few things you could do at boarding school that were no one's business but your own.

"He told me," Tally fibbed. "When I bumped into him on my way to the Tuck In the other day. He said the only thing he cared about having in his office was his beloved old book collection."

Alice narrowed her eyes. Maybe the story sounded feasible—but she wasn't satisfied. Her memory flashed back to last Saturday night, when Tally had nicked that arty girl's rose pin off the pavement—taken it without a second thought. First that, now this. Like everyone, Tally had a thousand faults. She was a mess, she was a flirt, she was a liability—but until now there was one thing she had never been: a thief.

Alice dug her nails into her palms. Several times in the weeks since Mr. Logan had shown up, she'd felt alienated from her best friend, like she hardly knew Tally at all. Now the reason why was obvious: Mr. Logan was corrupting her. Tally had already resorted to stealing on his behalf. What next?

CHAPTER FOURTEEN

"Girl I passed you on the street.
You saw me,
Wouldn't meet my eyes.
All those things you told me—
Tell me now they weren't lies.

Once you were my best friend but
Your secrets
Set my soul on fire.
Friend, what are you hiding?
Don't pretend you're not a liar.

It's true
I think about you
In my room alone.
You're chewing up my heart
Like a rottweiler chews a bone—"

"Whoa, T, hold it!" Seb burst out, interrupting Tristan's rendition of "Secrets and Liars," the new song he'd written for the Paper Bandits. "What's up with the bloody rottweiler in the chorus? Bit psycho, don't you think? Does he have to be in there?"

"All right, all right, calm down." Tristan clamped a hand over his guitar strings, looking put out. "I was only trying to make it gritty, mate, you know? Keep it real." He ran his fingers though his tousled hair, racking his brain for alternative lyrics.

It was six thirty on Sunday evening and as usual, T, Seb, and Rando were in the middle of a jam session in one of Hasted House's practice rooms. Outside the wind was creaking through the trees, but in here everything was toasty and warm. That was because the music block was a new building, which meant it had wall-to-wall carpeting and central heating that actually worked, unlike the drafty stone piles that made up the old parts of school. Of course, those historic bits were what kept money flowing into the Hasted House coffers. Nouveau riche parents, not to mention loaded foreign ones, were complete suckers for the air of English romance in the echoing chambers and vaulted ceilings, the covered porticos and wrought-iron gateways. But if any of them actually had to try living here, Tristan suspected, they'd get over that crap pretty fast.

"Right!" He snapped up his head, pulling his guitar into position. "I've got it. Listen to this."

Shutting his eyes, he stroked his fingers over the strings. "Mmmm," he hummed:

"It's true
I think about you
When I'm in my room.
Suffocating, like a pharaoh
Sealed in my tomb."

Tristan paused expectantly as the music died away.

"Ummm, yeah." Seb blinked, putting on the kind of voice you might use to talk to a crazy person. "That's really poetic, T. But maybe you should try writing something a bit more . . . upbeat?"

Tristan stared at him.

"I mean, I think your songs are great and everything, I really do," Seb rushed on. "It's just that they're all about . . . you know, how fucking miserable love is. It's like, don't people deserve a fucking break?"

"No, they don't!" Tristan blurted out before he could stop himself. "People deserve the truth. And the truth is, love *is* miserable. It's full of deception and heartache. And people who you thought were your friends suddenly turning out to be hiding things in the most devious ways." He jumped up and walked to the window. *Mate, get a grip.* Did he really want to be the kind of guy who spilled his guts to everyone? That was so uncool. Peering through the windowpane, T strained to see past the glaring reflection of the practice room into the blackness farther off. He'd tried to put Alice out of his mind yesterday afternoon—and again last night, and again today—but it was impossible. He couldn't forget the funny feeling he'd had outside the pub in Hasted as she'd disappeared down the street. A strange sense of loss had bitten him, of longing, as if he were standing on the shore of an ocean, watching a ship sail away without him on board.

"Oy, T," Seb called from the other side of the room, "pay attention! We haven't got all night." He appealed to Rando. "Help me out here. Tell T we should come up with some catchy, happy love songs. Simple stuff. Just one or two."

Rando shrugged from his perch at the drum kit. "Sorry, Ogilvy, but I'm siding with T on this. When it comes to romance, you've got no idea what you're talking about."

"*Excuse* me?"

"Yeah, you only think love's simple because you've never *been* in love. It's your own fault. Why don't you ever make a move on anyone?"

Seb's pale face, already the color of talcum powder, turned a shade paler. He forced a smile. "*Please.* Don't be ridiculous," he scoffed, reaching into his jeans pocket for his whiskey flask. "You don't exactly have a girlfriend either, do you, Casanova? When's the last time you ever made a move?"

He took a swig, wishing he'd kept his mouth shut about bloody love songs. It always got uncomfortable when the conversation veered toward women, and now he'd had to come up with a nasty response like that.

Seb felt T looking at him. "Want some?" He thrust out the flask.

Tristan shook his head, scrutinizing his friend's face. Seb had always been a drinker, but lately, T had noticed, he seemed to be taking it to the next level, constantly glugging from that Jameson supply in his pocket and knocking back bottle after bottle of the wine they kept in their room. It couldn't be healthy. Not that T was the booze police or anything, but he was allowed to worry about his friend—especially since nobody else seemed to bother. Seb's mother had moved to Scotland when he was six years old and had barely been heard from since. His father, Sir Preston Ogilvy, was a trust-funder who'd inherited family money. He traveled the world buying expensive wines and sending them back to the cellar of his vast house in Chelsea, where Seb rattled about alone during the school holidays, throwing mad parties and swilling his father's drink and smoking his cigars, and taking himself off to art galleries in Soho and vintage films at the ICA.

Such behavior explained why most of their crew thought of Seb Ogilvy as completely independent, completely self-contained. Tristan knew he was one of the only people who suspected how lonely his friend was at heart. He was closer to Seb than anyone else: The two of them had been inseparable ever since their first year, when T had been drawn to Seb's wry, observational manner and the hilarious wild streak underneath it. Oh, and the fact that when you talked to him, you felt like you were talking to the most decent, most loyal person in the world.

He watched Seb take another slosh of booze and stow

the flask in his pocket. As soon as he could find a moment, Tristan promised himself, he'd have a word with his friend. But not now: best to wait and catch him on his own.

"Speaking of girlfriends,"—T changed the subject, turning to Rando—"how's it going with you and Tally?"

"Oh." Rando fiddled with his sheet music, straightening the pages on their stand even though they were perfectly straight already. "Yeah, fine. I saw her at the gig in Formica—god, she looked stunning." His face went a bit glum. "I just don't see her enough. Not ideal."

Tristan rolled his eyes. "Well, there's an easy way to fix that, you dope. Ask her out."

"No way! What are you, an idiot? I can't just do that."

"Why on earth not?"

"Because . . . because you've got to be delicate about this stuff. We're in the same social group and everything. Imagine if I text her—women can't keep secrets! She'll tell all her giggly girlie friends and show them my message and soon it'll be, like, the biggest joke at St. Cecilia's." Rando shuddered. "Anyway," he mumbled, "I already did ask her out."

"*What?*"

"Yeah, a few weeks ago. I texted her. She didn't reply."

"You dog!" Seb cried, slapping his hand across his bass guitar. "Now it comes out!"

Tristan shouted with laughter. "Mate, in that case I don't blame you for being cagey. I'd be cagey about a blatant brush-off like that as well!"

Seb shook his head in disbelief. "You mean she didn't reply at all? That is *harsh*."

"Oh, piss off, both of you." Rando scowled. He grabbed his drumsticks and chucked one at each of them.

"Ouch! No, but seriously," T relented, rubbing his arm where it had been hit, "maybe she didn't get the text. Plus, Tally's flaky. Honestly, if I were you, I'd try again."

"Yeah, go on, mate," Seb agreed. "It's not like you've got a crush on anyone else. What have you got to lose?"

Rando narrowed his eyes.

"No joke," Tristan urged. "We're not trying to make you look bad."

"No way."

Gradually, a hopeful smile nudged the corners of Rando's mouth. "Well, I'll think about it," he said. And maybe he would. After all, girls like Tally Abbott didn't come along every day.

CHAPTER FIFTEEN

arely batting an eyelid, Mimah elbowed her way through the screeching horde in the dining hall, past a cluster of eighth graders jammed three-deep round the coffee urns. After five years at St. Cecilia's, you got used to the teatime chaos. Every weekday afternoon, as soon as the end-of-lessons bell rang at four o'clock, the crush was on. Mobs of students swarmed into the Quad from all corners of the school, clattering along the portico outside the dining hall, through its arched doorway, toward the iced buns and loaves of white bread and industrial-size jars of Nutella, strawberry jam, and Marmite that the dinner ladies placed along the room's long, wooden tables. This was feeding time. Not to mention prime gossip time, when the day's best news was exchanged.

"Move it, move it, coming through!" Mimah barked.

"Piss off," someone retorted under their breath.

A short, chubby seventh grader shot Mimah a middle finger.

But for once in her life, Mimah didn't bother to retaliate. She was in too much of a hurry to reach the middle of the hall, where Alice, Tally, and Sonia would be clustered round their usual toaster. She had dirt to dish.

"Hey, girls," Mimah panted, finally standing up. "Fuck, I can't believe I'm out of breath."

"I can." Alice handed her a piece of toast. "It's because you gave up lacrosse at the beginning of term."

"Yeah," Sonia agreed, eyeing the toast enviously. She never ate anything at tea, especially now that they were going to Rome in just a few weeks—it would spoil her slim waistline, not to mention her salad-only diet. *If a rabbit wouldn't eat it, I won't eat it*: that was her mantra. If only rabbits ate toast.

"You've got to rejoin the team!" Alice went on. "How else is St. C's going to win against Malbury Hall this year?"

Malbury Hall, an elite school about an hour's drive away, was St. Cecilia's main rival for sports titles—as well as for the Hasted House boys. Mimah nodded noncommittally. She'd always been one of the most talented lax players at St. Cecilia's, but she'd quit the junior class sQuad a few weeks ago in a particularly rotten mood. She knew her absence was starting to take its toll, not only on the team's wins, but also on her own toned figure.

"I suppose you two have a point." She grabbed a tub of butter and set about spreading it on her toast. "But Miss Colin was pretty pissed off when I quit—I'll have to grovel to her if I want to be captain again."

"Captain?" Sonia objected. "You can't expect her to make you captain after you deserted everyone like that. You'll have to start at the bottom. That's democracy."

"Give it a rest, Sone." Alice rolled her eyes. "There's no democracy in sports—it's all about winning. Mimah's their star player—Colin would have to be a total moron not to make her captain again."

"Yeah, well Colin probably *is* a total moron." Sonia smirked. "I mean, she's a fucking gym teacher. Do you even need to go to college for that?"

"No." Tally tittered. "You just need a tracksuit and a butch haircut."

"And a name like Colin." Mimah grinned.

"OMG, we are *such* bitches!" Alice clapped her hands to her cheeks. "I love it!"

"Anyway," Mimah announced once the laughter had subsided, "listen up, people. I've got major gossip."

"Silence for the gossip!" Tally drummed her hands on the table.

"Heyyy, it's not about your dad again, is it?" Sonia was stirring her tea so hard that it sloshed into her saucer. "That was juicy."

Mimah glared at her. "Gee, thanks, Sone. Thanks for being so sensitive. Thanks for bringing that up again." She turned to Alice. "It's about Boy."

"What?" Alice halted her piece of toast halfway to her mouth. "What is it? Who told you?"

"My second cousins at St. Swithin's. Do you remember Alexandra? Well, she has this friend, and the friend's older sister's friend went out with Boy Stanley-Soames. For the whole of senior year."

"And?"

"Apparently he cheated on her. It's, like, the worst story ever."

"Shit." Sonia's eyes were popping out of her head.

"What happened?" asked Tally through a mouthful of iced bun.

"Well," Mimah began, "the girl was turning eighteen, and she decides to throw a house party. All her friends were there and everything. She's all dressed up and excited and in love. But suddenly, in the middle of the party, Boy just disappears. So she starts looking for him. She looks everywhere, all over the place, in the garden, in the kitchen, even in the basement. And then, finally, she finds him. Guess where he was?"

The other three shook their heads.

"In her bed. Shagging someone else."

"In her bed?" Sonia gasped. "What a bastard! She'll never be able to sleep there again. Jesus, Ali, stay away from him."

"For fuck's sake," Alice snapped. "As if I believe that rubbish."

"What do you mean?"

"People are always making up rumors that aren't true. Anyone as hot as Boy is bound to have a million stories flying round about him."

"But Mimah's cousin *knows* this girl," Sonia insisted. "It's a reliable source."

"Oh, yeah," Alice sneered. "Mimah's second cousin's friend's sister's dog's maggot. Sure, you can't get more reliable than that. I mean, for goodness' sake, Mimah, I thought you'd know better than to spread rumors. Remember when that story went round over the summer about you paying Seb to have sex with you? That wasn't true." She leaned in. "Was it?"

Everyone looked at Mimah, who threw down her toast.

"Of course not! God, are you people still talking about that? I mean, okay, fine, maybe I did offer to pay him, but—"

"Oh my *god*," gasped Alice.

"Are you a slut or something?" Sonia screeched.

"For fuck's sake, no. It was only a joke. Sort of. I mean, Seb never seems to fancy anyone, so I thought I'd give him a bit of encouragement."

"Financial encouragement." Tally grinned. "And did he take it?"

Mimah shook her head.

"Of course he didn't," Sonia sniffed. "That is so low-class. Just watch, I'll coax Seb Ogilvy into bed without any encouragement besides my natural appeal."

"What about your natural nose?" Mimah retorted. She'd fancied Seb since eighth grade, and still couldn't believe Sonia had claimed him for herself. But she left it at that—after all, she'd decided to put her feelings aside for the sake of the group.

"Anyway," Mimah continued. "This stuff about Boy—believe it or don't believe it. I don't care. All I know is, Alexandra insists it's true. She said it was, like, the most famous story at St. Swithin's and Boy's got a really nasty reputation all over the school."

"Well, that's probably because St. Swithin's girls are total sluts and they've all tried to sleep with him," Alice snapped, apparently forgetting that she was bad-mouthing several of Mimah's relations. "Anyway, Boy's been incredibly nice to me all week. His texts couldn't be more charming, actually, so I'm sure I don't know what you're talking about."

"Oh, wait, Boy's sending you charming texts?" Mimah widened her eyes in fake surprise. "Well then, that proves it—he *can't* be a womanizing dickhead, can he?"

Tally cleared her throat. "Umm, yeah, Al, what Mimah means is, isn't that the whole point? If Boy's a player, obviously he knows how to turn on the charm. How else would he seduce—"

"Oh my *god*." With an exasperated laugh, Alice thudded her mug on the wooden tabletop. "Could everyone please stop treating me like a moron? I think I know what I'm doing, okay?" She turned to Sonia. "Let's head back to Tudor. I've got to get a start on my French homework. Madame Celeste's assigned us an essay on *Candide*. Ugh." She paused. Then, without looking at Tally and Mimah, "Coming, you two?"

Mimah shook her head. "No, thanks. I think I might go for a run, actually."

"And I've got that History of Art lecture," Tally added. "Some curator from the National Gallery's coming to talk to us; Mr. Bianco says it's compulsory."

"Yeah, well," Alice sniffed. She still hadn't quite forgiven Tally for her stealing spree, and now Tally's patronizing speech had added insult to injury. "Try not to snore too loudly."

With that, she and Sonia wound their way through the emptying dining hall and set off across the Great Lawn, which was patterned with the trees' long shadows. Alice was very silent as they walked. So silent that, after a few failed attempts at conversation, Sonia took out her phone.

"Who are you texting?" Alice demanded.

"Who do you think? Seb!"

"Give me a break!" Alice cackled. "Don't you think it's time to give up? Didn't he stop replying, like, weeks ago?"

"No." Sonia looked hurt. "He replies to me . . . usually. Don't be a meanie, Al."

"Shhh!" They'd reached the beginning of Tudor House's first-floor corridor and Alice halted, pointing, a catlike grin on her face. A few meters away, the door to Sonia and Dylan's room was ajar and the tune of "You're The One That I Want" from *Grease* was echoing down the hallway.

"You have got to see this," Alice whispered, squinting through the crack. Dylan Taylor was standing in front of the full-length mirror, wearing a towel and striking poses as she piled her straw-colored hair on top of her head.

Sonia doubled over. "Could she be any lamer?"

"Hey, Dilly!" Alice cried, flinging open the door.

"Ohmygod," Dylan yelped. "Who's there?" Her towel half fell off as she made a dive for her iPod.

"Oops, sorry." Alice said. "Not interrupting, are we?"

Dylan glared, her cheeks burning fuchsia.

"Oh, good. Because we hear *someone* has a date with Jasper von Holstadt tonight, and we wouldn't want to hold you up. Where's he taking you, then?"

Dylan's eyebrows shot toward the ceiling. She should have known the details of her love life would fly round this gossip hive. Not that she cared: A date with Jasper could only raise her social profile. "For your information, I don't know. Jas wanted to make it a surprise."

"Oh, *Jas* did, did he?" Alice picked up the gold star pendant that Dylan had laid out and twisted it through her fingers. "Isn't that sweet. Well, in that case, I'm absolutely certain he'll do it. *Surprise* you, I mean."

She nodded to Sonia, who sloped after her out of the room.

No sooner had the two girls reached the hallway than they made a dash for Alice and Tally's lair, where they slammed the door and collapsed against it, shaking with laughter.

CHAPTER SIXTEEN

*S*o much for trying to warn her," groaned Mimah, as soon as Alice had disappeared from the dining hall. She slapped Nutella over her second slice of toast and set about spreading it with a vengeance. Neither she nor Tally bothered budging from their table, even though the dinner ladies were now circulating with trolleys, nudging girls aside as they attempted to clear things and set up for dinner. "I should have known she'd react badly. Alice is so damn stubborn."

"Tell me about it." Tally poured a stream of white sugar into her coffee. Alice's snippy treatment of her ever since Saturday afternoon at the bookshop had not escaped her notice, and it really wasn't fair. Not that she was about to let Mimah in on that little episode, of course. "It's like, Alice is an expert at telling everyone else what to do and how to do it, but if *you* try to give *her* advice, you're fucked."

"Agreed." Mimah cut her toast into two triangles and

chomped off the corner of one. "The thing is, though," she whispered, adopting a sympathetic-friend tone, "I'm seriously quite worried."

"What about?" Tally leaned in, her tone confidential too.

"About this whole Boy situation. With Ali. I think she might be in way over her head. I mean, it sounds like Boy's the kind of guy who goes out with stunning 'It' girls and just wants to have a good time. Yeah, obviously Ali's great and everything—she's in the right social scene and she's fun—but she's not exactly . . . well, *experienced*." Mimah gave an innocent shrug. "I'm not trying to be a bitch or anything—it's just true."

"Of course, not at all." Tally nodded. "Telling the truth doesn't mean you're a bitch. You can't help it if that's the way it is."

"Exactly. It's not *my* fault that Ali's a virgin. You know, I think having sex makes a big difference. It's like you're in the club. Not to be nasty or anything, but I sometimes feel there's loads Ali doesn't understand."

"Oh, totally!" Tally stretched her hand toward Mimah on the table. "I know exactly what you mean. It's like, if I had a boyfriend or I wanted boy advice, I'd definitely talk to you about it rather than her. She just wouldn't get it."

"I know." Mimah smirked. "You could always talk to Sonia, though. She'd *totally* get it."

Tally snorted, almost spraying coffee through her nose. "Yeah right! *Sebby! Sebby! Wait for me!* God, poor Sone. I hope he asks her out before she dies of stress. But honestly"—she

scooped some crumbs round her plate with her index finger—
"I do wish things had worked out with Ali and T. They would
have been so romantic together, and it would have been such
a confidence boost."

"Yeah." Mimah pouted sympathetically. "She's still really
cut up about that, isn't she?"

"Absolutely. He dumped her so suddenly, she almost had
a nervous breakdown." Tally dropped her voice to a whisper.
"She was planning to lose her virginity to him that night."

"Really?"

"Really. Don't tell anyone, though. That's the thing with
Al—she never shows how upset she is, but she's loads more
vulnerable than she looks." Tally twisted a lock of hair round
her fingers. "Quite frankly, I'm a bit worried as well—I think
she might be so obsessed with the idea of losing her virginity
right now that—"

"What?"

"That she's gonna make a terrible mistake." Tally shook
her head and stuck a fragment of iced bun in her mouth,
seeming to have conveniently forgotten that the whole sex-
with-Boy plan had been her brainchild in the first place.

"God, that'd be awful!" Mimah scrunched up her face. "I
just find it so weird, though: Al's got so many guy friends,
and she's really pretty—okay, not supermodel-pretty, but
whatever—and she's, like, cool. Why on earth hasn't she ever
just had sex before? It's not like we don't go to enough parties.
I lost my virginity under a shrub in Bathsheba Fortnum's

garden!" She laughed uneasily. "I mean, not that I would have planned it that way, I guess."

"Hmmm." Tally twirled her hair sagely. "I guess not. Anyway, I think you're forgetting two words where Al's concerned. 'Control freak.' She's a classic case. I mean, can you imagine her shagging under a shrub? You know what she's like about planning things. And homework. And keeping our bedroom tidy."

"Shit. You're so right; I never thought of it like that. She's just like her dad, isn't she?"

"Exactly." Tally gave a significant look. "How could you *not* be uptight, coming from the Rochester family? Have you seen the pressure they pile on Al and her brothers?" She glanced behind her. "I mean, of course, I'm only saying this because I adore Alice. She's, like, my best friend in the world."

"Oh, obviously, me too," Mimah added quickly, releasing the table's edge. "I'm just worried about her, that's all. Like I said, I'm not trying to be a bitch."

"No way," Tally agreed.

"Oy, girls!" someone squawked. "What do you think you're doing here? Move along!" One of the dinner ladies had pushed her cart right up to them and was threatening to bulldoze them off their chairs. "How do you expect us to have supper on the table by six if you don't let us clean up?"

"All right, all right," Mimah grunted, dropping her spoon with a clatter. "What's for dinner, anyway?"

"Turkey stew. And steak-and-kidney pie."

"Kidney? Ugh. Why do they have to serve that crap?"

"Clean your mouth out, young lady! And I'd count myself lucky, if I were you."

"Shit!" squeaked Tally, causing the dinner lady's forehead to crease still further. Tally had been squinting at the clock on the wall, and now grabbed her bag and jumped up. "I'm late for the History of Art lecture. Gotta go, see you later! Byeee!"

Mimah grinned in amusement as her friend dashed off down the hall, then picked up her own satchel and headed for the locker rooms. Time to start whipping herself into shape.

CHAPTER SEVENTEEN

The Hasted streetlamps were just bright enough for Dylan to glimpse that the figure up ahead, pacing back and forth like a bored tiger, was Jasper von Holstadt. He was waiting for her in front of Caffe Nero just like he'd promised. Thank goodness for that. Dylan relaxed her grip on her Marc Jacobs bag a tiny bit. Ever since last week, she'd been forcing herself to remember that this whole date thing might be just another sick prank—one of many that had been played on her by Sonia and Alice and their band of bitches ever since she'd arrived at their pathetic little school.

But Jasper looked for real. He also looked ridiculously hot. Underneath his chocolate-colored blazer, his blue check shirt was unbuttoned to the top of his smooth, taut chest. His faded jeans were slung low over his nonexistent boy ass. His dark brown hair, swept back from his chiseled, aristocratic face, had that devil-may-care look about it that made him so deadly attractive to every girl within eyeshot.

Jasper was taller than Dylan remembered, and right now he was staring impatiently down the street in the opposite direction.

"Ummm, hi," she said, tapping his forearm awkwardly.

"There you are!" Jasper whipped round and gave her a quick once-over as he bent to kiss her cheek. "You look stunning. No wonder you're so late—I can see you've made an effort."

"An effort?" Dylan recoiled slightly. What kind of shitty compliment was that meant to be?

But Jasper didn't seem to have heard, and she decided not to push it. Best to avoid talking about why she was late, since the actual reason involved her crouching in a bush for ten minutes, getting crawled on by nasty bugs and mauled by dried leaves. Stupid English countryside. Yes, Dylan's escape from St. C's had been a total hassle, to put it mildly. Just as she'd been sneaking past the front windows of Tudor House on the way to the Great Lawn, Miss Sharkreve's ground-floor light had snapped on. Dylan had dived headfirst into some shrubbery, almost ruining her especially blow-dried hair. Trapped, panting, she'd crouched there, expecting the housemistress's accusing voice to screech out "Detention!" at any second. After all, at seven thirty on a Tuesday you weren't supposed to be skulking around the back of school wearing red lipstick and Tory Burch ballet flats. You were supposed to be in your bedroom. Or in the library, hard at work. But no voice came. At last, Dylan poked her head up through the leaves and saw that the light in Sharko's window was still on. But the housemistress wasn't looking at her at all. She was too preoccupied by the tall, shadowy guest in her living room—unidentifiable through the curtains—who was pouring out two glasses of wine. Dylan hadn't been able to make out who it was.

"Come on!" Jasper interrupted the recollection. "Ready? Let's go."

"Go?" Dylan's forehead creased delicately. "Where? I thought the plan was to have a drink in there." She pointed across the street to Hasted's shiny All Bar One, a bland, brightly lit chain pub. "I thought that's why you wanted to meet on this street."

Jasper gave a dismissive laugh. "Oh, no. No, no. Only Hasted townies go to that dump. It's where they wine and dine their girlfriends when they're trying to be posh. I'm taking you somewhere far cooler than that. Far more private. Come on."

He flashed Dylan a smile, letting his ice-blue eyes linger over her as they walked. Dylan's cheeks were slightly flushed in the night air. Her short red jacket hung open, and underneath it, her little black dress clung exquisitely to her hips and to those perfect, round breasts—so exquisitely that Jasper could hardly suppress the urge to bury his face in them, right then and there on the street.

Jas smiled to himself. Yeah, T's ex was definitely beddable. Ideal for a quick fling. He wasn't going to pretend there wasn't a touch of competitiveness, of one-upmanship with his best friend in wanting to get Dylan in the sack. But that was only natural, all part of the game. The thing was, Jas wasn't the kind of guy who had girlfriends. He was the kind of guy who screwed every hot girl in sight (or tried to, at least) and then hardly ever looked at them again. Love 'em and leave 'em—that was his recipe for fun. Tonight was going to be a piece of cake.

"Let's hurry." He slipped his hand onto the small of Dylan's back and nudged her forward. In his other hand he held a crumpled paper bag about the size of a bottle.

"Hey." Dylan giggled, nervously fiddling with an empty packet of gum in her pocket. "Where exactly are you taking me?" The pressure of Jasper's palm was making her feel half sexy, half like a shopping cart being wheeled through a supermarket aisle. "What's up with all the secrecy?"

Jasper, shrugging, eased a cigarette from his pocket. "You'll just have to wait and see. Oh, sorry. Last cig. You don't really smoke, do you?"

Dylan eyed him wryly. "Guess not."

"Excellent. 'Cause it's hard to smoke if you can't see."

"Can't see? That doesn't make any— What the fuck?" Dylan stopped in her tracks as Jasper produced, from his jacket, a long, red, silky strip of material, which he jiggled between two fingers. She took a step back. "What on earth is that?"

"Exactly what it looks like. A blindfold."

"A *what*?"

"I made it especially for you."

"Are you crazy?" Dylan backed away. "I don't wear blind-folds on first dates! It's perverted!"

"Oh, go on. Pleeease?" Jasper's face drooped into a puppy-dog look. "I'm not trying to be dirty, I promise." *Not yet*, he added silently. "It's all part of my surprise. I don't want you to know where we're going till we get there—otherwise it won't work."

Jas's cigarette was dangling from the corner of his mouth in his habitual give-a-shit pose. He looked insanely sexy—like a movie star in the middle of a Hasted street. And how could anyone resist a movie star?

"It goes with your jacket," he wheedled.

"Oh man, fine. Fine!" Dylan lolled back her head.

"Yesss!"

"But promise you won't tie it too tight," she ordered as Jasper spun her round. "Otherwise I'll get claustrophobic."

"I'll leave you plenty of room."

Dylan shook her head. "How the hell do I let myself get talked into these things?"

"Easy. I'm just too charming for you to say no."

"Please. Don't flatter yourself." Dylan elbowed Jasper in the stomach. "The only charming thing here is me."

Laughing, Jasper smoothed the red ribbon over her eyes. Dylan's eyelashes tickled as they fluttered against the silk and she giggled a little, breathing in Jasper's boy smell of cigarette smoke and rumpled clothes. His fingers brushed the back of her neck as he tied the soft material, and made her breath catch. Goose pimples ran down her skin.

"Okay!" Jasper declared at last. "That should do it. Promise you can't see anything?"

"Promise."

"Really and truly?"

"Yes! Dude. Come *on*, I'm getting cold." Dylan tingled as she felt Jasper's hand enclose her upper arm. He was so cute to think of a surprise. Where would they be when the blindfold came off? The Palms, Hasted's coolest bar? No, too boring. It had to be something better than that, something she'd never be able to think of herself. Maybe some kind of private room, filled with strawberries and champagne.

"This is so weird." She giggled with excitement. "I feel like I'm completely at your mercy! If we ever go out again, *I'm* choosing what we do. And it'll be something normal, like going to a restaurant. Or maybe I'll cook for you—if you're lucky."

Jasper chuckled. "That depends on what you'd cook."

"Roast chicken. My specialty. It's so easy—all you have to do is stick it in and leave it there."

Jasper smirked. "Stick it in and leave it there?" Dylan was obviously talking in code, letting her dirty side hang out. "That doesn't sound right. In my experience it's better if someone . . . moves it about."

"Moves it about?" Dylan's forehead creased in confusion. "I don't know what you mean, I've never tried it that way."

"I'll show you"—Jasper leaned in—"if you want."

Dylan jumped at the voice next to her ear. But before she

could say anything, Jasper led her round a corner and the sound of their footsteps echoed. It was like they were somewhere big, empty. Dylan reached for the blindfold.

"Oh, no you don't!" Jasper swatted away her hand. "Come on, just a few more seconds. Come closer, I've got to lift you up."

"What? Why? No." Suspicion sprang into Dylan's voice. "Is this some kind of stupid joke? Listen, Jasper: If I open my eyes and all your friends are here laughing at me, I'm gonna be furious. Jasper? Jasper!"

"I'm right here! Whoa, paranoid." Jas laughed again. This was fun. More fun than he'd expected—Dylan was sparky. And she was game, and open, and strong-willed. It made a refreshing change from the uptight girls he was used to. He encircled her waist with one strong arm and scooped the other behind her knees. "Ready? Up you go!"

"Wheee!" Dylan felt herself against Jasper's chest, in the air, flying—and then back on earth. The ground was softer now. There was a fresh smell in the air. A cool breeze brushed her skin. Dylan was still smiling as Jasper took her hand and guided her over what felt like grass. Maybe he'd made a garden wonderland for her in his favorite hideout, all decked out with fairy lights and a pagoda and lush plants—

"Here we are!" he said. "Ready?"

"Yes."

He untied the blindfold and let it flutter off Dylan's face. She blinked. There were no fairy lights, no pagoda. They were standing in the middle of a scrappy park with a swing set and slides at one end. It was quiet and dark. But not that dark. Through the gloom, Dylan managed to make out dim shapes on several of the benches. She squinted—and opened her eyes wide. A few meters away, two people were busy sucking each other's faces off. Just beyond that, a woman was straddling a man's lap, gyrating back and forth.

Suddenly, Dylan felt Jasper's body behind her. He slipped his hands over her hips and pressed his crotch into her butt. Dylan was sure she could feel something *bulging*. Down there.

"You're sexy," he whispered, grazing his lips against her ear. "I've wanted you ever since I first saw you."

"What are you doing?" Dylan elbowed him away. "Where are we? Is this the town pickup spot? Have you brought me to Hasted's red light district?"

"Of course not." Once again, Dylan was doing exactly what Alice had said she would—pretending to be offended when she was secretly loving it. "Hasted doesn't have a red light district."

"What is that supposed to mean? Who exactly do you think I am? The slut from New York who'll put out for anyone?"

"No! Not for anyone. Just for some people," Jasper chortled. "Look, calm down. We won't do anything you don't want to. I even brought you a present!" With a flourish, he produced a bottle of Veuve Clicquot from his paper bag and thrust it into Dylan's hands, letting the bag fall to the ground.

"Litterbug! Pick that up. And this is *not* a present for me. It's a present for you, to get me drunk and have your way.

What is wrong with you? I thought you were a gentleman."

"Oh, right, gentleman." Jasper reached for Dylan again. She was pretty good at this whole hard-to-get thing. "Gentlemen are overrated, aren't they? Being a *gentleman* implies that a woman wants to be treated like a *lady*."

"I *do* want to be treated like a lady, you jerk! How dare you assume I don't!" Dylan retreated, deftly unwrapping the foil on the champagne and shaking the bottle vigorously. She aimed it at him. "Apologize!"

"Dill, babe, chill. I didn't mean anything by it. I thought this was your thing."

"I am not your babe!" Dylan cried. "I will not chill, and this is not my thing. Take that, creep!" She popped the cork. A jet of golden liquid burst from the bottle, blasting toward Jasper, and hit him full between the eyes.

"Aaargh!" he gasped.

"Serves you right," Dylan howled, flinging away her weapon. She darted over the grass to the park's edge, leaped the low metal fence, and disappeared from sight.

Sputtering, Jasper fell back against a tree. Forget sparky— Dylan Taylor was downright dangerous. He stuck out his tongue, catching a trail of champagne as it dripped down his face.

CHAPTER EIGHTEEN

*A*li, sweetie, would you move your elbow to the right, just a teeny tiny weeny smidge?" Sonia wheedled as she glided forward over the gray school carpet, her video camera glued to her face. "It's in the way of my shot." She swiveled her lens to the mirror above the sink, where Alice was carefully brushing her eyelashes with Christian Dior Blackout mascara.

"Perfect, perrrfect," Sonia cooed. "I am just *loving* the detail."

She moved in even closer. The side of her camera nudged Alice's cheek.

"For fuck's sake!" Alice snapped. "Get that thing out of my hair. It's seven o'clock on fucking Wednesday morning. The last thing I want is a camera up my nose."

"Well, sorr-eee. I was only trying to make some real-world cinema. You'll thank me when I'm famous. God." Sonia switched off her camera and plopped onto Tally's unmade bed. Tally was in the shower and would probably be late for breakfast, as usual. That was why Sonia always made a point of dropping into their room at this time of day—she was guaranteed to have Ali all to herself.

Ping ping. Alice's iPhone vibrated on her bedside table. Snatching it up, Alice giggled.

"What? What?" Sonia bounced in curiosity. "Who's it from?"

"Oh, just Boy. He's started texting me on his way into work. He says I'm, like, the only person he knows who gets up as early as him. It's quite sweet, really."

"Sweet? It's totally adorable. Read it to me, go on, go on."

Alice giggled again. "*Mornin' beautiful,*" she began in a deep voice. "*Can't wait for our date. Do you like river views? xB*"

"No way!" squealed Sonia. "He loves you. But why the hell is he talking about rivers?" She rolled her eyes. "That is like, a total non sensitor."

Alice stared at her. "*Non sequitur.* And no, it isn't. Boy's obviously thought of somewhere to take me, and he wants to make sure I'll love it. Duh."

"Oh my god." Sonia slapped her hand over her heart. "Ali, you're so right. He's gonna take you somewhere on the water! Just imagine—what if he's hired out one of the compartments of the London Eye for a private dinner? How romantic would that be?"

"Romantic? Yeah, right, being wined and dined inside some glass bubble on a glorified Ferris wheel sounds just great. Not tacky at all. As *if* Boy would do something like that."

Despite her acerbic tone, Alice smiled inwardly. It was

unexpected, but she was getting genuinely excited about her upcoming date. Maybe because she kept playing the memory of Boy's deep, long kiss over and over in her head. Or maybe because the less she saw of Tristan, the easier it was to try moving on. Of course, Alice still thought about T all the time. Her throat tightened. She missed the way they used to chat on the phone every day. The way they'd sneak out to the fields to get stoned on lazy Saturday afternoons. The way they used to stay up all night together during the holidays, T strumming his guitar and Alice improvising ridiculous lyrics, until they fell asleep next to each other on the same pillow, his soft, tempting lips only inches from hers. Alice had been too stupid to realize it back then, but her friendship with Tristan had made her feel special—like she had an ally, like there was someone she could phone any hour of the day or night, who cared about her more than anyone else in the world. What she had with Boy didn't replace that, of course, but it was making her feel just a little bit special again.

"Anyway." Tossing back her hair, Alice glanced at the gold seventies-style watch that she'd bought in Paris. "We'd better get to breakfast. Ooh, wait! What's the word on Dylan and Jasper's date? What did she say last night when she came in?"

Sonia smirked. "Not much. But she got back pretty early. And she was in an utterly foul mood."

"Are you sure?"

"Of course I'm sure. What do you think I am—unobservant?" Sonia smoothed the front of her already impeccable school sweater. "She kept stomping round and muttering to herself like some lunatic. And when I asked her how Jas was doing, she told me to shut up. It was, like, rude."

"Brilliant!" Alice clapped her hands. "I knew it would work. Some people are so predictable. Hang on a sec," she exclaimed, a sly gleam lighting her eyes. "I've just thought of the most amazing idea." Dashing over to her desk, she leaned over her laptop and typed furiously into Google.

"Babe." Sonia stared as Alice reached for her phone. "What on earth are you doing?"

"Implementing phase two of the Date a Dylan plan, naturally," Alice grinned. "What else?"

CHAPTER NINETEEN

"Hmmph, yes, well played, Jemimah," grunted Miss Colin, St. Cecilia's head gym teacher, at the end of lacrosse practice later that afternoon. She regarded Mimah severely, then turned back to her clipboard.

Wednesday was elective day at St. Cecilia's, when lessons ended at lunch and girls were supposed to focus on their extracurricular activities—rehearse plays, start clubs, write for the school newspaper, be nice to old people, blah blah blah—and Mimah had chosen today to try worming her way back onto the lax team.

"Thanks," she panted. She stubbed the ground with the end of her lacrosse stick and searched the teacher's face. Miss Colin (despite her mullet-and-tracksuit ensemble) was a pretty imposing character. She was sharp-tongued and strict and demanded respect—and she had *not* appreciated Mimah ditching lacrosse out of the blue. This afternoon, Mimah had played as hard as she could to get back in Colin's good books. She was on pins and needles.

"Er, Miss Colin?"

"What?"

"Sorry to interrupt. But . . . just wondering . . . how did I do?"

"Ah, yes, how did you do." Miss Colin stopped writing and started tapping her clipboard against her bulging thigh. "Well, you certainly still have what it takes to captain the junior class team. Without a doubt you're the strongest player we've got—you always were."

Mimah grinned cockily. But Colin held up her stubby hand.

"However! Sports are about dedication and team spirit—especially school sports. And after your recent behavior, I'm not so sure you have those things."

"But I do!"

Miss Colin pursed her lips.

"I promise! Really." Mimah couldn't believe she was actually having to grovel. She wouldn't have bothered listening to Colin's lecture, except that she really did want to get back on the team. "Honestly, Miss Colin, I miss lax so much. I dream about it every night."

"You need to get a life then, Jemimah," Miss Colin sniffed. But her voice was less severe. "All right, I'm prepared to give you one more chance. I'll put you into our next match after half term. But if you let me down again, mind you, you're out for good."

"Thank you, Miss Colin! I understand. And I won't let you down. Definitely not."

Her mood high with the victory, Mimah took off across the field to the long, glass building that housed the locker rooms and the heated indoor swimming pool. Now she could look forward to crisp afternoons of practice while the autumn winds whipped her hair and snapped her skirt and drowned out her teammates' calls to each other as they hurled the ball back and forth. She could look forward to the matches, too. Competition had always been one of Mimah's passions, ever since she was six years old and used to make her sister, Charlie, race her up and down the wood-paneled gallery of their Wiltshire manor house.

Which reminded Mimah: How was Charlie, anyway? Her wayward younger sister had practically been in hiding for weeks, and that horrific article about Daddy last Monday had only made it worse. Most mornings, Charlie ran off straight after chapel. She'd stopped appearing on the Great Lawn at break. And Mimah was sure that the only reason she showed up in the dining hall for meals was because it was compulsory for anyone below the junior class. These days, Charlie didn't eat much. She and her new BFF, Georgie Fortescue, mostly got their sustenance from drinking booze and smoking weed. Mimah frowned. She wasn't against having a bit of fun, obviously, but this was different. It was her little sister. And she was only fucking fourteen.

"Oy, Mime!" called Flossy Norstrup-Fitzwilliam from across the locker room, as Mimah towel-dried her hair after showering and slipped into a pair of gray St. C's tracksuit bottoms with two yellow stripes down each leg. "What are you up to? Want to sneak out for a cig?" Flossy's curly blond hair and cherub-like face made her smoking habit a standing joke throughout the junior class.

Mimah shook her head. "Nope. Can't. Gotta go check on my sister. Oh, Floss, hold it," she called, flinging a pashmina over her shoulders. "I'd keep out of the woods if I were you. Mr. Vicks caught Felicity and Zanna smoking there this morning. Try behind the parking lot instead."

Flossy waved. "Thanks for the tip! Will do."

Fifteen minutes later, Mimah was scaling the staircase of Locke House, home to the ninth grade. Hard to believe it was only a year and a half since she'd lived here herself. She glanced round at the overflowing bulletin boards and familiar violet-painted walls tattooed with squares of sunlight from the windows. On each landing, she peeped through dormitory doors into the rooms where she and her friends used to sleep. None bore any traces of her life—the bright duvets, soft toys, photos, and piles of clothes were familiar yet foreign. They made Mimah feel strangely old and detached—as if time had recycled itself here, but she'd been pushed on.

Finally she reached the attic, where Charlie's door, unlike most others on the low, sloping-roofed corridor, was shut tight. Mimah knocked.

"Yeah?"

"Charl, sweetie, it's me."

Something rustled, then the door flew open. "Jemimah,"

Charlie growled. "My roomies will be back soon. What do you want?"

Mimah didn't answer. She was too busy giving her sister the once-over. She and Charlie had the same raven hair, dark eyes, and pale complexion, but that was where the similarities ended. Charlie had grown skinny over the past few months, with circles under her eyes and hollows under her cheekbones. Her hair, once glossy, was now dull and stringy, and those laddered tights she was wearing sagged around her knobbly knees. She looked like one of those heroin-chic models in fashion spreads—except that in real life it was more pathetic than cool.

Without waiting for an invitation, Mimah pushed into the dorm. "How you doing, sis?"

Charlie shrugged defensively. "Fine."

"Really? Then why haven't I seen you out and about much?"

"How am I supposed to know?" Charlie glared at Mimah, her hair falling straight from her middle part down the sides of her face. "Maybe you weren't looking hard enough. And, by the way, if you're here to do your 'caring sister' routine, you can leave it out."

"Christ, hold it. No need to be bitchy." Mimah kept her voice light despite a flash of annoyance. She and Charlie had always been just as stubborn as each other, but she hadn't come here to fight. "I only wanted to say hi. I miss you, Charl. You never come see me anymore."

"No shit. Believe it or not, I have better things to do than chase you all over school." Charlie rolled her eyes, but let her gaze rest on Mimah's for a beat longer than necessary. It was weird, but Mimah could have sworn that was Charlie's twisted way of trying to connect, without conceding anything.

"Yeah right." She punched Charlie in the arm. "What better thing could you possibly have to do than come see darling old me? Clip your toenails? Squeeze your zits? Download porn onto your computer?"

"Snap your lacrosse stick in two and shove it up your ass?" suggested Charlie, finally breaking into a smile. She launched herself onto her bed (one of the two nearest the windows) and crossed her feet underneath her.

Mimah laughed. Typical Charlie, being able to change moods at the drop of a hat. In her sister's bright expression, there was a trace of the cheeky fourteen-year-old she'd been just a few months before.

"By the way, it's a good thing you came," Charlie carried on mischievously, "because I almost forgot: Alexandra called and told me you've been nosing round about Boy Stanley-Soames. Wooo! Do you faaancy him?"

"No!" Mimah cried. "God, gossip travels fast on the cousin network. Can't I ask about a boy without fancying him?"

"Of course not. Ha! You've gone red: You luuurve him! You wanna shag him! I'm gonna tell him—then you'll be embarrassed."

"You'd better not tell him, because it's not true!" Mimah flopped onto the bed and dug Charlie in the ribs with her big toe. "Hang on a minute—how could I fall for that trick? You don't even know who Boy Stanley-Soames *is*."

"Do so."

"No you don't. How?"

"Not telling. First admit you have a crush on him."

"But I don't." Mimah groaned in exasperation. "I was asking for Alice. They're having this intense flirtation. I think they might even have snogged, and now she's got a date with him Saturday night."

"Serious?" Charlie's eyes widened. She'd looked up to Alice ever since she was a toddler and the Rochesters would come on holiday with the Calthorpe de Vyle-Hanswickes to Spain. *That was the one good thing that had happened over the past few weeks,* Charlie thought. *Mimah and Alice had got over whatever stupid fight they'd had last term.* "Wow, score for Ali. You know, I can get Boy gossip without having to go through Alexandra at all."

"Seriously? How?"

"You know Georgie, yeah? My friend Georgie Fortescue?"

"Mm-hmm."

"Well, her parents live in Singapore, just like the Stanley-Soameses, and Georgie's older brother, Felix Fortescue, is best friends with Boy."

"Whoa, random." Mimah sat up straight. "So what's the scoop? What do you know?"

"Well, for starters, everyone fancies Boy. Georgie totally does. But he's really secretive. He's always disappearing, and he'll never tell any of his friends where he's going. Or who he's seeing."

"Shit." Mimah bit her lip. "That sounds suspicious. What's he trying to hide?"

"No idea. Drugs? Girls? Look, Mime, maybe you should tell Alice to be careful."

"I tried! But she basically jumped down my throat." Mimah grabbed a pocket-size bottle opener from Charlie's bedside table and spun it round her finger. "Hey listen, if Georgie knows so much, maybe you could do me a favor. I think we should do some spying. Could you tap her for info every couple of days?"

"Every couple of days?" Charlie tugged the bottle opener back. "That's way too weird—Georgie'll think I'm obsessed. *Hey, how's Boy today? What's he doing? Who's he going out with? Tell me, tell me.* She'll think I'm a freak."

"Not if you ask subtly." Mimah pawed Charlie's arm. "Come on, pleeease? I'd do the same for you."

Charlie heaved a sigh and shut her eyes in a long-suffering kind of way. "Whatever. Maybe. I'll see what I can do."

"Wicked! I knew I loved you." Mimah jumped up to leave. "Oh and, Charl?"

"Yeah?"

"Don't tell anyone about this. I'm going to loop Tally in, but no one else." She wrapped her charcoal-gray pashmina round her neck and set off into the darkening afternoon. If Boy was up to anything funny, she was going to get to the bottom of it.

CHAPTER TWENTY

*D*ylan was just cracking open her French grammar textbook on Thursday afternoon when someone banged on her bedroom door. The interruption was more than welcome—French wasn't exactly Dylan's favorite subject these days, to put it mildly. In New York she hadn't been bad at it, but at St. Cecilia's she sucked, thanks to the fact that her entire fucking class owned mansions in St. Tropez and had been spoon-fed by Parisian au pairs since before they were potty trained.

"Come in," she called, tossing back her straw-blond hair. Just because there weren't any boys for miles around didn't mean it wasn't important to look good.

Arabella Scott poked her head round the door.

"Oh," Dylan mumbled. "Sonia's downstairs." She turned back to her work. Bella, like most of the junior class's in crowd, had hardly bothered addressing a word to her since she'd arrived at St. Cecilia's, and there was no point hoping for any change. "She's in the common room. Watching *Neighbours* or something."

"I know. I'm looking for you."

"Me?" Dylan's head shot up.

"Yeah, you've got a package. Down by the pigeonholes."

"Really? What is it? Who's it from?"

"How am I meant to know? Sharko just asked me to come tell you. Get a move on and go see for yourself." Bella left, slamming the door shut with a tiny twinge of guilt. To be honest, she felt sort of sorry for Dylan—the girl didn't seem that awful, after all. She probably just needed a few more friends. Not that Bella was about to offer herself up for the job—Alice Rochester absolutely despised Dylan, and Alice manipulated the opinions of so many people (especially the Hasted House boys) that if you got on her bad side, you were basically social history.

Dylan crammed her grammar worksheet back into her French file. A package . . . For her . . . Who could it be from? Definitely not her mom—her mother was too busy shagging Victor Dalgleish to even remember that Dylan existed. She'd probably even forget Dylan's birthday in a couple of months. But her dad—maybe it was from him. Dylan knew her father felt guilty for letting her be dragged off to dreary old England. She and her sister, Lauren, were going to visit him in New York at half term, and he'd promised to take them shopping and treat them to delicious dinners every night.

Obnoxious Australian accents assailed Dylan's ears as she descended the staircase to the foyer. Peering into the common room, she saw Alice, Tally, and Sonia curled up together on one of the big red couches, Sonia plaiting a strand of Alice's sleek brown hair while Alice kept her eyes fixed on the TV. Tally raised her head as Dylan walked by. She nudged Alice.

But Dylan didn't even notice. She'd just seen the reason why she'd been called downstairs.

Tudor House's pigeonholes, where the junior class's mail was deposited every morning by the school porters, were built into an alcove opposite the front door. Next to them stood a wooden table reserved especially for packages, and on the table lay the most stunning bunch of roses Dylan had ever seen. There were twelve of them, all the same deep, rich red and coiled together in an elegant black square bag that read JANE PACKER on the outside. The arrangement was so beautiful that tears sprang to Dylan's eyes. She ran the rest of the way over the polished parquet floor.

Embedded between the velvety petals, she saw a small square envelope and tore it open. Lines of delicate calligraphy gleamed back at her:

> Gather ye rosebuds while ye may,
> Old Time is still a-flying:
> And this same flower that smiles to-day
> Tomorrow will be dying.
>
> Robert Herrick

Dear Dylan, I'm desolate that I disrespected you. Life's too short for fights. Please let me make it up to you: meet me at nine o'clock tonight by the statue in the center of town. Wear a rose in your hair.

XOX,

?

Breathing fast, Dylan turned over the note. There was no name anywhere. She felt her heart melting. Wow, how adorable of Jasper to spend so much time and thought on an apology after his mess-up the other night. He really must have been nervous to behave like he did. Poor, embarrassed boy.

"Oy," Sonia whispered to Tally in the common room. "Move your head. Can you see anything?"

"Shhh! Yeah, she's reading it. She's smiling."

"Loser!"

"Wait, now she's sniffing the flowers."

"How does her face look? Does she seriously believe they're from him?"

"Of course. Why wouldn't she?"

"Yesss!" Alice squashed her head into a cushion to stifle a giggle. "My plan is *so* working. Sone, are you ready for your part? You'll have to stay in your room tonight—you know, to keep watch that she actually sneaks out."

"Nooo," Sonia whined. "Why me? Mr. Carter said he was

going to help me edit some footage for my Paper Bandits documentary this evening. Why can't Mimah keep watch?"

Alice shot her a glare. "Because Mimah doesn't share a room with Dylan. You do. Tell Carter you can't make it. You can't back out now. Someone has to alert Miss Sharkreve when Dylan sneaks out, or how else is she going to get caught and majorly screwed?"

"Oh, shit," interrupted Tally. "Al, look, she's getting out her phone."

Alice turned pale. This was not part of the plan.

Ring ring. Ring ring. Dylan listened through her earpiece, biting back a smile, waiting for Jasper to pick up.

"Hello?"

"Hi. Jas. It's me."

There was a pause. "Dylan? Hey . . . Um, how are you?"

In the background, someone guffawed. "Dylan? That's *Dylan*? Wooohooo!"

"Shut it!" Jasper hissed.

Dylan bit her lip. Jasper must have told all his friends about his grand romantic gesture. They were probably sitting round him for moral support, waiting for her to call! "Anyway, I guess I just wanted to say thanks for the flowers. It's a really nice surprise."

"What?"

"Yeah, they just arrived. I'll be there tonight."

"Huh? You'll be where?"

"Exactly where you said." Dylan examined the card again.

"Oh, I get it. Silly boy. Just because you didn't sign it, you thought I wouldn't know who it was from."

"Who *what* was from? Hang on, did you say you got flowers?"

"Y-yeah . . ." Dylan frowned. Come to think of it, it didn't make much sense for Jasper to play dumb. Not this dumb, at least. What the hell was going on?

Bang!

Dylan whipped round. The front door of Tudor had just slammed shut, and out in the yard, through the window, she could see Alice, Tally, and Sonia doubled over with laughter. Alice lifted her hand to her ear in an impression of someone talking on a mobile. Fucking bitches! No wonder Jasper sounded confused. Dylan's knuckles turned white as she gripped her phone.

"Never mind," she croaked, punching end call. She didn't even feel upset. All she felt was a burning fury as she pounded over the parquet.

"Wait, wait," Jasper spluttered on the other end of the dead line. Shit. Whoever had sent Dylan flowers was a goddam genius—he should have thought of it first. Instead, he'd been kicking himself pointlessly for ruining things with a girl who'd actually turned out to be pretty cool. He had to get back in her good books. There must be a way.

CHAPTER TWENTY-ONE

*S*torming into the neat front garden outside Tudor House, Dylan marched across the grass toward Alice, Tally, and Sonia. The light was fading, but she could clearly see their little cluster giggling under the enormous oak that shaded half the building.

"Would you like to tell me what's so funny?"

Alice smirked down at Dylan, over whom she towered by about three inches. "Umm, no thanks. Not really." She turned her back.

"Tough!" Dylan drew closer, nearly tripping over a hose that was snaking along the lawn. "And fucking face me when I'm talking to you!"

"Excuse me?"

"You heard me, bitch!" At the back of her mind, Dylan knew she'd clicked into one of her dangerous rages—the kind she'd been struggling to get under control ever since she was a kid—and she also knew she was too far gone to stop. Once the anger switch snapped inside her head, she was at the mercy of the current.

"Whoa." Alice turned mockingly to Sonia. "I think *someone* needs to chill. Anyone got tranquilizers? Dylan needs one jabbed in her fat ass."

"Don't you *dare* talk about me like I'm not here!"

"Oops, sorry. Wishful thinking."

"What the fuck?" Dylan's eyes sparkled with fury. "You listen to me, Alice Rochester—I'm sick and tired of you treating me like this. Ever since I got here, all you've done is mock me and exclude me and undermine me and make bitchy remarks behind my back. I'm a stranger in this country—you should be welcoming me, not slapping me in the face. Bitch! What are you so fucking afraid of? That I might steal all your boyfriends? That your darling Tristan might come running back to me? Well, I wouldn't blame him if he did—you're such a shit, I can't believe he could even stand the sight of you. But don't worry, I wouldn't take your sloppy seconds, even though you took mine. And by the way, I'm sure Tristan'll find someone way better than you. In fact, I fucking hope he already has—that way, you can get yourself a new enemy, because I am *Fed. Up!*"

Dylan drew out the last words of her tirade with a shriek of frustration and blindly shoved at Alice, whose face was frozen in shock—no one had ever accused her before with such raw feeling. Knocked breathless by the force of Dylan's hands, she stumbled back. Her shoes tangled in something—the hose.

"Shit!" Alice lost her balance and crashed into a bed of pansies. "What the—?" She jabbed out at Dylan with her foot.

Dylan's leg buckled and she tumbled on top of her nemesis.

"Get ooooff!" Alice screeched. "Ugh. Your freakish boobs are murdering me. I'm being suffocated by silicone. Gross!"

"Silicone? My breasts are real. Not that you'd know what real ones look like, since you're as flat as two peas on an ironing board. Take that!" Dylan yanked a chunk of Alice's hair.

"Ow!" Alice sank her teeth into Dylan's arm.

Sonia trotted backward, wringing her beautifully manicured hands. "Ohmygod, ohmygod. Catfight. Catfight. Someone call the police."

Tally rolled her eyes. "What is wrong with you? Pull yourself together and help. Grab one of Dylan's legs. I'll get the other."

"No way! Dylan's a beast. What if she kicks me in the face? Dr. Essex said that if my nose gets broken again, he might not be able to fix it. He said I have to be careful of my bones."

"Gee, that's some sophisticated medical advice, that is. Get out of my way. I'm going in."

But before Tally could join the fray: "Girls!" bellowed a furious voice.

Everyone froze.

Miss Sharkreve pushed past and glared down at the tangle of limbs in the flower bed, her hands on her hips. "Alice Rochester, Dylan Taylor, what on *earth* do you think you're doing? Get out of there! Get up. How old do you think you are?"

Alice and Dylan rolled away from each other. Sullenly, they scrambled to their feet. Smudges of soil streaked Alice's cheeks and forehead, and dead leaves stuck to Dylan's clothes and hair. Rows of purple pansies were crushed.

"Miss Sharkreve," Alice bleated piteously. "Thank goodness you're here. I am *so* sorry. But it wasn't my fault, I promise. Dylan attacked—"

"Oh, shut up, Alice," Miss Sharkreve snapped.

Alice flushed red. Teachers never spoke to her like that.

"I don't care who started it. You were both scuffling round in the dirt, so you're both to blame. I don't even expect this kind of behavior from sixth graders, let alone juniors." The housemistress flicked her pale blue eyes from one girl to the other and back, then gave a slow, calculating nod. "Whatever's between you two, you're going to have to sort it out. And I know just how to make that happen."

CHAPTER TWENTY-TWO

*A*lice slouched into an armchair in the entertaining nook that she and Tally had outfitted, kicking her fluffy white slippers onto the equally fluffy white sheepskin rug. Could this evening get any worse? Not only had she been forced to take her second shower of the day after Dylan's assault in the flower bed, but Sharko had refused to disclose the specifics of whatever stupid punishment she was planning. How was Alice meant to talk her way out of it if she didn't even know what *it* was?

As if that wasn't bad enough, Dylan's words kept echoing in her head. *Tristan'll find someone better than you. He probably already has.* Alice shuddered. What if that were true? She hadn't seen Tristan properly in ages. He could have been sleeping with half the girls' schools in the country, for all she knew. No, T wouldn't do that, he was too sensitive. But maybe those bitches from the gig at Formica had become his groupies and he'd hopelessly fallen for one of them. Shit, shit, shit.

Wrapping her arms round her knees, Alice stared forlornly at her copy of *Othello*, which was resting on the wooden trunk in front of her, bristling with color-coded tabs at every key point. Next to it, she'd lined up her highlighters and colored pens and sharpened pencils, all ready to write one of her brilliantly organized, teacher-friendly essays. But she couldn't bring herself to work. Where the hell was Tally? Yet again, Tally seemed to have taken off on one of her mysterious dinnertime library visits, wearing red lipstick for no apparent reason. Who was she trying to impress— *Encyclopaedia Britannica*? One of these days, Alice was going to take a trip to the library herself to check out what was so bloody exciting.

Anyway, it didn't matter; she knew what Tally would say if she were here: "Ring Boy. It'll take your mind off things." Alice clasped her hands and nodded. Okay, yes, she probably should. Their date was on Saturday—only three days away— meaning they really needed to make a plan. She weighed her phone on her palm for a moment, then dialed his number.

Boy picked up on the ninth ring.

"Sexy. Hi there. What's up?"

"Not much." Alice gave a little grin. Boy's nickname for her really was so sweet. "Chilling and stuff. How are you?"

"Fine, babe, fine. Busy. I'm still at work."

"I didn't mean to interrupt. I was just wondering—do you

know what time you'll be here Saturday? I can't *wait* to see where we're going."

Boy was silent for a second. Then he sighed. "Yeah. Shit. I've been meaning to tell you, turns out Saturday's not so great."

"S-sorry?" Alice couldn't believe her ears. They'd arranged this days ago—and *Boy* had suggested it. And he'd just texted her about it yesterday.

"Yeah, something's come up at work."

"For Saturday night?"

"I know. Total drag. But . . . hey—I guess that's life."

"Umm, I guess so." If it had been T on the phone, Alice would have informed him how rude and unacceptable it was when people canceled things this late. But there was no way she could do that with Boy.

"Aw, Sexy, I'm sorry," Boy crooned. "Listen, I'll make it up to you. It turns out I *am* gonna be in Rome the weekend of your cousin Coco's party, just like I thought. How about I take you out then? We'll do something ten times better than London would have been."

"I don't know." But Alice's smile was already reappearing. "Promise?"

"Promise. I'll plan a wicked surprise."

"Okay . . . I guess you can't really help having a work thing. Rome sounds fun."

"It will be. Have a good weekend, babe. Don't do anything I wouldn't do."

Alice hung up, humming to herself. Boy was so charming.

Seeing him in Rome might help her forget her shattered plans with Tristan. Not to mention the fact that if T saw them together, it'd drive him out of his mind with jealousy. Ha. Served him right.

Alice stretched out her arm for *Othello*—but before she could open it, the door flew open and Tally burst in. As usual when Tally entered a room, the place turned into a bomb site within seconds. Coat, yellow silk scarf, bag, files, and books fell in her wake as she dashed over to the entertaining nook and flung herself into the opposite chair. Alice frowned suspiciously. The library must have been pretty damn special to make Tally glow like that.

"You're looking cheerful," she remarked.

"And you're not, you grumpy little grouch. What's that glare for? Still upset about the fight?"

"Maybe."

"Forget it, sweetie," Tally said. "Just focus on your date with Boy—it's so soon!"

"*Was* so soon."

Tally's eyes widened. "What do you mean?"

Alice examined her fingernails. She couldn't bear for Tally to know Boy had canceled on her. Tally could be so cocky: She'd think it meant she was right about Boy being a player—even though it only meant he was a genuine working man. "Oh, I canceled that. Earlier on. Turned out I had too much homework to do."

"You canceled a date because of homework?"

"So? Got a problem with that? Anyway, Boy's gonna be in Rome over half term so I said I'd see him then."

"Babe, are you serious?" Tally bolted to the edge of her chair. "You mean, like, you'll be *seeing* him seeing him? Like, in his hotel room?"

"What do you think I am?" Alice batted her with a bright pink cushion. "No! I mean I'll be seeing him for *dinner*. Like, in a *restaurant*."

Tally felt a current of relief. So Alice hadn't decided to sleep with Boy for certain—she and Mimah still had time to investigate any incriminating evidence against him.

"Anyway," Alice went on, "if you can keep your one-track mind off sex for one minute, can we please do our *Othello* essay? Thank god this is the last thing we have to write on that damned play. I can't wait to start *The Portrait of a Lady* after half term—at least people who aren't dead Elizabethans might be able to understand it."

"Um, yeah, sounds great." Tally cleared her throat. These days, she was having to lie more and more often to keep her little secret. How much longer could the concealment go on?

CHAPTER TWENTY-THREE

"Tristan! For fuck's sake, wait up," wheezed Seb, dragging himself after his friend, who was jogging toward the Hasted House boat lake with a ridiculous amount of energy.

Tristan tossed a grin over his muscular shoulder. "I'm running as slowly as I can."

"Congratulations. Ever hear of walking? I think it's something Einstein invented."

It was Saturday afternoon, and weekend athletics practice had just ended. Tristan and Seb had spent the past two hours doing ghastly things like shot-putting and hurdle leaping and javelin throwing, and Seb, for one, was about ready to lie down and die. Not that he hated sports or anything—he was up for the gentlemanly kinds that complemented a glass of Pimms, like tennis and golf, but athletics was something else. What the hell was the point in throwing yourself over poles and chucking big bits of metal, just to prove that you were a better man than everyone else? They weren't cavemen, for god's sake. Well, most of them weren't. George Demetrios left some room for doubt, Seb thought, chuckling to himself. George's infamously hairy chest, loud, grunty voice, and prehistoric technique with women might be clues: He could be the evolutionary missing link.

"Here we are. Looks like they're empty," Tristan said, slowing to a halt in front of the old boathouses on the farthest side of the lake. Thanks to his rigorous daily training for the junior class rugby team, he wasn't even out of breath.

Seb, on the other hand, was.

"Thank god for that," he panted, surveying the row of ramshackle sheds. They were set back slightly from the water and almost completely strangled by weeds. Last year, as a special treat for the award-winning Hasted House rowing team, the school had replaced these dumps with shiny new boathouses nearer the main lawns, which meant that no one really came here anymore, except for the occasional groundskeeper on his rounds. Oh, and clever boys who wanted to get stoned.

Digging into the pocket of his navy tracksuit, Tristan located one of the joints that he'd pre-rolled this morning before breakfast. He sprawled onto a cracked wooden bench under a tree and, basking in the warm, slanting afternoon sun as it fell through the branches, lit up. Smoke coiled in the crisp air. The breeze caught it and whisked it away in a thin, hazy thread. A bird flapped its wings in the lake, raising a shower of cold, silvery droplets. T exhaled luxuriously.

"Here." He passed the joint to Seb, not bothering to hide the thing. On the rare occasions when teachers came poking round these parts, you could see them approaching from miles away.

"Thanks, man." Seb took a few puffs and passed it back. After a second, his hand crept into his hoodie top and he slid out his hip flask. Tristan stared.

"What?"

"You brought that thing with you to athletics practice?"

"So?"

"Are you mad?"

"Mate, what are you chatting about? You brought the *joints* with you."

"Yeah, but joints are small. And I don't crash on my ass the whole time when I'm hurdling. I can't believe that thing didn't fall out and get noticed by Mr. Gibbs. You would have been in such shit."

"Well, I'm not, am I?" Seb grinned. "And now we can have a nice afternoon booze-up."

Tristan watched pensively as his friend unscrewed the cap. He still hadn't spoken to Seb about his drinking habit, and now seemed like the perfect time. Well, perfect except for one thing: He had no idea how to broach the subject without sounding like some kind of inept school counselor.

"Er . . ." Tristan cleared his throat. "Isn't it a bit early to start drinking?"

"Excuse me?" Seb guffawed, pointing at the joint in T's hand. "Oh, right, that's not hypocritical at all, mate."

"This is different. We're smoking weed *together*. It's a social thing."

"Yeah, well we could drink whiskey together too. Want some?"

"No. Come on, you know what I mean. You break out the booze at every opportunity. It's like, I'm all for having fun, but your habit's getting a bit extreme." Tristan ran a hand through his golden brown hair. "Look. I'm not trying to be a dickhead. I guess—I mean, I just want to check that you're okay. If there's anything on your mind, I hope you know you can always talk to me about it. Whatever it is." Tristan gave a snort. "Fuck, listen to me, I sound like a total gay."

Seb winced and stared down at his knuckles, white around his flask.

"Yeah . . ." He sighed, turning away from Tristan. "Thanks, man. I appreciate your concern. But you don't have to worry about me. I'm fine. I just like the taste of this stuff, that's all. I can stop any day I want."

Tristan was silent. The joint had extinguished itself in his hand. For the first time in their six-year friendship, it felt like Seb was lying to him. Or, no, not lying—holding something back. T had no idea what it was; all he knew was that a crack seemed to have opened between them, like a chasm on a mountaintop. He studied his sneakers, the silence rushing in his ears. Maybe he should give it one last try—but at that moment, Seb's phone beeped.

"Oh, Christ," Seb groaned, rolling his eyes.

"What?" T smiled with relief as the tension ebbed.

"See for yourself. I swear, if you had to deal with what I have to deal with, you'd be driven to the bottle as well. Look what Sonia's sent me now."

Sebby Webby, I have some GOOORGEOUS footage of u for my documentary. U look like Brad Pitt. Oh my god yes u do. Let's arrange a private viewing. Sxxx

"Brad Pitt?" T scoffed. "Is she blind?"

"Oy, shut it!" Seb grabbed the phone, grinning. "I could be Brad. You can barely tell us apart."

"Oh yeah, sure. You're practically identical twins—except for the fact that you're ugly and he's not."

"Dick!" Seb punched T in the arm.

"Seriously though, mate, Sonia is full-on."

"That's what I've been trying to tell you!"

"But I still don't get why you don't just go on a date or snog her or something. Everyone thinks she's hot. And you never know, maybe you'll like her."

"Yeah, yeah, she's pretty," Seb mumbled. "I get it." He should have kept his text to himself. Now he had to devise a way to get Tristan off his back. Without thinking, he shrugged. "Whatever. I guess I'll ask her on a date."

"Finally! Do it. Now."

"Hold your horses, not *right* now," Seb stalled. "After half term. When I have more time."

"Brilliant." Tristan clapped him on the shoulder. "I'm holding you to that. And if it doesn't work out, so what? You can't spend your whole life waiting for the perfect girl, or you'll never give anyone a chance."

"That's rich, coming from you." Seb plucked the joint from Tristan and lit it up with T's vintage gold Zippo. "You're still moping round thinking about Alice. I saw you last night, gazing at that photo of her Rando found on the floor. What's up with you?"

"I'll tell you," T said. "Fuck it all. I've decided I need some new action. New girls. Maybe some actual sex for a change. Time to move on."

"Are you serious?"

"Dead serious. I've been thinking—I've had enough of staying in on weekends. It's been ages since we went out in London. Next Saturday, let's do it. I'm gonna give some Malbury Hall girls a call, and we'll make shit happen."

"Okay." Seb stretched himself out on the bench. "Whatever you say. Sounds like a good plan to me."

"*Good* plan? You mean great plan." Tristan dug the tip of his sneaker, hard, into the ground. He couldn't wait to get Alice Rochester off his mind.

CHAPTER TWENTY-FOUR

At quarter to nine on Monday morning, all 250 St. Cecilia's students spilled out of chapel after suffering through yet another of Mrs. Traphorn's snore-inducing speeches, and swarmed down the tree-lined avenue to the Great Lawn. They clotted together as they reached the grass, chattering and squealing and jostling each other in a tangle of bags and coats and ponytails. This was news hour, the daily fifteen-minute gap before the beginning of lessons, when everyone scrambled to catch up on the gossip of the morning and the evening before.

A slight sneer twisted Charlotte Calthorpe de Vyle-Hanswicke's pale face as she watched. There had never been anything subtle about the St. Cecilia's social hierarchy—telling who was in and who was out was as easy as telling a bird of prey from a rodent. The losers mostly stood on the fringes of the crowd, wearing uniforms that were slightly too big, with sensible shoes, and socks pulled up to their knees. The cool crews congregated on and around the wide, low, redbrick steps leading to Quad. This allowed them not only to see the rest of the school, but to *be* seen as well. They wore their skirts short, their heels high, and their hair messy and loose. Designer bags dangled carelessly from their shoulders. Perfume wafted from their clothes. They looked round confidently, like they owned the place. Which they did.

Charlie took a deep breath. For the past few months, she hadn't bothered to turn up at stupid news hour. Who needed to be stared at and talked about (which was exactly what had happened to her after Daddy's sex scandal had hit the press)? It was way more appealing to run off to the woods for a quick joint with Georgie Fortescue, one of the most loaded and reckless girls in her year. The two of them were daring social renegades, laughing from a distance at all these lame suckers who tried to fit in. But sometimes Charlie got a bit bored of spending her entire time with one person. And besides, today she had a mission.

Gritting her teeth, she plunged into the horde. On its outskirts, a gaggle of knobby-kneed sixth graders were clustered round the latest issue of *Horse and Pony*, whose cover showed a grinning prepubescent girl in braces, leading her chestnut darling by the halter. Charlie's face softened. Just a few years ago, she and her friends used to go mad over that magazine too—it was like a rite of passage until you grew out of ponies and into boys. Well, Charlie smirked, either way, some kind of riding was involved.

A little farther on, a cluster of three juniors stood under a fiery-leafed oak. Charlie brushed past the first two, Farah Assadi and Emilia Charles, but slowed down to get a better look at the third. It was that new girl, Dylan Taylor—the American who used to go out with Tristan Murray-Middleton until he'd dumped her for Alice, and who everyone seemed to hate. Dylan was pretty, in a wholesome, Clearasil-ad kind of way—in other words, not the sort of bitch you wanted to be competing with over boyfriends. No wonder Alice Rochester couldn't stand her. Just then Dylan raised her arm to gather back her hair, and Charlie noticed some kind of red welt on her wrist. It looked like there were teeth marks round the edge. Bizarre—and rank. Maybe Dylan had found herself a freaky new boyfriend and that was his idea of a love bite.

By now, Charlie had reached the steps to the Quad. She raised her eyes to the top, where every morning Alice Rochester reigned supreme with her posse of the most gorgeous girls in school. Alice's straight brown hair looked particularly glossy today as she shook back her head and glanced imperiously at the scene below. Next to her, Tally Abbott was the picture of effortless cool. Tally's vintage leather satchel was slung haphazardly over her shoulder and a giant knitted scarf was coiled round her neck. Tendrils of her white-blond hair flew in every direction. On Alice's other side, Sonia Khan kept shuffling as close to her idol as possible, her almond-shaped black eyes darting round jealously, presumably to ward off any competition. And finally there was Mimah, leaning on her lacrosse stick, her face glinting with mischief as she mouthed some sly remark to the others.

Slowly, Charlie braved the steps, desperately plotting how to get Mimah away without distracting Alice.

Just as she reached the summit, Alice turned and tapped Cherry Rupert-Greene on the shoulder. Now. Charlie pulled a pen out of her bag and chucked it toward Mimah.

"What the fuck?" Mimah scowled, her dark eyes flashing in annoyance as the pen bounced off the back of her navy cashmere jacket. She swung round.

"Hey," Charlie whispered, beckoning furiously. "Mime. Over here."

Mimah gave a quick nod and wrenched the sleeve of Tally's sweater.

"What?"

"Shut up! This way. I think Charlie's got something to report."

They slipped through the throng, following Charlie round the side of one of the buildings of Quad.

"What's up, Charl?" Tally cried, flinging her arm round Charlie as soon as they were out of sight. She'd hardly seen Mimah's little sister all term, and not having any siblings herself, she liked to make the most of other people's. "How are you? How's ninth grade going?"

"Fine, thanks. Although I think someone could have warned me how much work—"

"Blah, blah, blah," Mimah butted in. "You two can chitchat later. It's almost lesson time. I assume you've got news?"

Charlie nodded. "I just heard something weird in chapel."

"About *you know who*?"

"Yeah. Didn't you tell me Alice was meant to have a date with him on Saturday?"

"She was," Tally said. "But then she canceled it."

"Oh. Weird. I thought maybe *he'd* canceled on *her.*"

"Why?"

"Because Georgie Fortescue just told me Boy had a visitor in town all weekend. Some girl."

Mimah shot Tally a glance. "A visitor? From where?"

"Don't know. Spain? Germany? I don't think she was English. Georgie heard about it through her brother, Felix, but Felix didn't even meet the bitch."

"Was it a girlfriend, or what?"

"I told you, I don't know. But apparently they hardly left Boy's flat. I bet they were shagging. Friends with benefits."

"Shit, guys." Tally bit her thumbnail. "This is *so* not good. But maybe Boy made the plan with that other girl after Alice canceled? Maybe he felt rejected."

"Rejected?" Charlie scoffed. "I think not."

"Yeah, right," Mimah agreed. "I bet he has a whole phonebook full of girls who he rings up whenever he wants a date. What a sleaze. Tals, we have got to warn Al."

"No! Not yet. You saw how she reacted last time. And this could be nothing—we're hearing it, like, fourthhand. I vote we wait and see."

Mimah frowned. "Fine. Charlie, I want you to keep your ears open. I think Boy's getting more suspicious by the day."

CHAPTER TWENTY-FIVE

Mr. Logan drew his curtains shut against the shadowy trees and lawns, looking absurdly sexy as he turned back to his study. It was almost criminal. The lamplight cast a warm glow onto his boyish face, illuminating his blue eyes, his full lips, and the adorable cleft in his chin. His faded corduroys and scuffed loafers made him look like a serious academic with a lofty, exquisite soul. Tally sighed and buried her nose in her glass of pinot noir. This was their fifth tutorial in two weeks, and Mr. Logan still hadn't ripped off any of her clothes. What the hell was he waiting for?

"Dublin's only three days away," Mr. Logan singsonged, settling into the armchair next to hers. "Tomorrow, Thursday, and then Friday evening we're off. All ready to go?"

"How can you even ask?" Tally smiled, twirling her pencil in her fingers. She wasn't about to tell Mr. Logan, but she was so ready she'd even chosen what clothing to bring—

practically unheard of for her, since Tally usually left packing till the very last minute, at which point she tossed whatever items happened to be handy into her beat-up Louis Vuitton weekend bag. The pièce de résistance for Dublin was her new purple lacy bra from La Perla with matching lacy hot pants. Tally had laid them out in her drawer, all ready to debut on Saturday night. Hopefully she wouldn't be the only one who'd get to see them. If only stupid Miss Baskin didn't get in the way.

The central heating pipes clanged. It was warm and stuffy in here, and Tally's face felt flushed. Maybe from the red wine. Or maybe from fucking frustration. Uncoiling herself from her armchair, she peeled up the bottom of her gray St. Cecilia's sweater—but as she lifted it over her head, she felt the wool create a storm of static, sending her already messy hair shooting out in all directions. Great. She looked like some kind of retarded hedgehog, she thought, hastily trying to smooth it down.

"That's a nice top," came Mr. Logan's voice. Tally started, realizing his eyes were glued to her. Looking down, she saw that she'd left her school blouse almost entirely unbuttoned under her sweater, revealing the flimsy strappy top she'd thrown on that morning—and a whole lot of B-cup cleavage.

She blushed. "Thanks."

"I find it amazing how well you girls spice up your uniforms. I went to a state school where we didn't have uniforms. We weren't that posh. They must get so constricting." Mr. Logan's eyes glinted as he ran a hand through his curly brown hair. "Sometimes, don't you just want to tear them off?"

"Y-yeah." Tally stared at him. "I do."

At that moment, her Prada phone vibrated in her pocket, just as Mr. Logan stood and walked over to his bookshelves. Feeling like she was about to faint with the sexual tension, Tally slipped out her mobile. The message was from Alice:

*WHERE R U??! Got a wicked idea, want ur advice.
U in the library? Ax*

Whatever. Tally let the phone fall back into her pocket. Alice could wait half an hour until her tutorial finished and she got back to their room. Meanwhile, Mr. Logan was heading back to his chair.

"I think we'll try something different today," he said, holding out a slim book. Tally read the title: *Songs of Innocence and Experience*, by William Blake. She caught her breath. Was that supposed to be some kind of hint? Innocence and experience: her and Mr. Logan. How obvious could you get? But soon, if things went according to plan, she wouldn't be so innocent anymore.

CHAPTER TWENTY-SIX

Alice glared at her flute, which was lying like a dead worm on her music stand next to a pile of convoluted sonatas. She hated her parents for making her take lessons even now that she was sixteen. The flute was, like, the geekiest instrument ever. There was nothing lamer than the sight of someone puckering their lips to blow into it, twiddling their fingers and rocking back and forth like some demented leprechaun.

Alice swiped up her phone. Tally still hadn't texted back, which was annoying, since she wanted to discuss her new plan: underwear shopping over the weekend. She needed some gorgeous panties for her date with Boy in Rome, and Tals would know exactly the kind to buy. Tally's underwear collection was the most treasured part of her wardrobe—it was the only stuff she owned that she bothered taking care of. She'd be away in Dublin this weekend, but that didn't mean she couldn't plot with Alice about the best places to hunt.

The Great Clock struck seven. Alice had a flute lesson tomorrow morning with the dreaded Miss Cox, but practicing any more Bach right now was out of the question. Library. Right. That was where she'd go. It was about time she discovered what Tally found so bloody thrilling there.

Throwing on her new beige pashmina, Alice set off into the crisp evening. The air smelled of wood smoke. Squares of light shone from classrooms, bedrooms, and kitchens. A swirl of clouds blocked the moon. Trickles of girls hurried across the Great Lawn, but most people were inside at this hour, scoffing a last bite of supper, finishing up school clubs and societies, or watching TV in the common room before study hall began officially in fifteen minutes' time.

Alice scaled the steps at the far end of the Great Lawn and swept under the archway into the Quad. A muffled din emanated from the dining hall, and her footsteps echoed on the stone path as she strode through the courtyard. The main floor of the front of the building was occupied by the library, an elegant spread of drawing rooms dating back to the eighteenth century, when St. Cecilia's had been a private manor owned by Lord and Lady Cornwallis.

Ascending the entrance hall's sweeping spiral staircase, Alice passed Mrs. Driscoll, the librarian, and entered the main reading room. Green reading lamps lit the rows of long wooden tables. But there was no sign of Tally, so she crossed into the first of the drawing rooms. It was furnished with clusters of velvet armchairs round the fireplace, antique tables in cozy nooks between shelves, and an old-fashioned couch with curved wooden feet. Still no Tally.

There was Zanna Balfour, though, lounging on one of the window seats with her face stuck in a geography textbook. Zanna was one of the biggest library geeks in the junior class. She hated doing homework in her bedroom. "There's no way I can work and sleep in the same place," she maintained. "It's bad karma." But Alice knew the real reason wasn't bad karma—it was bad smell. Zanna's roommate was Sophie Granville, and Sophie's relationship with deodorant was sporadic.

"Oy," hissed Alice in her fake library whisper.

"Hey!" Zanna started. "Funny seeing you here. You don't usually work in the library during study hall."

Alice brushed her fingers over the tasseled curtain rope. Of course Zanna knew her movements and habits. Everyone at St. Cecilia's did. "I'm aware of that. I just came to find Tally."

"Who?" Zanna asked in surprise.

"Tally? You know, blond girl? My best friend?" Alice rolled her eyes. "Which room does she usually work in?"

"None of them. Tally hasn't been to the library in ages."

"Ummm, yes she has. She comes at least twice a week, just after Supper."

"No way. She doesn't."

Alice narrowed her eyes.

"I'm always here at that time," Zanna insisted. "Right in this seat. I'd have seen her."

"Are you positive?" Alice demanded. "Maybe you're not as observant as you think."

"Course I'm positive. The only reason I sit here is for the people-watching. Tally did come once, a few weeks ago. She was over by the poetry shelves doing some English essay. But she definitely hasn't been back since then. Ask Mrs. Driscoll if you don't believe me."

Alice's palms turned sweaty. Something fishy was going on, some kind of deception. And it felt like she was the victim.

"Fine," she said, turning on her heel. "Have it your way." Stalking over the oriental rugs on the floor, Alice clenched her fists. She was going to find out what was really going on. And she was going to find out now.

CHAPTER TWENTY-SEVEN

The Quad was deserted as Alice emerged from the front hall. Supper was over. The last bit of gray roast beef had been scraped into the trash can, the final custard tart had been shoved into someone's mouth, and almost everyone had legged it back to their dorms for study hall. Alice skirted the edge of the courtyard, hugging the buildings rather than striking out through the center, so teachers would be less likely to spot her and tell her off for being out and about. She could come up with some sort of excuse, obviously, but why take the risk?

Suddenly, passing one of the doorways along the side of the Quad, Alice heard a clattering down the wooden staircase. A figure in a St. Cecilia's uniform hurtled out and rammed her, almost knocking her flat.

"Ow!" she snarled. "What the hell do you think you're doing? How dare you crash—" Alice stopped. "Tally! Finally. What the hell were you doing in there?"

"Al! Hey . . . this is a surprise. Um, nothing."

"What do you mean, nothing?"

"Well I-I thought I'd left something in one of the class-rooms. I was on my way back from the library and thought I'd check."

"Oh, the *library*." Alice gave a thin smile. "Of course. How could I forget?"

"Don't know, babe." Tally flicked back a wisp of her hair. "Shall we go back to Tudor and make some tea?"

"Hang on." Alice blocked her way. "It's funny, you know. Speaking of the library, I was just up there."

Tally's light gray eyes wavered, then steadied.

"I bumped into Zanna Balfour. She said you hadn't been there in weeks."

"Really? What is she, Big Brother?"

Alice said nothing.

"Whatever." Tally waved her hand dismissively. "Zanna's such a loser. As if she'd know where I've been. She probably skulks in one of the back rooms where I hardly ever work. Come on, let's go."

"Liar," Alice growled.

"Excuse me?"

"I said you're a fucking liar! I happen to know that Zanna sits in the front room, right by the window."

Tally turned pale. "So?"

"So she can see everyone who comes and goes. It's obvious you've been lying all term." Alice took a step forward. "What are you trying to hide? Your behavior's really hurtful, you know. It's like you're trying to get away from me."

"Of course I'm not."

"So, what, then? Are you in some kind of secret society? Oh my god, are you in a *cult*?"

"No!" Tally gave a nervous laugh. "Honestly, what do you think I am?"

Shaking her head, Alice let her eyes slip past her friend to the doorway from which Tally had just emerged. Nailed to the entrance was a list of the classrooms and offices the hallway contained, and absentmindedly she skimmed it.

BURSAR ~ ROOM 10

SCHOOL NURSE ~ ROOM 21

MR. LOGAN, ENGLISH ~ ROOM 44

"Oh my god." Alice gasped, a look of shock freezing her face.

"What?"

"You haven't. You can't be. That is disgusting."

"What? What are you talking about?"

"Oh, right. Like you don't know."

"Ali, you're scaring me! I have no idea what you're talking about."

"Mr. Logan, you idiot! You're shagging him. Don't think I don't know. All this time you said you were going to the library, you've been sneaking up to his office to do rank things. Fuck. I can't believe this is happening." Alice whipped round and practically flew out of the Quad.

"Hang on!" Tally chased her. "You've got it wrong. Let me explain."

"Explain what? That you're sleeping with a teacher? That's all I need to know, thanks very much." Alice slapped the cold stone wall of the archway as she walked past. "You *swore* to me in Paris that you weren't, but I knew it was you I saw with Mr. Logan in the pub in Hasted. I was such an idiot to let you convince me it wasn't. Thanks a lot, Natalya Abbott. I really love looking like a total fool."

"But you're not a fool. It really wasn't me!" Tally was almost in tears. She couldn't remember the last time Alice had called her by her full name. "I swear."

"Ha!" spat Alice. "That's even worse. Because if it wasn't you, then he's having an affair with you *and* someone else at the same time."

"No way. He's not having an affair with anyone else. *Or* with me," Tally added hastily.

Alice kicked loose a few pebbles as she stomped down the redbrick steps to the Great Lawn. "You've been lying to me for weeks. Why should I believe you now?"

"Because it's true. Honestly, Al, you're jumping to conclusions. You have to listen to me!" Tally's face was wild. She hated arguments, and there was no way she could lose her best friend. She groped for a new tactic. "Anyway, I'm the one who should be pissed off at you—for spying on me!"

Alice stopped short. "Spying?" she shrieked. "Spying? I only came to find you in the library because I got lonely all by myself in our room. Remember? Our room? The one we're sharing because we're meant to be *best friends*?"

Tally sighed shakily and looked at her feet in the dark grass. "You're right," she murmured. "I'm sorry. I have been lying. But not in the way you think. There's nothing dodgy going on, I swear."

"Prove it."

"Fine." Digging in her bag, Tally pulled out her dog-eared copy of *The Portrait of a Lady* and held it up like a shield. "I've been having tutorials with Mr. Logan. That's the truth. He offered to help me because he thinks I'm"—she blushed— "talented. At English." Tally winced and rushed on. She knew how much Alice hated being outdone. "But it's only because he can see what a mess I am. You do amazingly in every subject, Al, but I don't. I'm always forgetting to do homework and stuff, and Mr. Logan's the only teacher who's ever taken me seriously. So, anyway, he's been helping me read this book in advance."

Alice grabbed the volume and flicked through it. Her forehead creased as she scanned the pages and pages of highlights and annotations in Tally's scrawling script.

"What the hell? This is, like, total favoritism." Alice waved the book. "It's such a cheat! If you do better than me because of your private sessions, it'll be so unfair."

Tally rolled her eyes. "Umm, Al, that is so not the point.

This isn't about who does better on exams. It's about my life—I've finally found a subject in school that I actually like."

Alice folded her arms. It was true. Tally was the coolest, most adventurous person she knew, but she'd always been kind of messed up and directionless. And now she seemed to be serious about something that could actually benefit her future. But still. "Why didn't you just tell me this was what you were doing?"

"Because I knew you'd disapprove. You hate Mr. Logan. You've hated him from the second he arrived."

"With good reason," Alice sniffed, drawing herself up straight. "He's corrupting you."

"How?"

"It's so obvious. Have you forgotten your little kleptomania binge? *Ooh, I know, how about I steal this for Mr. Logan? He just loooves illegally obtained presents.*"

Tally blushed fiery red. "That had nothing to do with Mr. Logan. I just wanted the book and I didn't have cash. I'm sorry, okay? Can't we forget about that?"

Alice crossed her arms. "Maybe. Maybe not. What do you love so much about Logan, anyway?"

"I've told you before. How clever and sexy and gorgeous and sensitive he is." Tally's eyes started to shine. "How he's the only adult who's ever believed in me."

"Oh, come on." Alice shifted uncomfortably. Talking about cheesy feelings wasn't her strong point. "I doubt that's true."

"It is," Tally insisted. "I know it. And there's nothing sleazy going on. He's never tried to kiss me or anything, honestly. But I hope he does. I think something might happen in Dublin."

"Oh god, no. This is too weird."

"It's not that weird. Some of the greatest literary figures in the world were into younger women. Like Yeats. He's one of Mr. Logan's favorite poets. I looked him up on Wikipedia and guess what? His wife was less than half his age."

"Yeah, well he was, like, a historical person. This is different. This is the twenty-first century. The fact is, Mr. Logan's twenty-five and you're sixteen. It's creepy."

"It's not. Sixteen's legal in this country. And if we're in love, we're in love. Al, I would have thought you'd understand. You know what it's like to be in love with someone who people would never expect. When you first got together with T, it probably seemed so weird—he was like a brother to you, you'd known him your entire life. But it was amazing, right? And I was glad—because I've always wanted the best for you, and I've always helped you try to get what would make you happy. Why can't you do the same for me? If Mr. Logan and I got together, it'd be my dream come true."

Alice's face had softened, and Tally pressed her advantage. "Can't you see? Sometimes love happens in the strangest places. It takes us by surprise. That's life, and whether it's good or bad—well, does bad really exist if no one's getting hurt?" As she looked at Alice, tears welled onto her cheeks.

"Shit. Babe." Alice hugged her. She loved Tally, and couldn't bear to see her cry. "I didn't mean to be unsupportive. Of course I want you to be happy. Really, I do."

But as she drew back, she regarded her friend with worried eyes. She couldn't help thinking that someone *was* going to get hurt. And it was clear who it would be.

CHAPTER TWENTY-EIGHT

Tudor House's garden was so bloody freezing on Wednesday afternoon that crystals of frost crunched on the grass and glinted on the leaves. Dylan shivered and flipped up the collar of her red wool jacket. Didn't the weather know it was only fucking October? That meager grilled cheese she'd cobbled together in the kitchen definitely hadn't been enough to sustain her out here in the Arctic. She glanced at Alice Rochester, who folded her arms and stared pointedly in the other direction. Alice's nose was already bright red.

"Right, girls, ready?" Miss Sharkreve was rubbing her hands together, puffing out white clouds of breath, and looking extremely smug. "You both know why you're here. The other day, not only did you put on one of the worst displays of juvenile behavior I have ever seen, but you also crushed the famous Tudor House flower beds. So today you're going to give up your electives to fix the damage you've done. And perhaps, in the meantime, you'll learn to get on with each other and iron out your differences."

Alice suppressed a snort. What was this, an Enid Blyton novel? People didn't suddenly kiss and make up just because some stupid teacher tried to "teach them a lesson." Christ.

Sharko pointed to the trays at her feet, filled with pansies and wallflowers and snowdrops and hellebores. "I want you to plant all these flowers according to this scheme drawn up by the gardeners, and I want you to mark each row of flowers with the labels prov—" She sighed, as Alice jumped up and down and waved her hand. "Yes, Alice?"

"Excuse me for interrupting, Miss Sharkreve, but my family's gardener says you can't plant things when the ground's frozen. And he's a professional. Don't you think we should do this another day? Or maybe we should wait till the spring."

Miss Sharkreve smiled vindictively. "Nice try, Alice, but this is only surface frost—the ground hasn't frozen yet. I'm sure your gardener would agree that now is the perfect time to plant our winter flowers." She turned away. "I'll be back to check on you soon. And oh, girls, if you're going to get this done quickly and come out of the cold, you'll have to work *together*."

Yeah right, Alice thought, edging away from Dylan as their housemistress disappeared inside. Sharko was probably going to make herself a nice warm cup of tea while she spied on them slaving away outside the window. Alice stooped and snatched up a trowel. "This is the most inappropriate punishment I've ever heard of. My parents don't pay to send me here so I can learn to be a gardener. I swear, if I get ill, Sharko will be hearing from my father."

Saying nothing, Dylan dragged a tray of pansies nearer the flower bed and began studying the diagram. She felt guilty about getting violent the other day. Normally she'd apologize for losing it like that, but she wasn't about to say sorry to Alice Rochester, who'd made her life miserable for the past month. Still, maybe this little gardening hour might be an opportunity to establish some sort of peace.

"Pass me a pansy, please," Alice droned in a monotone, not looking at Dylan. She'd chipped a small hole in the soil and was holding out her hand.

"Oh, let me do that," Dylan offered. "Why don't we divide up the work? You dig the holes and I'll plant the stuff. It'll go faster that way."

"Wow, thanks, *Stalin*." Alice threw her a filthy look. "I'm not a Communist, you know. We're not, like, working on some kind of communal farm." Alice smirked. She'd studied the Russian Revolution at GCSE, and it really was quite genius of her to reference it now. "Anyway, why should *I* dig the holes? Why don't you do the dirty part?"

"Look around," Dylan snapped before she could stop herself. "I think you'll find there's dirt everywhere. This is a garden, not a spa. We're not getting a manicure, you know."

"Fucking right. You're the last person on earth I'd ever get a manicure with." Alice shoved the pansy into the soil and whacked the earth around it. A hostile silence descended, and as the minutes ticked by, her expression grew darker and darker. She sniffed. God this was boring. The rush of girls to and from Tudor had thinned out now, meaning most of the afternoon activities had begun. Suddenly, the sun was sucked behind a cloud and a freezing gust swept over the lawn, rendering the afternoon even bleaker.

"Oy, Farmer Al," came a husky voice.

Alice twisted on her knees. There was Mimah, wearing a lacrosse uniform and a broad grin across her face.

"Oh, no you don't," Alice threatened mockingly. "If you laugh at me, I'll bury you."

"Farmer Al, how can you say that? I'd *never* laugh at you. The work you do is very serious. Someone has to make the flowers look pretty for us girls."

Alice snatched a pebble and threw it at Mimah.

"Ooh, vicious. If you were my gardener I'd fire you. Anyway, gotta run, just wanted to say I got your text and yes, I can come to London on Saturday. Bring on the underwear shopping! I might bring Charlie along too, if that's okay. I'm trying to straighten her out a bit."

Alice nodded. "Fine. As long as she doesn't mind helping me pick out the perfect panties."

"I'm sure there's nothing she'd rather do. See you later. And don't forget to make the garden grow." Mimah took off.

"Underwear shopping?"

Alice whipped round. Dylan was addressing her with a hopeful look, trying to make conversation. *As if.*

Then again, another few hours of this silent dirt-digging might drive Alice mad. Unlike Tally, she didn't deal well with alone time.

"Yeah," she replied nonchalantly. "Underwear shopping. For my date in Rome at half term."

"I didn't you know you had a date."

"Oh *really*? How weird—I usually confide all the details of my personal life to you." Alice rolled her eyes. "And by the way, it's not with Tristan, in case you were wondering. I've found greener pastures."

Dylan pulled a dead pansy out of the ground. "With who?"

"A guy on his gap year. He's eighteen."

"Name?"

"For fuck's sake." Alice adjusted her gloves, pretending to be put out by Dylan's nosiness but actually quite enjoying bragging. "Boy Stanley-Soames, if you must know."

"Stanley-Soames?" Dylan scratched her chin. "That's two words, huh?"

"Clearly."

"Hmm . . . How interesting. Alice Stanley-Soames . . . You know what that means, right?"

"Um, that you're taking an unhealthy interest in my love life?"

"Nope. That if you married him, your initials would be A-S-S." Dylan giggled. "Suits you."

Alice snorted. But she had to hand it to Dylan: The girl

had attitude—unlike most people, who shriveled up and collapsed in the face of Alice's insults. Her comment had even been vaguely amusing.

"Fucking right it suits me," Alice retorted. "I've always thought I had a nice ass. So what about you? Any word from Jasper?" She concentrated on planting a clump of wallflower, not quite sure why she was bringing up that whole thing. Or, for that matter, why she was taking an interest in Dylan's life, considering it was Dylan's attack that had landed them here in the first place.

"Are you crazy?" Dylan raised her eyebrows. "Don't you think you sabotaged our date effectively enough?"

Alice brushed a trail of soil from her tights. "Maybe. Look, it wouldn't have worked anyway. Jasper doesn't have girlfriends. He just likes to use people for a shag. So I did you a favor."

Dylan studied her nemesis, confused. A sarcastic retort hovered on the tip of her tongue, but she hesitated. Was Alice's tone pleasanter than usual? Had their bitching turned into banter? Impossible. Right?

At that moment, Miss Sharkreve emerged onto the lawn, wearing a blue coat with a yellow silk scarf round her hair. The outfit suited the housemistress's pale, freckled complexion. In fact, she actually looked pretty, which was bizarre. It was always disconcerting when you started to think of teachers as real people.

"I'm glad to see you two making progress," Sharko remarked, scanning the flower beds.

"Oh, thank you, Miss Sharkreve." Alice stroked a pansy petal. "I've started to really enjoy myself. And I just wanted to say again how sorry I—"

"Well, well, isn't this a pleasant gathering," interrupted a male voice.

Alice turned. Ugh. Mr. Logan was strolling through the gap in the hedge at the end of the garden, wearing a shabby jacket with faded elbow pads. He'd probably come to find Tally. Dirty sleaze. Despite Tally's impassioned defense of him last night, Alice still couldn't get over her revulsion.

"Hello, Alice." Mr. Logan gave her a cold nod. "Miss Sharkreve." Teachers always addressed each other formally in front of students—school rules.

Miss Sharkreve brushed a hand through her pale blond hair. "Hello, Mr. Logan."

"That's a nice coat. Is it new?"

"It is indeed."

"Suits you." He looked her up and down. "A lot. Have you got time for a quick word?"

"Of course. I always have time for you, Mr. Logan."

Excuse me? Alice shot Sharko a look and noticed she'd gone pink. Maybe it was from the brisk air. Or maybe not. As the two teachers moved off, she glanced at Dylan, who was staring back with her mouth open.

"Were they just *flirting?*" Dylan gaped.

"What the hell? It looked that way. Why does every woman around here seem to have a crush on Mr. Logan?"

"Gross. *I* don't. He's a creep. And so pretentious."

"Exactly! Thank you! Finally someone agrees with me."

Dylan grimaced. "How could anyone *dis*agree? What a poser. Just look at his hair—I bet he spends hours every day trying to get it to look perfectly messy like that. Reminds me of my mom's stupid boyfriend, Victor Dalgleish."

Alice tittered. "Oh my god, totally. Poor you, having to put up with that washed-up loser. I can't believe I used to love his TV show when I was younger."

"Are you serious?"

"Yeah. Thank goodness I grew out of that."

She and Dylan caught each other's eyes. Were they actually having a sort of okay time together? Alice wheeled round and dug her trowel into the earth.

CHAPTER TWENTY-NINE

"Friday nights at school are the worst," grumbled Rando. He was perched on top of Seb's desk, swinging his ankles back and forth into its wooden sides to produce a kind of discontented drumbeat. He and the rest of their gang were hanging out in Seb and Tristan's room, digesting the bangers and mash they'd just been served at dinner.

"If only there were girls here," Rando went on. "Any girls at all. It'd be so much better. I'm getting worried about myself—I'm even starting to fancy Mrs. Ashe. Help."

"Ugh, Ashe the Tash?" Jasper grimaced. "What turns you on about her—the way she waxes her moustache? The way she gets chalk all over her sleeve when she's writing up the physics equations?"

"Hold it, hold it," interrupted George Demetrios. "I'd like to say two words in Ashe's defense: nice tits. They look hot under those tight sweaters she wears."

"Bloody hell," Tristan groaned. "You lot have got to get a grip. Look, just wait till we get to London after lessons tomorrow, okay? Then you'll be able to see some real girls— ones under thirty years old who don't have bowl haircuts."

He polished off the last of his Snickers bar, tossed the wrapper at the trash can, missed, and picked up his guitar. "Anyway, I wanted to play you guys my new song. I think it's pretty apt, considering the ridiculous levels of sexual frustration in this room."

Rando sighed. "Go for it."

"I'm calling it 'Just Say Yes.'" Tristan struck a chord:

> *"Oh baby you taste so good*
> *And you smell so fine.*
> *Your body's driving me*
> *Out of my mind.*
> *But all we do is kiss*
> *And hold hands—*
> *When the fuck you gonna let me*
> *In your pants?*
> *I want more sex—*
> *And less romance.*
> *I said*
> *I want more sex—*
> *And less romance."*

"Yes!" roared George Demetrios. "Hear, hear. More sex, less romance," he chanted. "More sex, less romance. Girls, if you're listening, it's time to let us in your goddamn pants!"

Rando slapped the desk. "Seriously, T, you are so right. Why does every girl on the planet just want to kiss and snuggle? We want action."

"Not want," George ranted. "*Need.*"

"Yeah," Jasper jumped in, "what's the point of all this bloody testosterone if we can't even use it?"

"Ummm . . ." Seb was looking round in amusement. "Can everyone calm down for one second? It's starting to sound like the fucking army in here. Anyway, T, none of your lyrics rhyme. 'Fine' and 'mind'? 'Hands' and 'pants'? And 'romance'?"

"Whatever." T shrugged. "They almost rhyme. And it doesn't matter anyway—music's all about rhythm and sounds."

"Exactly." George chuckled. "Just like sex. At least, when *I* have sex."

Seb shook his head in disgust. "George, man, really, we don't want to know. So, T, what exactly are these weekend plans of yours? What've you got on the cards for us?"

"Well." Tristan grinned. "Jasper and I have mustered up a pretty hot group. We've tapped the Malbury Hall pool. Bathsheba Fortnum said she'd come, and Cecilia Stiles—"

"Cece's hot," Jasper attested.

"Yep. Really hot. And Hattie Wakefield. Oh, and the Wyndham-Rhodes sisters." T snuck a look at George Demetrios, who'd tried, and spectacularly failed, to have a threesome with those two at his notorious birthday party last month.

"Can't we get Tally Abbott along as well?" Rando panted.

"I know she's St. Cecilia's and not Malbury Hall, but I think one exception—"

"No." T turned away. "Sorry, mate. Tally left this afternoon on some weekend trip to Dublin."

Tristan neglected to mention the fact that he wouldn't have invited Tally in any case. If he had, he'd have had to invite Alice Rochester, too, and that would have defeated the purpose.

CHAPTER THIRTY

"Ali, these are so you," giggled Charlie Calthorpe de Vyle-Hanswicke, dangling a pair of white satin nipple tassels from her fingertips. She and Mimah were prowling round the Agent Provocateur flagship in Soho, helping Alice seek out the ideal date-night underwear. The shop's interior was totally bordello-chic, complete with flowery wallpaper, black velvet armchairs, and pink oriental lanterns. Wire models hung from above, modelling sexy bras, corsets, stockings, and suspenders. Wooden display cabinets showcased kinky and fabulously expensive handcuffs and whips.

Charlie held the tassels against her chest and shimmied so they jiggled back and forth. "Perfect for giving Boy a lap dance. Wooohooo!"

"Charlie!" Mimah scolded.

Alice giggled.

"Ladies. May I help you?" sniffed a lipsticked sales assistant with a peroxide pixie cut. Her cleavage bulged out of her very tight, very pink, nurse-style uniform.

"We're already being helped," Alice informed her airily. "In fact, I'm about to try some things on." Turning away, she snatched a leopard-print bra off its hanger, making sure the server got an eyeful of her Chanel handbag. Alice was used to dealing with shop assistants. If they knew you had money, they treated you with proper respect. "Girls, I'll be in the changing rooms."

Mimah waved. "'Kay, babe. Give us a shout when you've got something to model. And if you don't find anything we can go to Myla or something instead."

"Oh, I'll definitely find something—Tally said I would. This is her favorite lingerie shop in London, and she knows her stuff."

"Tally must have some pretty kinky taste, then," Charlie muttered as the dressing-room curtains swished shut behind Alice. She was examining a pair of panties with a red opening sewn into their crotch.

"Hey," Mimah whispered suddenly, seizing her sister and dragging her behind a display case. "I need a word with you. This is urgent."

"Whoa! No need to be so rough."

"Fine. Sorry. But listen—you can't say a word to Alice about our Boy suspicions."

"Why on earth not?"

"Because we haven't really filled her in yet."

"Are you serious?" Charlie almost dropped the panties she was holding. "Then what was the point of all my spying?"

"So we could protect her if we found out anything for sure. But Tally and I have discussed it: We don't have any proof at the moment, and we think it's time for Alice to get over T. If you let anything slip about Boy, she might go running back to Tristan before she gets to lose her virginity."

Charlie stared. "Alice Rochester is a *virgin?*"

"Shhh! Only her best friends know. I'm only telling you because you're my sister. And because I trust you." Mimah gave Charlie a look.

"Girlies!" Alice trilled, sticking her head through the curtains. "Where are you? Oh, there. Advice please. Come in, come in."

Mimah and Charlie parted the purple silk curtains and crowded inside Alice's cubicle. Over her Calvin Klein thong, Alice had tried on a pair of skimpy blue lace boy shorts decorated with bows. On top, a matching blue lace bra was sort of sagging off her chest.

"Whoa, Al," Charlie gushed. "Those panties are awesome— they give you amazing butt cleavage!"

"Butt *what?*"

"Butt cleavage. You know, when underwear doesn't cover the whole of your butt crack and you can see a bit of it peeking out the top. Sooo sexy."

Mimah was staring at her little sister. "How on earth do you know anything about that?"

"I know lots of things."

"Oh, really?"

"Yeah, really. Test me."

"Maybe I will."

"Truce, truce," Alice cut in. She'd twisted round and was staring at her skinny backside in the mirror. "I'm not sure butt cleavage is going to help—Boy won't see it till he's already got most of my clothes off. I need some *real* cleavage to tempt him with." She looked at Mimah, who'd had the biggest boobs in their clique ever since they were thirteen. "You're such a lucky thing. You've actually got some."

"You've got some too!" Mimah squinted at Alice's A-cup chest. "Well, I mean, you could. Just buy a massively padded bra. I saw a cool polka-dot push-up one outside—want me to get it?"

Alice tweaked one of the bows on her shorts. "I don't know. Isn't that false advertising? I mean, what's the point in making Boy think I have big boobs? If he sees them naked—"

"*When* he sees them naked . . ."

"Whatever—*when* he sees them—he'll be pissed off at how small they are. He'll think I tricked him."

Mimah scoffed. "I doubt it. I bet most guys don't give a crap when they get to that point. They're just so excited to have your panties off. They're concentrating on other things." She gave a suggestive wink.

"No, Ali's right," Charlie piped up. "I read a survey in

Cosmo. Thirty percent of men said they get disappointed when a girl has way smaller boobs than they'd expected."

"Well, then men are dicks," Mimah declared. "And what kind of men answer *Cosmo* surveys, anyway? Losers. Tell me you're not getting your love-life advice from there." She turned back to Alice. "Look, I'm not saying you should stuff chicken fillets in there or anything. And definitely stay away from those gel bras. Just get one with a little lift."

"But that's the kind I wear all the time anyway." Alice sighed. "I wanted something different for my date."

"Then don't wear any underwear at all. Just put on a short skirt and a see-through top. That'll get him."

"Maybe." Alice giggled. "Except that we'll be in Rome. I mean, hello? Vespas?"

Mimah tittered.

"Wait." Charlie looked anxious. "I don't get it."

"Think about it. What'll Alice do if she has to, like, straddle the seat?"

At that moment, Alice's phone rang. As she reached for it, Mimah grabbed her arm.

"Wait, wait, if that's Boy, tell him you're underwear shopping. It'll make him totally horny!"

"It's not Boy. It's Jasper. Hey, Jas."

"Al, babes, hi," came Jasper's posh, drawling voice on the other end of the line. "How's things?"

"Fine."

"Fantastic. Look, I've got a favor to ask."

Alice perched herself on the ottoman in front of her mirror. "What about?"

"Your cousin Coco's party in Rome next weekend. Think there's any chance I could invite a guest?"

"A guest?" Alice narrowed her eyes suspiciously. "It's a bit short notice. Why? Who did you want to ask?"

"Oh, just Dylan."

"Dylan *Taylor*? But I heard your date went horribly!"

"Who told you? Did she tell you that?"

"Ummm, possibly." Alice cleared her throat. "I can't remember. Who cares? Why are you still trying with her?"

"Because the fuck-up was all my fault and I feel bad about it," Jasper said. "And you should feel bad too, since you gave me shitty advice."

"I did not! I told you Dylan liked manly men. It's not my fault if you acted like a total date rapist."

Jasper sighed. "Fine, whatever. Anyway, I wanted to make it up to her. I've realized I actually quite like her, Al—more than I've liked anyone in ages. I thought an invite to the party of the season might convince her to give me another chance."

"Sorry, no can do." Alice pursed her lips. But for some reason, she didn't feel as pissed off as she usually would at a request like this involving Dylan. "Aunt and Uncle Frisk finalized the list months ago, and it's not like Dylan's family is important enough for an exception to be made. Also, the party's being thrown by Italian *Vogue*, so they'll probably have a strict door policy. Anyway, gotta go, I'm trying on underwear in Soho."

"Soho? In London?"

"No. Soho in Australia. Duh. I'm with Mime."

"Wicked. We're in London too—the whole crew. Why don't you come join?"

Alice's heartbeat quickened. The whole crew—that meant T was there too. Why hadn't she known about this little trip?

"Oh, right." Alice tried to keep her voice steady. "That might be nice. Where are you?"

"The usual pub on the King's Road."

"I guess we could hop in a cab when I'm finished here."

"Yeah, great. Perfect."

"See you soon."

Alice dropped her phone back into her bag. Maybe it wasn't such a great idea to spend Saturday night in the same place as T. But she couldn't resist. At least this way she'd get to check out what he was up to.

CHAPTER THIRTY-ONE

*A*n evening drizzle spattered the windows of O'Leary's Guesthouse in Dublin, where Tally was standing in front of the mirror in her lamp-lit bedroom, speedily tracing on eyeliner. The bed-and-breakfast, nestled down a narrow cobbled street just south of the River Liffey, was every bit as romantic as Mr. Logan had promised. Its high beds were piled with woolen blankets and warm patchwork quilts. Its furniture was heavy and old-fashioned. The room Tally was sharing with Cherry Rupert-Greene even had a fireplace. Fine, it had been bricked up and filled with an electric heater, but still, it added to the sense of history.

In fact, Tally thought, Dublin was proving pretty historical all round. After arriving late last night and falling into bed, the St. Cecilia's group had spent today doing cultural things, like visiting the Dublin Writers Museum and the National Gallery of Ireland. Miss Baskin had insisted on the art part despite the fact that everyone had been famished and tired.

"Gabby Bunter has expressed an interest in Irish landscape painting," she'd said. "We'll do a full tour."

Snore. The gallery's only saving grace had been the fact that Mr. Logan really did know about Irish art, which only added to his sexiness.

Tally glanced at her watch and brushed on silver eye-shadow. As usual, she was late. All eight students on the trip were meant to be downstairs in the living room at quarter to seven, which was exactly one minute ago, and she wasn't ready at all. Unfortunately, being on time tonight was important, since the whole group was going on some kind of literary pub crawl that Mr. Logan had booked in advance. The idea was to traipse round the drinking spots that great writers used to frequent, getting pissed as the two tour guides acted out famous bits from Irish books and plays. Sounded geeky. But whatever—as long as booze and Mr. Logan were involved, Tally was game.

"Hurry up, let's get a move on," came Cherry Rupert-Greene's voice from the bathroom. Cherry's father was a music producer, meaning he was the kind of person who could name his daughter something dumb like Cherry and get away with it.

"Hot outfit, babe. Where'd you get the dress?" Tally asked, trying to buy herself more time as she burrowed in her suitcase for her digital camera. She was always losing everything.

"Dior." Cherry tossed her long, highlighted hair. She'd paired the extremely short, low-cut pink number with black leggings and heels, and her lips were glistening with gloss. The whole getup was more club-worthy than pub-worthy. Not that there was anything out of the ordinary about sexing yourself up on a school trip. All the St. Cecilia's girls did it. Style was a game of one-upmanship, and winning affected your reputation for weeks.

"You look good too," remarked Cherry, casting a glance at Tally's skintight black jeans, high ankle boots, and slinky halter-neck studded with Swarovski crystals. "Good" was an understatement. It wasn't exactly easy being stuck sharing a room with Tally Abbott. She always looked stunning whatever she was wearing, and ridiculously gorgeous when she made an effort like tonight.

Ten minutes later, the group of eight St. Cecilia's juniors and two teachers left O'Leary's, heading into busier streets a few minutes away. The pub crawl was due to begin at the Duke pub, where—Mr. Logan had informed Tally—James Joyce used to get his alcohol fix when he wasn't writing masterpieces. Tally didn't know who James Joyce was, never mind what masterpieces he'd written, but apparently he was Mr. Logan's favorite Irish author. First thing tomorrow, she was going to buy one of his books.

The drizzle grew more insistent.

"My hair," lamented Cherry Rupert-Greene as they entered a lively alleyway.

"At least yours doesn't frizz up," retorted Zanna Balfour. "It stays completely straight. Mine's turning into a bush."

"Hardly," chimed in Felicity Foxton, who was sharing a room with Zanna. "Anyway, we are *so* getting wasted tonight, and then you won't care."

"If only I had hair like Tally's," Zanna moaned, "always perfect. By the way, Tals, are you invited to Coco Frisk's engagement party next weekend?"

"Of course Tally's invited, idiot." Felicity pouted at her own reflection in a shop window as they passed. "She's Alice Rochester's best friend. Coco's invited all of Alice's crew."

"Gosh, you lucky thing," gasped Zanna. "I'd give anything to go to that bash. The Italian actor who Coco's marrying— Lorenzo da Fonseca—he is sooo hot."

"Oh my god, I know. Have you met him? Tally?" Cherry nudged her. "Have you?"

Tally nodded, even though she had no idea what Cherry was chattering on about. She was too busy staring ahead at Mr. Logan, who was deep in conversation with Miss Baskin. Tally hadn't quite appreciated how annoying Miss Baskin was until now. Or what bad style sense the woman had. She was wearing a long, hippyish skirt—the kind that only an art teacher would ever try to pull off—with a flea-bitten sheepskin vest that she'd probably bought at some nasty charity shop. Tally frowned. Mr. Logan was most likely chatting to Miss Baskin out of politeness, but that didn't make up for it—every second the two teachers spent together was a second of this trip wasted.

"Now, girls." Miss Baskin turned and faced the group as they reached the pub, barring their way through the door.

"Budge it," Felicity grunted under her breath. "I'm cold."

"I expect everyone to act responsibly tonight," Miss Baskin continued. "Stay with the group at all times. And no alcohol for anyone underage. Do you hear me? None. And that means all of you."

A collective groan rose up. Cherry and Zanna rolled their eyes. As if you could forbid people from drinking on a fucking pub crawl. Luckily Miss Baskin wasn't the sharpest tool in the box, so they could probably slip a few past her.

Inside, the four girls settled round a small table, and Tally whipped out her Canon.

"Smile, gang. Everyone say 'Dublin.'"

"Dubliiin," the others singsonged, flashing their perfect teeth.

"Adorable! That is *so* cute."

"Speaking of cute." Felicity leaned in. "Mr. Logan looks pretty sexy tonight, don't you guys think?"

Tally's eyes shot to her face. *Stay away from Logan!* she wanted to scream. *He's mine!* But she didn't. Instead she shrugged and rolled her eyes, as if only a freak could possibly find a teacher attractive.

"Yeah," Zanna jumped in. "His blue sweater totally brings out his bright blue eyes."

"He has such a cheeky smile."

"Do you think he has a girlfriend?"

"No," Tally snapped. "I mean, not that I've ever thought about it, but I doubt it. He's too dedicated to his work."

"That's rubbish. He must have some kind of sex life. He's not that old."

"I'll bet he's shagging one of the teachers," Felicity whispered. "Or lots of them. They're probably all dying for some action."

"They probably take turns lining up outside his office!"

"Everyone except Mrs. Traphorn. That frigid old trout wouldn't know a man if one hit her in the face."

"Shhh!" tittered Cherry. "Here he comes."

"Hello, girls," Mr. Logan cut in, sauntering up to their table. "How's everyone? Taking pictures, I see?"

"Lots of them," Zanna answered. "Oooh, Mr. Logan, let's get one of you." She grabbed the camera. "Give us a pose."

"Well . . ." The teacher swung up a chair next to Tally's and tossed his curls. "I suppose I can manage that. How's this?" He draped his arm over the back of Tally's seat and grinned dashingly.

Flash!

"Gorgeous."

"Mr. Logan," Cherry asked, "what exactly happens on this pub crawl? Have you been on it before?"

"I have indeed." The teacher nodded. "See that map over there?"

"Yeah. So?"

"It shows all the places they take us."

As Zanna, Cherry, and Felicity turned to look, Mr. Logan leaned toward Tally. "Come on," he said in a low voice. "I'll buy you a Guinness. You've got to try at least one while we're in Dublin."

"But you're not allowed to let us drink. Miss Baskin said."

"It'll have to be our little secret, then." Mr. Logan winked. "Won't it?"

CHAPTER THIRTY-TWO

Try to look old. And confident," Mimah ordered Charlie as the girls walked up to the Bull & Butcher, their crew's regular pub on the King's Road. "And keep your mouth shut—let me and Al order the drinks."

"Chill, Mime," Alice interrupted. "Everything'll be fine. None of our crew have ever been ID'd here. Why should they start now?"

"We hope." Charlie crossed her fingers. This wasn't the first time she'd been to the pub or anything, but it was the first time in months Mimah had invited her out with her friends—and if anything went wrong, it might be the last. If the bartender noticed Charlie was underage, he might notice that Mimah and Alice were too—and that would really piss them off.

A roar of conversation hit the three girls as they entered the main bar. Even though it was only six o'clock, the place was packed. Mostly with boarding school types, Charlie noticed—you could tell by the girls' big, chaotic hairdos, cashmere tops, and designer handbags, and the boys' quiffs, baggy jeans, and check shirts.

"Whoa, no way!" Mimah stopped short as she caught sight of their crew's regular table by the fireplace. "Great, Al. Thanks for warning me *they* were gonna be here."

"Who?"

"The Malbury Hall bitches."

"*What?*" Alice elbowed Mimah out the way.

"You try and get rid of them," Mimah muttered. "I'll buy us drinks."

"Hmph," Alice grunted, barely hearing. She'd taken it for granted that Tristan, Jasper, Seb, Rando, and George Demetrios would be alone in the pub, bored shitless and grateful for the slightest hint of female company. After all, without her and her gang, what kind of social life did those Hasted House boys have?

A pretty fucking feisty one, from the look of things.

"OMG, Tristan Murray-Middleton, you are so naughty!" Cecilia Stiles gave a laugh that sounded like the tinkling of tiny bells and dipped her head toward T. Her fluffy brown hair tumbled forward and the scent of fruity shampoo wafted up his nostrils. Tristan grinned. So far, his plan was running smoothly. He was feeling relaxed after two pints, Cece was lapping up his stories, and for the first time in ages he was out enjoying himself without having to worry about Alice.

He'd thought.

"Psst, T." Seb chucked a coaster at him from the other side of the table. "What are *they* doing here? What's going on?"

"Who?"

But there was no need for Seb to answer, because just then, T caught sight of a familiar figure—tall and angular—wearing a familiar brown leather jacket and standing less than a meter from their group. No way . . .

"Oy." He elbowed Jasper. "What the fuck is Alice Rochester doing here?"

"Take a wild guess." Jasper wasn't in the best mood. For the past half hour, he'd been making a halfhearted effort to chat up Bathsheba Fortnum. The problem was, Bathsheba was dullsville compared to Dylan. And things were looking hopeless with Dylan now that he couldn't invite her to Rome. "Maybe she's thirsty."

"Thanks for being so helpful," Tristan retorted. "Who the fuck invited her?"

"Me. Why? Got a problem?"

"No." Tristan sighed. "I just thought we'd agreed to have a night out without that lot for once. That's all." As he said this, his eyes fell on Charlotte Calthorpe de Vyle-Hanswicke who was hovering behind George Demetrios's chair. She was twisting her fingers, looking for somewhere to sit.

"Charlie," he called. Mimah's little sister was a sweetheart, and besides, she might be good for some info.

Alice watched as Charlie skipped over to Tristan and plonked into the chair he'd pulled up. It was thoughtful of T to include her. It reminded Alice of how lovely he'd always been to Hugo, her fourteen-year-old brother who went to Hasted House. She strained to catch what he and Charlie were talking about, and frowned as George Demetrios's voice drowned out everything in earshot.

"Hi, T," Charlie grinned. "Thanks for rescuing me."

"No problem. Haven't seen you in ages, Charl. How's things?"

"Fine."

"Come on . . ." Tristan nudged her. "You're not getting off that easily. How's the old love life? Any crushes at the moment? I give very good advice."

Charlie reddened.

"Uh-ohhh—I can tell there's *someone.*"

"Well . . ." Charlie bit her nail. "I mean, sort of. There's this guy at Glendale named Benji. But he doesn't know I exist."

"Course he does! Tell me the truth—that's why you came to London, isn't it? You were following him round."

"*No.*" Charlie rolled her eyes. "We were underwear shopping for Alice."

"What?" Tristan gulped his beer. "For goodness' sake, doesn't Alice have enough underwear?"

"Yeah, the normal kind." Charlie giggled. "But not the sexy kind. She wanted some new lacy panties for her date with Boy in Rome. I mean . . ." Charlie slapped her hand over her mouth. "Oh, look," she squeaked. "Uhhh, here comes Mimah. Better go help her with the drinks."

Tristan didn't reply, his face stormy as Charlie scuttled off. He drained the rest of his pint.

"T?" Cece said. "Tristan, hello? You've been ignoring me for the past five minutes. Are you okay?"

"Yeah," T replied, looking straight into Cece's big, full eyes. He slipped his arm round the back of her chair. "Yeah. Everything's fine."

"Cheers." Rando clinked Alice's rum and Coke, which Mimah had just deposited on the table. "This is a nice surprise. T said he'd only invited Malbury Hall girls tonight."

"Oh, really?" Alice gripped her drink. "How nice. I hope you're all having jolly good fun."

"Yeah, thanks, we are." Rando cleared his throat. "So, how's Tally? I hear she's in Dublin."

"Hmm?" Alice sneaked another glance across the table, even though it was painful. Somehow, she felt the need to keep an eye on Tristan—maybe because staring at him was as close as she could get to controlling what he did. Or maybe because she couldn't bear to be the last one to know if he got together with . . . anyone else. Alice glared. Cecilia Stiles was dangerously cute. Her big hazel eyes, upturned nose and giggly voice made all boys think she was the sweetest little angel in the world. Ugh. And, tonight, the bitch looked fabulous. She was wearing a purple jersey dress that scooped halfway down her back, a gold chain belt around her waist, and knee-high Chanel boots. Suddenly Alice felt like a total tramp. Why hadn't she gone home to change into something sexier than her white wool roll-neck dress, which, by the way, was beginning to itch? Then at least she might have been some competition for the Malbury sluts. They were baring enough flesh to open a strip club.

"Hey, Al," Rando prodded. "Are you listening?"

"Of course. Duh. What do you want?"

"Nothing. I mean . . ." Rando picked at the sleeve of his green sweater. "Listen, please don't tell Tally I asked you this, but—well, do you think I have a chance?"

"What, with her?" Alice shut her eyes. She'd known for ages that Rando fancied Tally, but really—did he have to ask such lame questions at a time like this?

"Is that a yes?"

"Did it look like a yes?"

"I don't know. Just be straight with me. Please!"

Something about Rando's tone caught Alice off guard. She studied his face. It had a compelling quality—a boyish attractiveness combined with something more determined, more intense. It hadn't occurred to her before that Tom Randall-Stubbs might be sexy—when she'd met him, she'd been too preoccupied with T to notice another guy. But now she noticed how Rando's dark brown hair contrasted with his glass-blue eyes, how his dimples and pointy teeth gave his smile a cheeky, dashing air.

"I don't know." Alice shrugged. "Tally and I haven't ever discussed you. I guess you could have a chance. What exactly do you like about her?"

"Everything," Rando gushed. "What's not to like? Tally's so angelic. And so kind. And so sweet."

"Kind? Sweet?" Alice grimaced. Boys were so predictable—and not in any good ways. "What's so great about those things?"

"Huh?" Rando's mouth dropped in confusion.

"Come on. You only think Tally's kind and sweet because she's pretty and blond." Alice glared over at Cece Stiles again. She was getting fed up with the way boys thought. "Maybe you men should look below the surface for once."

"What do you mean?" Rando's face was more befuddled than ever. "Tally's a complete saint."

"Ha," Alice spat. "If you only knew. That girl's got so many problems." She dropped her voice, knowing it was a bit mean to talk about her best friend like this, but unable to help it. Rando needed to be shocked out of his stupid doe-eyed state. "She's so incredibly damaged. You know, like, messed up."

"Oh, please."

"I'm not lying. Just between you and me, Tally's life's a mess. Her mum lives in Moscow and basically kicked her out of the house when she was fourteen. That's why she lives over here. And her dad—he's a total cokehead. Everyone knows. I worry about her. It's exhausting."

Rando shook his head. "But she seems so happy and normal."

"No one's normal," Alice countered sagely. "But Tally Abbott's definitely not." She was practically whispering now. "The other day, she did something that shocked even me."

"Shit. What?"

"No." Alice folded her arms. "I can't. I mustn't tell you."

"Go on."

"Okay. But swear it won't make you think any less of her."

"I swear."

Alice took a deep breath. "Okay. So we were in this bookstore in Hasted. I was browsing round and Tally was in the back room, and the poor old half-blind lady who owned the place was snoozing off in her chair. I had no idea Tally was up to anything weird. But when we tried to leave, I found out—she'd stolen something. She'd stuffed this really expensive, really valuable book into her coat and was trying to smuggle it out. Like a common thief."

"No way. How did you find out?"

"The old lady caught her."

Rando gasped.

"She nearly phoned the police. I had to plead with her not to. Can you imagine if we'd been arrested? I've never been so embarrassed in my life."

"Fuck me." Rando stared at the wooden tabletop, slowly shaking his head.

"I know." Alice sipped her rum and Coke and eyed Cece Stiles again over the rim of the glass. "Bad, isn't it? Promise me you won't tell a soul."

*   *   *

"Round *numero dos*," Seb declared, placing one pint on the table in front of Mimah, and one in front of himself. "Cheers."

"Thanks," Mimah crooned. When she'd first joined the group, she'd managed to end up next to Seb by barging between him and Hattie Wakefield, much to Hattie's chagrin. Not that Mimah gave a shit. She hadn't spoken to Seb in ages, and now that Sonia was MIA, this was her chance. She watched his bony fingers nervously trace patterns on his glass.

"Have you seen the Rothko exhibition at the Tate Modern?" he asked.

"No, I'm not into Rothko." Mimah wiped a line of foam off her top lip. "He's a hack. He just paints clumps of color and sticks them on the wall. I could do a Rothko myself and sell it for a million pounds if I felt like it."

"No," Seb protested. "You couldn't. If you really understood Rothko's work, you'd see how emotional it is. It's . . . it's—"

"I'll tell you what it is." Mimah cut him off. "It's Saturday night. Why are we wasting time talking about art? I want to talk about something interesting. Like your love life. What's going on with you and Sonia, huh?"

"Nothing. Christ." Seb stared across the table to where Tristan was leaning in so close to Cecilia Stiles that their hair was touching. "Why is everyone always asking that?"

"Because she obviously fancies you. So if nothing's going on, there must be a reason. Like maybe you're into someone else." Mimah reached under the table and brushed a finger over Seb's knee. "Right?"

He jerked away his leg.

"I don't get you." Mimah pouted. "It's almost as if you don't like girls at all."

Seb shoved back his chair. "I'm going to the toilet," he mumbled, and strode away.

The lights had dimmed, the music had grown louder, and Alice was on her fifth rum and Coke by the time Tristan and Cece stood up and headed for the door. Where the hell were they off to? Alice's eyes stuck to Tristan so intently she thought they might burn a hole in his back. He pulled a pack of cigarettes from his pocket. Okay, that was fine—he and Cece were obviously going outside for a smoke. They'd be back in five minutes and everything would be normal.

But five minutes passed. And another five. Still no sign. Alice pulled herself to her feet. All that rum seemed to have made her legs numb, because she wobbled and had to grab Rando's shoulder for support. But he didn't notice—he was too busy playing footsie with Hattie Wakefield, on his other side.

"I'll be back," Alice slurred to no one in particular.

Hardly registering her own movements, she squeezed through the crowd, past the bar, and out the front door, where the icy air hit her like a cold lake. In her rush, she'd forgotten her jacket. But it didn't matter—the chill felt good on her hot cheeks.

T and Cece weren't in the crush of smokers round the entrance. Nor were they farther out on the pavement. Alice's heart pattered faster. A gust of wind swept past and she shivered. Something was wrong. She walked round the side of the pub, wobbling, and was suddenly struck by a wave of nausea. There they were, the two of them, pressed up against the pub's brick wall. T was kissing Cece, his eyes closed, his fingers running through her hair. Cece's hands were inside his blazer, wrapped round his waist. No! Alice tottered and reached for the rough bricks. She needed to sit down. There was no seat. She yanked her phone from her pocket and speed-dialed Tally's number.

Ring ring. Ring ring. Ring ring. Ring ring. Ring ring.

"Hi. This is Tally Abbott. Please leave a message."

Fuck. Alice raised her face to the starless sky. That indifferent, recorded voice was the loneliest sound in the world right now. What could her best friend possibly be doing? Why wasn't she picking up?

CHAPTER THIRTY-THREE

*D*ublin's early-evening drizzle had intensified into pouring rain. Damp and shivering, huddled under a gray stone archway in Trinity College, the St. Cecilia's flock and their teachers peered out at the courtyard where Oscar Wilde had supposedly lived during his days as a student here. Tally tried to give a shit, since Mr. Logan seemed interested, but it was hard to care about dead writers when the toes of your new ankle boots were getting soaked by streams of dirty water. Thank god this was one of the last stops on the interminable literary pub crawl. Tally's head was reeling from the two and a half pints of Guinness Mr. Logan had bought her along the way. Her slim figure had always made her a bit of a lightweight, and now she could barely concentrate on what their actor tour guides were babbling about. Only one thing was clear: She had to be with Mr. Logan. *Alone.*

"Rrright, everyone," boomed one of the guides, rolling his

r's and flourishing his bowler hat. "Brrrollies at the rrready! Onto the next stop—quick march!"

As people started shuffling forward with groans, Tally sidled up to her English teacher. "Mr. Logan?"

"Yes, Natalya?"

"Didn't you say that your favorite author, James Joyce, had rooms round here when he was at uni? I'd love it if you could show me."

Mr. Logan shook his head. "James Joyce didn't go to Trinity. He went to University College. Easy mistake, though."

Damn. No shit it was an easy mistake—Tally had been completely faking it. She racked her brains. They absolutely had to lose the others. "Well, how about you, Mr. Logan? Didn't you study here for a bit? I'm dying to see where you lived."

"Are you, now?"

"Yes. Pretty please?"

Mr. Logan's cheeks dimpled. They were flushed with alcohol and cold. "Now, how could anyone resist a face like that?" he said, glancing round. "Come on—we'll have to be sneaky, though—we're not meant to split off from the group. If Miss Baskin notices we're missing, she'll have my head."

Squeezing Tally's arm, the teacher drew her close, under his umbrella. She nestled her nose into his coat, as subtly as possible, breathing in his delicious warm smell. Her legs felt weak.

"Shhh, quietly," Mr. Logan whispered, his mouth right near

hers. His breath was warm on her face, and heavy with whiskey. Watching as the others sloshed into the courtyard, he tugged her backward until they rounded the other side of the arch and were hidden from view.

"This way." Tightening his arm round Tally's delicate shoulders, Mr. Logan hurried her through an open square. The rain drummed on his umbrella, cozily, like they were in a tent. They crossed that square, then two more, then, rounding the side of an imposing stone building, Mr. Logan halted and indicated a row of windows.

"Here we are. I lived on the third floor. That set of rooms, there."

"Wow." Tally gazed at the black panes of glass, picturing him scribbling away under low ceilings late into the night. "How old were you?"

"Nineteen." Mr. Logan sighed. "I remember it so well—how impassioned and eager I was. A bit like you." His eyes lingered on her face. "Not as ravishing."

"Oh, I'm sure you were," Tally exclaimed, then checked herself. "I mean, not that I was trying to say I'm ravishing or anything—"

"You are." Mr. Logan's eyes were brimming and soft under the lamps. "You're gorgeous."

Tally's chest swelled. Something echoed in the square. Footsteps. A night watchman wandered past and nodded, his shadow thrown large against the stone walkway.

"Is that the river, over there?" Tally whispered.

"No." Mr. Logan flicked his eyes off hers and pushed a hand through his dark brown curls. "It's farther off. Down there."

"I'd love to see it at night. Looked stunning from my window."

"It is." Mr. Logan's boyish profile was pensive against the haze. He lowered his head for a moment, then nodded slightly, as if he'd decided something. "Come with me. O'Connell Bridge is just a few minutes' walk. I want to show you one of my favorite views in Dublin."

Sheltering Tally under his umbrella again, he led the way out of the labyrinthine college and along a busy street. Lights from cars and windows and shop signs shimmered and fragmented on the wet pavement. Up ahead, round lamps floated on the bridge. As Tally and Mr. Logan waited to cross the road, a truck roared by and skimmed up a wall of water.

"Careful!" Mr. Logan lurched toward Tally in a clumsy attempt to shield her.

"Too late," she shrieked, laughing. "I'm already drenched!" Drunkenly, she stumbled backward and Mr. Logan caught her round the waist. He chuckled too, grinning, his blue eyes dancing. His fingers tightened over her body. "Are you sure you're okay?"

"Y-yes." Tally drew a shuddering breath, feeling the warmth of his hands radiate through her clothes.

"Good," he breathed, relaxing his grip after a second.

The rain relented as they strolled onto the bridge, and Mr. Logan leaned forward with his elbows on the balustrade, his gaze miles away. Neither said anything for a while—they let the river slip silently under them like a great snake gliding into the night. Tally heard the current without seeing it. She felt Mr. Logan next to her. The air between them seemed magnetized, pulling every atom of her body toward him. All her energy, all her thought, was trained on him. He had to be feeling the same. Sexual tension couldn't be one-sided, could it?

A lone seagull squawked.

"You must be cold," Mr. Logan murmured.

Tally shook her head, not daring to speak for fear of breaking the spell.

The teacher looked into his student's large, silver eyes. They were glowing in the moonlight, her blond hair framing her face like a halo, the rain glistening on her skin. The city shone around them.

"Someone should paint you, Natalya." Mr. Logan tucked a strand of her hair behind her ear. "Only a great artist could do you justice."

Tally inhaled the smell of his clothes, his skin. "I want to stay here forever," she breathed.

Mr. Logan lifted his palm to the side of her face, and cupped her cheek. Tally's heart was beating so fast she thought it might jump through her ribs. Slowly, he moved his lips toward her—brushed them against her forehead—drew away.

Tally shut her eyes. Suddenly, impulsively, she ducked forward and kissed him on the mouth. A pulse ran through her body. She'd imagined this moment so many times, but none of her fantasies could compare to his taste, to the feel of his lips on hers.

For a split second Mr. Logan kissed her back, then—"No!"—he pulled away. "What on earth are you doing? We can't. This isn't right. It's against the rules. It's against the law. And anyway, I . . . I . . . ," he trailed off.

"What?"

"I . . . Nothing. I just can't. This has to stop."

"But I thought you liked me," Tally croaked, her eyes filling with tears.

"I do like you. I like you very much. You're one of the most beautiful, talented girls I've ever seen."

"But—but that's not what I meant." Tally held her breath a moment to prevent a huge sob heaving out. "I love you," she whispered.

"Oh, Natalya, sweetheart. Don't cry. I'm sorry. Please." Mr. Logan stroked his fingertips over Tally's cheek. Then he leaned in and nuzzled away her tears. "Oh god, forgive me," Mr. Logan murmured, pulling her close again and kissing her passionately. Her heart swelling, Tally pressed into him as he half lifted her against the balustrade in his strong arms. He twined his hands in her hair and kissed her and kissed her. The wind howled around them but it didn't matter, because in his embrace she didn't feel the chill.

CHAPTER THIRTY-FOUR

N o way," Alice gasped. "No fucking way."

"Yes. Way." Tally stared into Alice's eyes across the table. It was Sunday evening and the two best friends, fresh from London and Dublin, respectively, had scheduled a debriefing in the dining hall, over dinner. "You'd better believe it. Would I make this up?"

Alice gaped. "But did you—" She peered round furtively, making sure none of the girls sitting near her and Tally was eavesdropping. "Did you *sleep* with him?"

"No. Not even close."

Alice heaved a sigh of relief. *Thank god.* At least not *every-thing* was out of control. "What happened?"

"Miss Baskin rang Mr. Logan's mobile while we were still on the bridge. He was so flustered, he almost dropped his phone in the river—but she wasn't even suspicious. Mr. Logan told her I'd got food poisoning and she totally bought it. Moron!"

"Why shouldn't she buy it?" Alice said loudly. "That story's a hell of a lot more likely than what actually happened—you two getting it on."

"Shut up!" Tally's eyes widened. "Quiet. No one can find out about this, not a single soul. I'm dead serious. Mr. Logan could go to prison if anyone finds out."

"He could not!" Alice argued, but she was whispering now. "I mean, maybe he could get fired. But you're sixteen. You said so yourself—you're over the age of consent in the UK, meaning it's not a *crime*."

"Wrong. It is. He's my teacher. No matter what age I am, and who kissed who, he'd still get blamed."

"Shit." Alice pushed away her plate of sausages and mash. This didn't sound like it could end well. At all. Actually, as far as she was concerned, it shouldn't even have begun—but she wasn't about to risk losing Tally over that old argument again.

"Hey, tell me," she breathed, cupping her mouth to Tally's ear so no one could read her lips. She hesitated, curiosity wrestling with disapproval. "What— what was it like? Snogging a teacher, I mean. It must have been *so* weird."

"It was! So weird. And amazing. It's the most amazing thing that's—"

"Wait, shhh! Here come—"

"Well, well, well," cackled Mimah, "what are you two little gossips whispering about? Keeping secrets, are we?" She crashed down her tray opposite Alice and Tally, followed by Sonia, whose plate was sprinkled with lettuce leaves and grated carrots.

"Secrets?" Sonia frowned. "I hope not. I thought friends didn't keep secrets."

"They don't," said Tally calmly, taking a sip of her orange juice. "We were just talking about Tristan snogging the awful Cece Stiles."

Mimah pounded her tray. "That bastard. I don't care how drunk he was at the pub—doing something like that is just plain rude."

Alice said nothing. She seemed to be concentrating very hard on scooping mashed potato onto her fork.

"Yeah," Sonia added. She wasn't about to let Mimah look like a better friend than her. "I'll never talk to Tristan Murray-Middleton again. None of us will, Ali. We'll be like the four musketeers."

"Um, Sonia," Mimah butted in, "I hate to shatter your image, but there were only three musketeers."

"Too bad." Sonia smiled smugly and squeezed a packet of nonfat salad dressing over her feast. "I guess you'll just have to leave."

Mimah rolled her eyes.

"Now, now, girls," Tally interrupted, "let's not get bitchy."

"Tell that to Sonia." Mimah sneered. "Oh! By the way, did anyone see those weird notices in Tudor? The ones from Miss Sharkreve? I think she just put them up this morning."

"No," Alice said defensively. She always liked to be the first to know about things from teachers. "What do they say?"

"Some bullshit. Apparently Sharko has an 'important

announcement' to make on Thursday night." Mimah put air quotes round 'important announcement' to show how unimpressed she was. "We all have to be in the common room at eight o'clock."

"Important announcement? What can be so fucking important that it can't wait till after half term?"

"Who cares, Al?" Tally cut in. "Let's not get sidetracked by notices. The point here is your love life. We've got to plan your date in Rome this weekend—it's got to be absolutely perfect."

"Yes!" Mimah exclaimed. "Al, have you shown Tals your new lingerie? Boy's gonna *love* it. You'll have him salivating."

"Brilliant." Tally clapped her hands. "Now all we've got to do is come up with a plan for you to lure him back—to his place, not yours."

"Yeah, the Hotel de Russie might be a bit, you know, public."

"*And* we've got to pick out the perfect outfit."

"Ali, Ali, let me do your makeup!" Sonia cried.

"And don't forget to smother yourself in delicious-smelling Jo Malone body lotion!"

"Oooh, yes, rub it *everywhere*!"

Alice took a deep breath and closed her eyes. Her friends' transparent, overly cheerful chatter was starting to grate. Okay, they meant well—but having her personal life constantly spotlighted and arranged, like some kind of scene in a play, was getting exhausting. Jumping to her feet, she grabbed her tray. "Move it," she sighed. "I'm going to get pudding."

CHAPTER THIRTY-FIVE

*D*ylan inspected the selection of dining hall desserts melting on their glass plates under the hot lights. St. Cecilia's always laid out a good spread on Sunday nights—probably to cheer people up, take their minds off the whole long week of school about to begin. Which reminded her—double history first thing tomorrow morning. Ugh. More endless dictation on the Wars of the Roses. Why were the English so obsessed with studying nothing but *English* history? Hadn't they heard of the Declaration of Independence? The American Civil War?

Dylan focused on the food display. Chocolate chip cookies. Fruit salad. Some kind of meringue lump. Slowly, she chose a brownie, put it back, and slid out a lemon tart instead. Then she inched her tray, snail-like, along the metal rail toward the cutlery racks.

Prolonging the food-selection process meant delaying the moment when she'd have to face the vast room, full of chatting, laughing girls in twos and threes and fours, while she drifted aimlessly with her tray, desperate for a safe port. The only people Dylan would have felt comfortable approaching were Farah Assadi and Emilia Charles, but tonight those two had cooked themselves pasta with pesto on Tudor House's electric stoves and were eating a best-friends dinner in their dorm. Meaning Dylan would have to sit by herself. There was no way she could plonk down next to just anyone—at St. Cecilia's, that was unacceptable. In order to join a group, there had to be an implicit understanding that you were welcome—and if you weren't, it became clear pretty fast. Fingers of anxiety gripped Dylan's stomach as she remembered those two or three meals at the beginning of term that she'd spent eating in painful silence, while the girls around her nudged each other and pointedly ignored everything she said.

Oh god. Dylan stopped and slid her tray back toward the desserts. Maybe she wasn't ready to face the room yet. Maybe she did want a brownie after all. Stretching out, she grabbed hold of a plate.

But at exactly the same time, so did another hand, olive-skinned and neatly manicured, with a row of silver bracelets round the wrist.

"Oh." Dylan was in a daze and didn't look up. "You go ahead. Take it."

"I will," said the other person. "You've already got a pudding, anyway—what do you want two for?"

The voice that spoke this sentence was extremely familiar—and not in a good way. Jerking up her head, Dylan found herself staring straight into the eyes of—Alice Rochester. Great. Just what she needed. Actually, though, right now Dylan was beyond caring. She'd tried to make peace with Alice on far too many occasions, and the bitch always had some nasty comeback. This time, she might as well preempt her. Glaring at Alice, she put on a high-pitched voice, an obvious mockery of Sonia Khan's.

"I always eat two desserts," she mimicked. "How else do you think I grew my boobs this big?"

Alice stared at her, openmouthed. Dylan stared right back. Then, out of the blue, Alice burst into laughter. Not the smirking kind of laughter that Alice Rochester usually aimed at Dylan, but a genuine, warm peal.

"That was hilarious!" She grinned. "Oh my god, poor old Sone—you've got her down exactly."

"Ummm . . . Thanks."

"Honestly, I've never heard such a good impression—how did you do it?"

"Ummm . . ." This was incredibly weird. "Well, I do live with her. When you listen to someone that much, it just seeps into your brain. Osmosis."

"Love it. Have you got ones of anyone else?" Alice asked, then her face darkened. Dylan probably did have other impressions—and it wasn't hard to think who they might be of. She sniffed. "Actually, never mind."

Dylan looked at the scuffed floor. "Cool, well . . . enjoy your dessert. I hope you guys have fun in Rome this weekend."

"Oh. Thanks." Alice wavered. "I know you weren't invited—by my cousin, I mean. Not that you should expect to be, since they don't know you—or your family, for that matter." She cleared her throat. "Anyway. I think Jasper would like it if you were there."

"What?" Dylan nearly knocked over her water in surprise. Was Alice being genuine? Encouraging, even? Her face certainly looked sincere. "Really? How do you know?"

But Alice had already marched away.

CHAPTER THIRTY-SIX

*T*hirsty?" Mimah whispered, offering Alice what looked like a bottle of Evian.

Sitting at the next desk over, Alice snickered under her breath. She knew very well what was in that drink, and it wasn't water. It was vodka. Absolut. In order to relieve the monotony of lessons now that they were coming up to half term, she and Mimah had decided to get drunk in the middle of English. It was a fine art, smuggling alcohol into lessons disguised as other beverages: rum and Coke in a Coca-Cola can. Whiskey and ginger ale in a Sprite bottle. You had to be subtle and you had to be inventive, but it was worth it: Boozing in front of teacher's faces when they hadn't the slightest suspicion was utterly hilarious.

"Don't mind if I do." Alice tittered. She was about to reach for the vodka, when—

"No drinking in class, Miss Calthorpe de Vyle-Hanswicke!" Mr. Logan bellowed across the classroom, breaking off his boring monologue on iambic pentameter. "How many times do I have to tell you? Throw. It. Away."

"But, Mr. Logan." Mimah blinked back innocently. "How can you stop us drinking water?"

"No other teachers do," Alice piped up. "We could get dehydrated."

"Yeah. It's, like, abuse of our human rights."

"I'll show you abuse of your human rights, Jemimah! And, Miss Rochester, I don't care what other teachers do. Dehydration might do you some good. Jemimah, bring it here."

Mimah stiffened. No fucking way could she let Mr. Logan have the bottle. She'd get suspended if he found out what was in it.

"Oh, no, Mr. Logan," she bluffed, "it's my special bottle. Mummy gave it to me as a present at the start of term. I'll just put it in my bag."

Mr. Logan squinted. "Come again? Your mother gave you an Evian bottle as a present? What is this, *Oliver Twist?*"

"Really, I promise!" Mimah protested. "It's, um, a family tradition. We're very environmentally friendly."

"That's true," chimed in Felicity Foxton. "The Calthorpe de Vyle-Hanswickes recycle and everything."

"Recycling's important. And you shouldn't mock people's family traditions, Mr. Logan."

"Quiet!" Mr. Logan roared. "For god's sake. Fine. Jemimah, put the blasted bottle back in your bag. I don't want to hear another word about it. Now everyone pay *attention!*"

Alice rolled her eyes as Mr. Logan's voice rose to a fever pitch. The man really had to get his temper under control. Not only did it make him way more fun to wind up, it was *such* a sign of insecurity. That was one of the first things Alice's father had taught her when she was a baby: Only people who are unsure of their own authority lose their temper. Which was why she never did. Well, hardly ever, at least.

Next to Alice, Tally was barely listening to the uproar. She was too busy trying to catch Mr. Logan's eye, get some sign that he loved her. She hadn't managed to see him alone, or even exchange a single intimate look with him, since they'd got back from Dublin. That was three days ago already. And tomorrow it would be Thursday, and the day after would be Friday, and that was the beginning of half term and she wouldn't see him for almost two weeks. Tally took a panicky breath. She couldn't let that happen.

"Now, everyone," Mr. Logan was saying, "who can find me an example of a line of iambic pentameter in *Othello*?"

Iambic pentameter. Yes. Tally flicked through her play and shot up her hand. She'd never used to volunteer in class, but Mr. Logan had changed that.

He roved his eyes round the room.

"Anyone?"

Tally waved her fingers.

"Anyone *else*? *Besides* Tally Abbott?"

Tally flushed. What was going on? Mr. Logan hadn't even looked at her. He hadn't given her his dimpled, conspiratorial grin. And he hadn't called her Natalya.

"Gabrielle Bunter. You find one."

As Gabby scrabbled through the pages of her book, her fat face looking like it might explode with stress, Tally tried to calm herself. She turned to Alice, who was giggling with Mimah and sending a text—probably to Boy. The two of them had been messaging back and forth about their date all week, and Tally only hoped it turned out to be something special. Otherwise, Alice might become a wreck.

Just then the bell rang for the beginning of lunch, and the room filled with the sound of shutting books, snapping files, and zipping bags.

"I'll catch up," Tally whispered to Alice. "If you're making ham and cheese toasties, make one for me."

"Fine," Alice said, casting her a suspicious look.

Tally sidled up to Mr. Logan's desk, her tummy somersaulting uneasily. "Hi."

"Oh hello, Tally." Mr. Logan carried on packing his papers and books into his soft leather briefcase.

Tally watched him, her lip beginning to tremble. "Mr. Logan . . . Have I done something wrong?"

Hearing the tremor in her voice, Mr. Logan paused his hands and looked up.

"Natalya, no, not at all. Of course not." He waited for Tally to respond, but she didn't. "Listen, what happened in Dublin . . ." Mr. Logan glanced toward the hallway, and when he spoke again, his voice sounded urgent. "It's too dangerous to talk about it now. But I can't give you special treatment, or people might suspect."

Tally nodded slowly.

"We're agreed? Good. Then I think we'd better not mention the subject here again."

Tally mulled this over as she walked back across the grass to Tudor. Mr. Logan was right—they couldn't talk about their kiss in the classroom. But that didn't mean they couldn't talk about it (and more . . .) in his office. Which gave her an idea.

CHAPTER THIRTY-SEVEN

Tristan slouched over his desk in economics last thing on Wednesday afternoon, pretending to be taking notes on whatever Mr. Briggs was saying, but actually just doodling lines of zigzags.

He nudged Seb. "This is boring as shit."

"Well, I thought you were gonna give it up and take music instead. What are you waiting for?"

"Yeah." T shoved his toe against the table leg. "Guess I should get my ass in gear." He paused, and his voice became a sort of whine. "But I don't even know if you can change subjects this late in the term."

"So find out."

"Yeah . . ."

Seb watched Tristan pick up his pen and start to scratch away in his notebook. Typical T, abandoning the conversation. He was always ranting on about sticking up his finger at convention, following his passions no matter what stood in his way—but he rarely made the crucial move, the one that would actually rock the boat. Not to mention piss off his dad. It wasn't that T was all talk, or unadventurous, Seb knew. After all, he'd started a band. He partied. He broke rules. But he was also captain of the rugby team, was adored by most teachers, and (in Seb's opinion) would most likely be made Head Boy next year.

The scratching of T's pen sped up. Tristan stopped, hummed under his breath, then scribbled some more.

"Ahem." Mr. Briggs cleared his throat.

T kept writing.

"*Ahem.* Tristan Murray-Middleton! May I ask what you're doing?"

"Taking notes, sir."

"Oh, really? And may I ask why you're taking notes when we're doing an oral quiz?"

T chuckled apologetically and put down his pen.

"Oh no, Tristan," Mr. Briggs said. "I wouldn't want to stop you if you're writing something important. What is it?"

"Nothing, sir. Really."

"I can't believe that. Go on, read it to us."

T reddened. "No thanks, sir, that's all ri—"

"I *insist.*"

Tristan sighed. He eyed the bit of paper in his hand. "Honestly, Mr. Briggs, I think we should get on with the lesson."

"And I think you should read what's on your notepad! Or I'll read it for you."

"Okay, okay, sir. But I'm warning you, it's a s—" Tristan stopped himself. If he said "song," Mr. Briggs might force him to sing it. "Poem," he muttered, and cringed.

The room resounded with laughter.

"Oooh, Tristan," heckled Tom Huntleigh, putting on a mincing voice. "How romantic; you shouldn't have."

"Go on, Shakespeare; I hope you've written it in rhyming couplets!"

"Whatever." Tristan rolled his eyes. "It's called 'Not Watching You.' It's, um, about how people act when they fancy someone, but they're too proud to say so." He grinned. "I wrote it especially for you, Tom."

"Fuck off!"

"Quiet!" Mr. Briggs ordered. "Begin."

Great, Tristan thought. How the fuck had he landed himself in this situation? He held up his notebook and swallowed.

> *"I didn't watch you at the pub—*
> *Your eyes so dark, your dress so white.*
> *I didn't watch how your hair shimmered*
> *Under the soft light.*
>
> *Did you watch me not watching you?*
>
> *I ignored you when you sat and*
> *Sipped your drink, next to my friend.*
> *I ignored you, but I watched you from*
> *The start to the end.*

Did you watch me not watching you?

All night long you kept your back turned
So I kissed somebody new—
All night long you didn't notice how I
Wasn't watching you."

"Er." T looked up. "That's all I've done."

"Bravo!" cheered Tom, banging his desk. "Wooohooo! Let's hear it for the poet laureate!"

At his lead, the entire room erupted in stamping feet and cheers. T took a fake bow and blew kisses at his audience.

It was only when the noise died down that Mr. Briggs could be heard clapping hollowly, with a somewhat vindictive look on his face. "How wonderful," he intoned. "How charmingly adolescent. Hurrah."

Tristan looked at him doubtfully.

"I liked it so much," Mr. Briggs continued, "that I want you to write another poem—for me, this time. You can call it 'Ode to the Euro.' Discuss the pros and cons of the euro. In verse."

A guffaw burst from the back of the classroom.

"Sir?" Tristan gaped. "You're joking!"

"No, Tristan, not at all. Since your poetry's so popular, why give it up now? On my desk before half term, please."

Tristan groaned. Trust Briggs to be a dickhead just before the holidays. Most teachers would have overlooked his song-writing at this time of term, would have thought of it as a laugh. Plus, to make matters worse, those lyrics were about Tristan's private life. He damn well hoped no one would realize, or the ribbing would never end. Letting out a deep sigh, he crumpled up his new song and stuffed it into the pocket of his blazer. Would something in his life, soon, please like to go right?

CHAPTER THIRTY-EIGHT

Tally flitted over the Great Lawn, threading through the dark, silent trees. The chilly wind bit through her thin wool uniform but she hardly noticed—she was far too intent on her mission.

It was Thursday evening, and half term started tomorrow. First thing in the morning, a horde of parents, chauffeurs, and other household minions would descend on St. Cecilia's, collecting girls in all years, hauling away their baggage, leaving the school's classrooms and corridors to echo during the ten-day holiday. Tally and Alice were leaving with Marshy in the Bentley at seven thirty a.m. and would be in Rome by tomorrow afternoon. Alice's suitcases were already packed, of course, and sitting neatly by the door to their room. Tally's bags were still stuffed at the top of the wardrobe. Her clothes were still flung all round the dorm room. She'd pack later. Much later. After Miss Sharkreve had made whatever boring announcement she'd advertised earlier in the week.

The dewy grass swished over Tally's pink ballet flats, leaving a crisscross of damp marks across the suede. She padded into the Quad, breathing shallowly as she glanced up at the light in Mr. Logan's study. In the crook of her right elbow she cradled a package, which she stroked now and then as her footsteps echoed up his wooden staircase.

Arriving at the door, Tally gave a quick knock and went in without an answer.

"Hi there," she whispered.

"Hello." The teacher turned round with a smile on his face, which froze at the sight of Tally. "Oh! Natalya. Hello. I thought—I wasn't expecting you."

"I know." Tally bit her lip coyly. Mr. Logan looked hot. He was lounging in an armchair, his shirt unbuttoned to the chest, his sleeves rolled up to the elbow. She was struck by an urge to jump into his arms and kiss him, but she resisted. "I wanted to pay you a surprise visit before half term."

"Yes, right. That's . . . sweet. But shouldn't you be getting yourself organized to leave tomorrow?"

"I am organized! Very organized. I've brought you something."

Mr. Logan glanced toward the door. Then he looked at Tally's face, glowing from the cold and the brisk walk. "Natalya, thank you. But you shouldn't have."

"Yes I should." Tally took a step closer, tingling with her nearness to him. "It's only small. Go on. Open it."

With a searching look, Mr. Logan took the package. Tally

watched fixedly as he turned it over and slit open the pearly white paper with his strong, gentle fingers. Inside, swathed in tissue paper, was a small picture frame bound in green leather, the kind that folded in half so you could pack it in your bag and take it anywhere. And inside it was the photo of Mr. Logan and Tally at the Duke pub in Dublin. Even though it was for the hundredth time, Tally's look melted as she caught sight of the picture. Mr. Logan's grin was so spontaneous, and the way he'd flung his arm round her seat was so full of ease. Tally would never forget that night—how full of anticipation she'd been, and how happy.

"Keep it near you," she murmured. "That's why I put it in here. Look." She demonstrated. "You can close it up when other people are around, and everything about us will stay secret. Just like you said."

"Oh, Natalya, no. I didn't. That's not what I meant." Mr. Logan laid the frame back in its tissue nest and scrunched the paper over it. "Please, you'd better take this back."

Tally's face fell. "Why?"

"Because—" Mr. Logan dropped his voice to an urgent whisper. "We already talked about this, yesterday, after class: We have to forget Dublin. It shouldn't have happened."

"But . . . That's not . . . You didn't . . ." Tally felt light-headed.

"Come on, Natalya, be sensible. I'm a teacher and you're a student."

"But I thought that didn't make a difference to you! You

always acted like it didn't. When we were together, it was like we had this special thing going on."

"Well, yes, we flirted. Obviously." Mr. Logan dragged his hands through his hair. "But it's one thing to flirt. It's quite another to act on that flirtation. I thought we both knew nothing could happen."

"But something did! You kissed me back."

Mr. Logan looked like a cornered dog. "Listen," he said urgently, "we both drank a little too much and things spun out of control. That was partly my mistake, I know. But if I'd realized how seriously you were taking things— I mean, I thought you were in on the game."

"Game?" The word ripped through Tally like shrapnel. All the life seemed to drain from her body. *"Game?"*

"Natalya, calm down. Please!"

Tally sank into a chair, unable to choke out another syllable. She was completely shell-shocked.

"Listen, Tally, we've got to get past this. And there's something I need to tell you. I'm—"

Knock knock.

Mr. Logan's face went taut with stress. He jumped up.

"Hang on," he told Tally, hurrying to the door, cracking it open, and leaning out.

"Tom, darling," said a female voice.

Tally's eyes snapped to the entranceway. The voice had been nothing more than a hum, but did she know it?

Mr. Logan's athletic figure obscured most of her view, but

in the corridor's light, Tally caught a glimpse of a curvy female figure, a flash of bright yellow round her neck.

It was a scarf. A silk scarf—like the yellow Pucci scarf Tally had stolen from her mum.

A pair of arms wrapped themselves round Mr. Logan's neck. A pale blond head inclined toward his. The woman was—was *kissing* him.

Lightning struck Tally's heart. She bolted from her chair. A side table crashed over. A copy of *The Portrait of a Lady* spun to the floor. Mr. Logan whirled, his hand on the woman's sleeve—and as he moved, Tally saw with icy certainty who it was.

"Miss Sharkreve!" she half gasped, half sobbed.

"Tally!" Miss Sharkreve's cheeks blazed pink. "What are you doing here? Tom—I mean Mr. Logan—I—Oh, dear. Tally, you shouldn't have seen that. I'm sorry, it's very embarrassing. Teachers are supposed to keep their romances to themselves. Wait! Stop, where are you going?"

"Natalya!" There was a warning note to Mr. Logan's call.

But Tally didn't turn. Blindly, she pushed past the two teachers, hurtled down the staircase, and stumbled into the night.

CHAPTER THIRTY-NINE

Sharko?" Alice spluttered. "What do you mean he's going out with Sharko? How can he be going out with *her* when he kissed *you?* What a fucking bastard." She let go of Tally's arm, which she'd been stroking for the past five minutes, trying to get Tally to stop crying and start making sense, and took to pacing the room. "God, what a fucking *creep!*"

"Oh, Al," Tally choked out. "Help me. I don't know what to do. I feel so . . . completely . . . desolate." She threw her head into her pillow.

"Tally, sweetie, I know. But now you get it—maybe next time you'll listen to me. This is what I meant about him being a dickhead all along. I always knew he was bad news, from that first moment he was rude to me in class."

Tally hiccupped miserably. "That's—not—helpful."

"It's true, though. But I know, I know. I'm just so furious."

"Ohhh." Tally sniffled. "This is the end of everything. I

thought I was special, but I'm not. He doesn't care about me. He doesn't think I'm special."

"Who cares what he thinks?" Alice demanded. She couldn't let Tally relapse into hysterics again. "He's a loser. And you *are* special. It's Mr. Logan who isn't. I mean come on, have you ever seen his clothes? It's like he buys them at fucking T.J. Maxx." She glared at her English binder, which was lying neatly on her desk, and gave it a vicious shove. "Right. We have got to bring him down."

"B-bring him down?" Tally dabbed her eyes, looking scared. She'd never felt so helpless before. "What do you mean?"

"I mean he can't get away with treating you like this. He's got to pay! But not yet," Alice added hurriedly. "After all, it's half term now. We don't want to ruin our Rome trip: We've been looking forward to Coco's party for ages. And I've got my date." She glanced at herself in their full-length mirror. "But if Mr. Logan doesn't make things up to you fucking soon, then we'll work out some way to force him. And that way it'll be even better, because revenge is best served cold."

Two soft knocks came at the door.

"Who is it?" Alice called sweetly.

"Girls, it's Miss Sharkreve. I'm coming in."

"Oh no, one second, Miss Sharkreve! I'm just getting changed." Alice shot Tally a panicked look and motioned toward the sink. "Quick, wash your face. She can't see you've been crying. She'll think you're insane."

Alice waited till Tally had tied back her hair and cleaned up her makeup before she opened the door. "Sorry about that, Miss Sharkreve. I'm quite modest when I'm getting dressed, you know. Please come in."

"Thanks." Miss Sharkreve directed her gaze across the room. "Tally, dear, I'm sorry to interrupt. I just wanted to have a quick word. Alice, would you give us a minute?"

"No!" Tally said. "I mean, please, Miss Sharkreve, I'd prefer if she stayed."

"Fine," the housemistress agreed with a slight nod, perching on one of the armchairs. "Well then, girls, in a few minutes I'm going to be making a rather sad announcement to the junior class." She waited a beat. "I'm leaving St. Cecilia's."

"What?" Alice's eyes popped.

"Yes. I've been offered a very good job at a school in Scotland that I can't afford to turn down. I wanted to warn you, Tally, before I told the others."

Tally looked confused. "Why?"

"Because of what you just saw. I wanted to make sure you knew this had absolutely nothing to do with that. Or with you. It's been in the pipeline for a while. I've been planning to make the announcement all week. Oh, and, er . . ." Miss Sharkreve paused and rubbed her nose. "One other thing. Mr. Logan has probably told you this already, but he's going to be leaving as well."

"What, you mean he's going *with* you?" Alice snapped without thinking.

"No." Miss Sharkreve gave her a calm look. "Mr. Logan's

accepted a job at a state school up in Glasgow, a bit like the one he used to teach at in London before he came here. I really don't think boarding school is for him."

"But how long has he known about this?" Alice insisted. "He can't just . . . *leave.* Can he?"

"It's certainly unusual to make such a sudden decision, I'll admit. Originally Mr. Logan turned the Glasgow school down. Then he found out they were having a hard time filling the position, and he asked if he could still accept it. That was on Monday, just after he got back from Dublin. It really was all very sudden." Miss Sharkreve's eyes went dreamy. "It's nice for me, of course: We'll only be three or four hours from each other. Funny, this has all been such a whirlwind romance. You know, pretty much as soon as he arrived—I mean—oh gosh, sorry girls." She stood up. "I'm talking far too much. Tally, I'm sorry I didn't realize you were there before, in Mr. Logan's office. And please don't think either of us is leaving because of that."

Miss Sharkreve headed toward the door, stopped, and brushed an imaginary crease out of her skirt. "Oh, and girls, about me and Mr. Logan—I'm not going to ask you not to spread it around, or to keep it secret or anything. That wouldn't be fair. But please just remember, this isn't a soap opera—it's my private life. I'd appreciate it if it didn't become the gossip of the century." She moved her eyes from one student to the other, and shut the door behind her.

Alice leapt up. "What the fuck? This is mental. Sharko

leaving? *Logan* leaving? I mean, was he ever gonna *tell* us? Our last lesson with him was yesterday. And anyway, he just bloody got here. There's something totally suspicious going on. Don't you think? Tals?" She shot Tally a look of concern. Her friend was pale and pained, but seemed composed. "Babes, you okay? What are you gonna do? About Logan? Don't you want to, like, say good-bye?"

Slowly, Tally stood up. She went to the closet and eased down her suitcase from the top shelf. Then she shook her head.

"Don't need to," she whispered. "I've already said my good-bye."

CHAPTER FORTY

The ground floor of the Hotel de Russie in Rome was all cream marble and smooth leather and bright flowers curving out of metal vases. Seb Ogilvy slouched in a chair in the living room off the foyer, tapping his fingers in agitation. Next to him, George Demetrios was checking out two women in short skirts at a neighboring table. Tristan was flipping through a copy of Italian *GQ*—which, naturally, he could understand. Having a French mum and being bilingual meant he was pretty damn quick at languages.

Seb sighed deeply. Because of the balmy weather, the doors to the garden and patio remained open and the fragrance of blossoms floated in on the evening air, making it seem more like May than October. Most of their party had arrived at the de Russie in time for a late lunch on the terrace, and had spent the afternoon settling in, unpacking for tomorrow night's engagement extravaganza. Now the gang were going for a drink at Tristan's favorite place, somewhere called Bar della Pace. Or they would be going, whenever the hell the girls decided to show up.

"Finally!" Seb exclaimed, spotting Alice and Tally strutting in from the lobby.

"Wow." Tristan jumped to his feet as soon as he saw what the girls were wearing. Well actually, what Alice was wearing. Her black minidress hugged her long, angular body. Her high black heels made her long legs look like a supermodel's. As she walked, her hips swayed fluidly and the soft black cardigan draped over her thin shoulders rippled back and forth. The black evening bag in her hand swayed on its gold chain. She was the definition of timeless Italian chic.

"You look . . . nice," Tristan gulped. "Both of you, yeah. Very elegant for a relaxed drink."

Alice smoothed her hair and arched her swanlike neck to the side. Little did Tristan know that a relaxed drink wasn't all she had planned for tonight, or that she was practically shaking with nerves inside. Not that he *would* know, since she wasn't exactly talking to him—which was just what he deserved after his escapades with Cece "See My Tits" Stiles (as Tally had dubbed her). But, like everything else Alice did, she was handling the not-talking subtly. Flat-out ignoring someone was just so passé. And besides, it invited confrontation.

Seb clapped his hands and stood up. "Right. Come on, let's get a move on."

"But where are Jasper and Rando?" Tally asked.

George Demetrios chuckled. "They went to score some weed. Apparently Jas knows someone from that Italian exchange he did a couple of years ago. Bloody typical."

Seb lolled back his head. "Oh shit, what about Sonia and Mimah? Please don't tell me we've got to wait for them. I'm thirsty."

"No, don't worry, you lush." Tally ruffled Seb's hair. "Mimah's not getting here till midnight, and Sonia's gonna meet us later. She wanted to take a bubble bath and have her hair done. You know what she's like."

George chortled and the group set off through the lobby, Alice and Tristan both looking uncomfortable. Neither had bargained on it being just the five of them. Having a few more people around would have taken the pressure off a bit.

"Hey," whispered Tally, linking arms with Alice, "tell me again why Boy wouldn't meet you here at the hotel?"

"Huh?" Alice's nerves were getting worse now that the date was getting closer. "Don't know. Didn't quite catch it. He said something about it being safer not to meet me here. Tals, are you sure I should have worn this dress? Isn't it way too . . . slutty?"

"No way, babe. You couldn't look slutty if you tried. Anyway"—Tally winked—"a little sluttiness never hurt anyone. Especially on a night like tonight."

Alice giggled nervously.

"Have you brought the condoms?"

"Y-yeah."

"Good. Never trust a boy with that. They always want to do it without."

"Whoa," Tristan uttered in a low voice, stopping short. "Guys. Who on earth is that?"

"An angel," George Demetrios drooled. "It's got to be."

What the hell? Alice pushed past them. Right there, leaning over the concierge's desk, was one of the most beautiful, exotic women she'd ever seen. The woman had long black hair that fell in waves over her shoulders. Full eyelashes. Big, dark eyes. Creamy skin. Crimson lips. She was wearing a red silk shirtdress that revealed plunging cleavage and clung to her hourglass waist. Out of the bottom of the dress, as the woman leaned over, you could just see the tops of her stockings.

Alice rolled her eyes. "Oh. That's just Adrianna. Lorenzo's stepmother."

"As in, Lorenzo da Fonseca, Coco's fiancé?"

"Yeah. I met her at a lunch a few months ago."

"*That's* Lorenzo's stepmother?" George stammered. "That's gonna be Coco Frisk's mother-in-law? Fuck me. She's a hottie."

"A pissed-off hottie," Seb said, noting the somewhat fierce look on the woman's face.

"Whatever. She's annoying." Alice pursed her lips. "Can you believe she's only twenty-three and is married to Lorenzo's father? I mean, can you imagine having a twenty-three-year-old stepmother? Gross." As soon as she'd finished speaking, Alice sashayed forward over the marble floor. "Adrianna, darling! Hello!"

Adrianna straightened up. "Alice! Ciao. How are you? *Mwah, mwah.*" Adrianna spoke in perfect English, with a charming Italian accent. Expensive perfume wafted from her clothes.

"I'm very well, thanks," Alice said. "My parents are upstairs getting ready for dinner with the Frisks. And my friends and I are going for an aperitif."

"*Bellissima,*" Adrianna said. "Lovely." But the woman didn't look like she thought any of this was the slightest bit lovely. There was a pout on her face, and a crease in her forehead.

"Um, are you all right?" Tally asked.

"*Si, si.*" Adrianna waved her hand distractedly. "I think I have just misplaced something in the hotel. They will find it. You go. See you at the party tomorrow."

George Demetrios shook his head as the little group emerged onto the pristine Via del Babuino, where the faded stone buildings glowed in the late sunlight.

"Now that, there," he declared, glancing back at the lobby, "that's how a woman should look."

"Oh, shut up," Alice muttered under her breath. She and Tally sniffed and marched on ahead.

"*Un altro* . . . ummm . . . glass . . . *di Campari e*—oh, fuck it." Seb gave up on his broken Italian, and instead resorted to rattling his empty drink at the waitress.

"You would like another Campari and soda, sir?" she asked in perfect English.

Seb blushed. "Oh, uh, yes. Please. Thanks."

George Demetrios punched Seb as the waitress took off. "Nice one, mate. Smooooth."

Alice giggled. "Ugh. How can you drink that stuff, anyway? It's so bitter."

"Wrong. It's delicious. Really works up the appetite." Seb eyed the complimentary saucers of olives, crumbly cheese twists, and savory pastries that the bar served during cocktail hour.

"Whatever. Some people have no taste." Alice sipped her Martini Bianco and crossed her legs, trying to keep calm. They were sitting at a table outside the century-old Bar della Pace, which was tucked in a tiny, bustling square in the historic center of Rome. Inside, the place had wooden ceilings and an old-fashioned coffee bar, and was crammed with antiques. Out here, patrons crowded round small marble tables on the cobblestones, drinking and jabbering and watching Rome's most fashionable inhabitants hurry in and out of the connecting alleyways. The exterior of the building was wrapped in ivy and lit by old-fashioned street lamps. The whole scene was incredibly romantic.

"Hey, Al," Tristan said. He was focusing on her, trying to get her to look at him. He'd noticed, of course, that she'd hardly said a word to him since they'd arrived. Not in an openly hostile way, but with an oblique coldness that he couldn't quite put his finger on. When she was in a mood like this, he knew it was up to him to make the effort.

Alice looked up.

"Remember our trip to Italy this summer? When we sneaked off, just the two of us?"

Alice inclined her head, like she was trying hard to recollect. Then she nodded.

Duh. How could she forget that trip to her parents' villa in Positano? When her true feelings for Tristan had first dawned on her? It hurt to think about.

"This is the first time I've been back to Italy since then," T said quietly. "I had such a good time. I'm glad to be back."

Alice met his eyes. Something seemed to pass between them—that old connection sparking again. Her nervousness melted, and something deeper took its place.

Crash!

Everything on the table jumped as George Demetrios slammed down his fist.

"I'm hungry!" he announced. "These dainty little women's snacks won't help. I'm a growing boy."

Tristan's eyes flashed playfully at Alice. "Right, who's up for a pizza feast? Maybe in about half an hour?"

"Where?" George demanded.

"Just round the corner. I know a couple of places. Nothing fancy—I mean, they're not much to look at, but they serve up some of the best grub you've ever eaten. What do you think?"

Seb stuck up his hand. "You've got my vote."

"Fucking right," added George Demetrios.

"Girls?"

Tally nodded. "I'm in."

"Wicked. Al? I know you're not exactly dressed for slumming it, but still."

"Ohhh . . ." Alice ran a finger down the frosted surface of her drink. Actually, she would have loved to get pizza—she adored those packed, noisy places that T always seemed to know about. They were exciting. You felt so alive, so uninhibited, having to shove your way through the crowd and shout above the babble and grab for food. Plus, cocktail hour with her friends had suddenly got a lot better. It felt like old times. "Well . . . I've got other plans."

"Oh. Right." Tristan squinted a little and looked into the lamp-lit square. "With who?"

"With—"

"Alice! Sexy!"

Alice raised her eyes. A white Vespa had pulled up next to their table and was purring on the cobblestones.

"Babe. You are looking gorgeous." Boy took off his helmet and kissed her on the cheek.

Alice's heart sped up. Boy was incredible—so incredible that she couldn't believe he was here for *her*. Was the entire bar staring at him, or was it just her imagination? His slim-cut suit was a perfect fit on his tall, toned figure. His green eyes sparkled from his tanned face. Oh yes, tonight was going to be fun.

"Hey," she said. "I'm glad you're here. You've already met Tally, right? And this is George Demetrios, and Seb Ogilvy, and Tristan Murray-Middleton."

"Boy Stanley-Soames." Boy shook everyone's hand with a firm grip. Alice noticed the tense, proud look on T's face when their fingers touched.

"Sexy, you're a miracle," Boy told her. "That dress will be perfect for where I'm taking you." He handed Alice a helmet, climbed onto the scooter, and kicked up the safety stand. "Ready, babe? Hop on. *Ciao a tutti,*" he called to the others with a salute. Then, with his precious cargo, Boy wove off down the street.

Suddenly feeling like a complete and utter amateur, Tristan stared after them. As long as he could, he watched Alice's hair and her cardigan flutter in the breeze.

CHAPTER FORTY-ONE

*L*ooks like you need a top-off," Boy observed, reaching for the bottle of Montepulciano cooling in a silver stand behind his chair. He and Alice were sitting opposite each other at Il Gatto Nero, one of Rome's poshest restaurants. Fresh flowers and crisp tablecloths and dark wooden beams adorned the dining room. Soft music played in the background. The tables were spaced at least a meter apart, so you could gossip about your neighbors without danger of them overhearing.

"Oh dear." Boy winked. "That's the bottle gone. Better order another. Promise to drink quickly, though—I thought we'd go somewhere else for dessert."

As Boy signaled to the waiter, Alice scooped another forkful of her gnocchi and duck *ragú*. Delicious. *But don't eat too much*, she warned herself. She'd already scarfed most of the dish, and there'd be nothing worse than getting bloated and fat before . . . before . . . Setting down her cutlery, Alice watched Boy slice his swordfish across the candlelit table. He was so charming, so sophisticated. So *hot*. He'd known exactly which wine to order, and had obviously tipped the maitre d' to give them the best spot in the restaurant. But what would he be like later? In bed? Every time Alice tried to picture herself having sex with Boy, the image seemed to dissolve in front of her eyes. She couldn't help wondering what the others were doing right now. Stuffing their faces in some boisterous restaurant that smelled of wood smoke and crispy crusts and olive oil, George Demetrios stealing Tally's food, Tristan making sure everything ran smoothly.

Maybe she wasn't drunk enough. Alice downed her glass of wine.

"So," Boy asked, dabbing his mouth with his napkin, "who were those blokes I met you with before? At Bar della Pace?"

"Oh." Alice pushed a bit of gnocchi with her fork. "Just friends of mine. We've known each other forever."

"How sweet." Boy's smile was teasing. "Who was that last one you introduced me to? Tristan Murray-Middleton? He looked pretty fierce. Like he might bite me if I tried to take you away."

Alice blushed. "Did he?" she said as nonchalantly as possible. "No. He doesn't care." She pursed her lips. "He's . . . just a friend."

"Good. I thought I might be encroaching on his property. Not that I'd blame him for wanting to keep you to himself." Boy gave a dazzling smile. "You know," he continued, shifting his chair a little round their cozy table. "There's something I've been wanting to fix for the entire meal."

"What?" Alice's hand flew to her face. Oh god. She obviously had some big salad leaf plastered to her front teeth. Or—

"This." Boy leaned in and kissed her on the lips, a long, lingering kiss. "There," he murmured. "That should take care of it."

Alice smiled coyly, giddy with how close he was. Her mind had gone blank. "Mmmmm. I'm not sure. You might need to do it again."

"Gladly." Boy kissed her once more. "I'm glad we're finally here," he said. "I couldn't forgive myself for having to cancel on you a couple of weeks ago. I'd been looking forward to that date for ages." He paused. "This might sound cheesy, but it's not often I meet someone as beautiful *and* as smart as you. Usually with girls it's one or the other, but with you . . . well, you seem to be a double threat." He stroked her hand. "And I have a feeling our connection's going to be physical as well as mental."

Alice looked up at him, her cheeks burning. "Me too," she said, and knocked back another glass of wine.

"That's the way to do it." Boy grinned.

Alice giggled with the warm, confident feeling that was running down her body. Yes. She could definitely picture herself naked in Boy's arms. His lips were so full, so kissable.

"Shall we get out of here?" he asked.

"Sounds good to me." Alice rifled through her Dior evening

bag as Boy put down his Visa Gold card. She took out a pocket mirror and checked her makeup. Then she slid her fingers into the bag's back inside pocket—checking. Yes, the condoms were still there.

"Right," Boy said. "Ready for dessert?"

"Yep!" Alice smiled, clicking the bag shut. "I was thinking ice cream—I love gelato. I know this great place, right by the Trevi Fountain. Or we could just wander and find somewhere. There are so many good ones in Rome. Unless . . . you had something else in mind?"

Boy laughed. "Actually, I did. I was thinking more along the lines of . . . room service?" His eyes were on hers.

Alice's knuckles went white on her handbag.

"Only if you want to, of course. I hope I'm not being too forward. But my hotel does great desserts. And it'll give us some privacy."

Alice considered for a second, fear dancing with excitement in her stomach. So much for having to seduce Boy: He'd done all the seducing so far. Taking a deep breath, she poured the rest of her wine down her throat. *Now or never.*

"Your place sounds perfect," she said.

CHAPTER FORTY-TWO

The light flashed green on the door of Boy's hotel room as he slid his key card in and out of the slot.

"Welcome to my boudoir," he teased, his hand on Alice's waist, guiding her into the suite.

"God, what a dump." Alice grinned. Boy's suite was ridiculously lavish—much more opulent than her modern, clean-lined rooms at the Hotel de Russie. The rich hangings and drapes in the sitting area made the place look like some kind of nineteenth-century palace—at least, if you ignored the giant plasma TV and state-of-the-art sound system. Through a set of mirrored doors at the back, Alice caught a glimpse of another room, probably where Boy slept.

Tightening his arm round her waist, Boy drew her close. "How about that dessert?"

"Mmm. Yes please."

"And champagne?"

"Of course." Alice felt less nervous now that she was actually here, letting Boy take the lead. He obviously knew what he was doing.

Picking up the phone, he pressed for room service. "Yes, hello. I'd like some chocolate and pistachio ice cream with chocolate sauce on the side, and a bottle of Pol Roger on ice. Oh, and tell the waiter to leave the tray outside the door and knock." Boy stroked Alice's hip. "We don't want to be disturbed." Hanging up, he pulled her in and kissed her again, deep and lingering. "Mmm." His voice was husky. "Now I know why I nicknamed you Sexy. Come on. I'll show you round."

"The grand tour?" Alice giggled tipsily. "How exciting."

"I know. This is the living room. Does it meet with your approval?"

Alice smiled archly. "I suppose."

"Good." He kissed her on the nose. "This is a coffee table. Those are chairs. This is a couch—a very useful couch, I might add." Boy pressed Alice against the sofa's arm and nestled into the base of her throat. "Mmm, you smell delicious."

"Oh . . . thanks. So do you."

He led her through the double doors. "These are mirrors, so you can see how beautiful you are. Those are windows. Carpet. Lamp. Chest of drawers. And here"—he stopped— "we have the bed."

The bed was a giant, luxurious, four-poster affair. Boy

scooped Alice up and laid her on top of its red blanket, which had already been turned down for the night. A single white orchid had been placed on the pillow.

"For you," he said, brushing its petals over her lips. "I hope you don't mind if I . . ." The rest of his sentence was drowned as he kissed her insistently, then gathered away her hair and nibbled her neck.

Alice sank into the duvet. Boy kept going, seeming rapt. She didn't really know what to do with her hands, so she ran them over the back of his head. She felt stupid just stroking it, but it was better than kissing his hair and ending up with a mouthful of fuzz.

"Does this feel good?" Boy said, moving his mouth along her shoulder.

"Mm-hmm."

"Good." With his fingertips, he slipped off both straps of her dress and eased the black material down round her waist. Then he turned his attention to her bra—the leopard-print push-up one she'd bought at Agent Provocateur. He nuzzled it and worked his tongue teasingly round the edges of the silk.

"Take this off," he whispered hoarsely.

"Oh . . ." Alice wanted to, badly, but she moved her arms in front of her chest. Maybe Mimah had been right—maybe Boy wouldn't notice how small her boobs were—but she wasn't quite ready yet to find out. Not that this was the first time she'd had her top off with a guy or anything, but Boy was so experienced and seemed to expect so much. What if she disappointed him? She tugged at his shirt to distract him. "*You* take *this* off first," she whispered sexily.

Looking into her eyes, Boy unbuttoned it half way and then ripped it over his head. Alice drew in her breath. Boy's torso was brown and rippling. So were the muscles in his arms as he leaned over her and kissed her again. Alice could feel a bulge through his trousers rubbing against her thigh.

"I've been thinking about this for ages," Boy murmured, slipping his hand between her legs. "Wanting you." He stroked the rim of her underwear. Alice went rigid. She was tempted—well, kind of—but maybe it was a bit soon. Their dessert hadn't even arrived. Plus, he still had most of his clothes on. That didn't seem fair.

"Wait, wait, hang on."

Boy raised his head. "What?"

"I just . . ."

"Oh," Boy whispered. "I see. I have an idea. To make us both relax."

Relax. Yes. That sounded good. "What is it?"

"I've got a bottle of massage oil in the bathroom. Why don't I get it and give you a nice long back rub?"

"Okay. Yeah, I'd like that."

As Boy disappeared, Alice turned onto her stomach to prepare. She reached back and felt her bra strap. Maybe she should just take the stupid thing off. After all, it was pretty dark, and Boy was being so lovely and was so clearly into her, and how could he give her a massage with it on? She sat up and unhooked the bra with a shiver of excitement, peeking down at her small breasts. They didn't look so bad in the moonlight—they looked perky and nicely round. Casting her bra to the floor, Alice noticed she was facing the bedside table. A copy of *Elle* lay on the dark wood. How ridiculous. Chuckling, she shifted closer.

"I didn't know you read *Elle*, you big *girl*!" she was about to call to Boy, but as she opened her mouth, she caught sight of a Post-it note stuck to the magazine's cover, imprinted with a lipstick kiss.

What the fuck? Whose kiss was that? Alice grabbed hold of *Elle* for a closer look, and as she lifted it, gasped. Concealed beneath it lay a necklace and a pair of earrings, sparkling with diamonds and rubies.

Fuck. Someone else had been here. Another woman. And Alice was practically naked, exposed and waiting for Boy to come back. Blindly, she jumped up and pulled on her dress, then, snatching her new bra from the carpet, stuffed it in her bag. This was terrible. It was her worst nightmare! She had to get out.

"Sexy," Boy called, hearing the door to the suite slam shut. "Is that the champagne? Sorry, babe. I told them to leave it outside. Sexy? Alice!"

Boy bolted from the bathroom, wearing only his briefs and holding a bottle of massage oil. His eyes scanned the room, taking in the magazine and the Post-it note. "Shit," he muttered to himself.

Then he spotted the jewelry. "Fuck me. So that's where it is."

CHAPTER FORTY-THREE

Tally! Open up. Let me in," Alice called, pounding on her friend's bedroom door back at the de Russie. "Come on!"

Alice wasn't ready to brave her own suite yet—she didn't think she could face the silence, the lamplight, the empty bed, the minibar full of snacks and no one to share them with. She shut her eyes. This wasn't how she'd envisioned Rome during all those weeks at school. She was meant to be having fun.

But Tally clearly wasn't here to answer the door. Where was she? Her phone was going straight to voicemail, and there was no way Alice was ringing anyone else. Tally was the only one who'd understand. Alice checked her watch. Twelve thirty a.m. Great. It was early. The others could be anywhere—drinking in some bar in trendy Trastevere. Clubbing near the Campo dei Fiori. Cabbing it to some underground party they'd discovered.

Or maybe, if she was in luck, they were downstairs at the bar.

Alice tottered back down the hallway. Pausing by a mirror opposite the lift, she straightened her hair and slicked on more lipstick. Then, eyeing the corridor to make sure no one was coming, she struggled back into her bra. Alice would never have pulled a stunt like that sober—you never knew who might jump out of the lift. But she wasn't sober. Far from it. And anyway, her dress kind of drooped without the extra padding. Typical. She pressed the call button.

The hotel lobby still sounded lively when the doors pinged open. That was mostly thanks to the buzzing emanating from the hotel's Stravinskij Bar—which, the greasy concierge had informed them while they were checking in, was a real Rome hot spot. "Very young, very hip," he'd enthused in a heavy accent. Alice and Tally had rolled their eyes. Never trust an old person who claimed to know what was cool. Or who pronounced "hip" like "heap."

Alice wavered in the doorway to the bar. A pianist was playing cheesy music at a grand piano, serenading elegant patrons who lounged in red and beige chairs, flourishing different-colored cocktails. White sculptures stared out from alcoves in the walls. Alice's gaze traveled from table to table, cluster to cluster. Most people here were older, in their twenties and thirties, and her friends were nowhere to be seen.

She started to turn away. But wait—hang on. In a corner at the far end—was that . . . ? She took a step closer. Yes. Tristan. Alice's heart leaped. As she watched, T pulled a crumpled scrap of paper from his pocket, smoothed it out, and rested it on his knee, staring at whatever was written there. Alice's vision blurred a little. Maybe because of the booze. She brushed a tear from her cheek. T was here, by himself, just like her. Perhaps they weren't as distant from each other as she'd thought. Perhaps things could be the same again. Weariness washed over her, telling her the only thing she wanted in the world was to go lay her head on his shoulder and shut her eyes and let herself go. Seemingly of their own accord, Alice's feet started across the room.

Then, just as abruptly, they stopped. Someone had reached Tristan first. A glamorous girl in her early twenties was standing in front of him, touching his shoulder. Tristan hastily folded the paper and looked up, then shifted over on the couch so the girl could sit down.

A leadlike weight dropped through Alice's stomach. Defeated, she turned back toward the lifts. The moment was gone. They'd lost each other, after all. The only thing to do was curl up in bed, alone. Maybe she could cry herself to sleep.

"Ciao," announced Tristan's new neighbor on the sofa, holding out her hand. "I am Flaminia."

"Tristan." T squeezed out a smile. His impeccable manners never let him down. "Nice to meet you."

"*Si.* Of course. *Due* martini," Flaminia called, snapping her fingers at the waiter. "You will enjoy this, Tr*ee*stan. They are famous for their martinis here."

"Oh." T shook his head. "That's very nice of you. Really. But I don't think so. I can't."

Flaminia looked offended. "What do you mean, you can't? You have been *see*ting here by yourself all night. I have been watching you. It is impolite to refuse to have a drink with me. I am a w*oo*man."

Tristan rubbed his eyes. He'd weaseled out of exploring with the others by faking a headache, and had returned to the hotel for a contemplative—some might say sulky—drink on his own. Flaminia was pretty, but he just didn't feel like company tonight—not after Alice had taken off with Boy Stanley-Soames at the very moment he'd thought he had her back. And anyway, wasn't this kind of thing what Rome was for? Drinking solo and gazing into the river, sighing for your lost love? That sounded right up T's street. Maybe he'd pay a visit to the river in a little while. For now, he turned back to Flaminia.

"I know you're a woman," he said apologetically. "And I'm sorry. But I'd quite like to be alone."

"Then why did you invite me to *see*t down?"

"I didn't," T protested despite himself. "You asked if this seat was free and I said yes."

Flaminia grabbed her handbag. "*Ee*english men," she sniffed—"rude pigs"—and took off.

Tristan slumped his head against the couch, letting the piano music drift over him, and touched the worn paper in his pocket. It was the song he'd written about Alice in class. He should probably stop carrying it round.

CHAPTER FORTY-FOUR

O h my god, this place is, like, all my dreams come true!" Sonia squealed as the limo ferrying her, Alice, Tally, and Mimah joined a queue of posh cars outside an old palazzo in the center of Rome.

She rolled down the window and stuck out her head. A red carpet lined with paparazzi stretched through an archway into an ivy-hung courtyard. Beautiful people posed for pictures before venturing through the arch. Inside, Sonia spotted white marquees, under which guests were mingling and uniformed waiters were hurrying back and forth. She smoothed her long black hair. Some of the waiters looked pretty cute. Behind the tents, three sweeping steps led up to a portico, from which double doors opened back into what looked like a grand ballroom.

"Wow," Sonia breathed. Italian *Vogue* had really gone all out.

"Girls! Over here!" cried a photographer with an English accent as the four friends stepped out of the limousine.

"Gorgeous, stunning. Group together and smile."

Alice, an old hand at this, immediately positioned herself sideways to the camera (the best way to appear skinny in pictures) and beamed. Even though she hadn't exactly recovered from last night, she looked great. Her hair and makeup had been done by a professional at the hotel. Her high-waisted sequinned dress, the color of gunmetal, complimented her perfect olive skin.

Tally and Sonia posed on either side of her. Mimah hung back.

"Mime," Alice called. "Come on."

"Uh-uh," Mimah snarled, hovering at the edge of the red carpet. "No way. I fucking hate paparazzi. I'll kill 'em if they try to take a picture of me."

"But Mimah, these aren't the same ones that went after you and your dad. Come on—they just want glamor shots."

Mimah folded her arms.

"We'll probably be in *Tatler* . . . ," Alice wheedled.

"Come on, you look so pretty."

"It'd be so nice to have a shot of the four of us!"

Mimah rolled her eyes. "Okay, okay. *Fine.*"

She joined the group, and the flash exploded.

"Beautiful!" gushed the photographer, checking the image on his screen. He jotted down their names. "This is definitely one for the society pages."

"Eeeee!" Sonia bounced up and down. "Ali, did you hear that? He said 'definitely'!"

Alice glared at her and took a step backward. "Um, do I know you?"

"Huh?"

"For fuck's sake, Sonia, if you don't calm down, people are gonna think we've, like, never been to a celebrity event before. Puh-lease."

"Oh. Sorry." Sonia's smile faded, then almost immediately reappeared. "But Al, seriously, you *have* to introduce me to Lorenzo da Fonseca as soon as we get inside. I am so in love with him!"

Alice stared. "Okay, Sone? Remember the reason why we're here? Because Lorenzo is *marrying* my *cousin*. So would you mind keeping it down?" Linking arms with Tally, she marched down the red carpet. There was nothing more satisfying than being mean to Sonia when she was in a bad mood.

Tally squeezed her elbow. "How are you feeling, hon?"

Alice shrugged.

"Babe, listen to me. Boy's a total two-timing jerk. You wouldn't have wanted to lose your virginity to him anyway— you're way too good for him. We'll find you someone else."

"Yeah. I guess."

"Well, I *know*. Argh!" Tally rubbed her temples. "Damn hangover headache. Won't go away."

Alice poked her. "Serves you right for staying out till five a.m. at some crazy student night. Here, have one of these." She swiped two glasses of champagne off a tray. "Hair of the dog. The only cure."

"Thanks, babe." Tally took a glug. "Cheers! Let's both get plastered today and forget about our horrible men."

"Cheers!" Downing her glass, Alice surveyed the star-studded crowd. Fashion designers and actors mingled with artists, journalists, club owners, and the titled ranks of Roman and London society. Willowy women navigated the cobblestones in vertiginous heels. Messy-haired men in sharp suits slapped each other on the back, holding insidery conversations. Free copies of Italian *Vogue* sat on tables next to every food and drink station. Glossy placards proclaimed, in English and Italian, "Please join Italian *Vogue* in congratulating Lady Caroline Frisk and Lorenzo da Fonseca on their engagement." Flowers bloomed everywhere. Candles and lanterns flickered, ready for when it got dark in a few hours' time. Violinists were playing in the center marquee, and later there'd be a surprise appearance by some hot band, but it was a big secret which one.

Alice shook her head. "I know this sounds like something Sonia would say, but this party makes me totally want to marry a film star."

"I'm with you, babe." Tally knocked back most of her champagne. "Ooh. That feels better."

"Wicked. Look, there's Coco. Let's go say hi."

Hand in hand, Alice and Tally wove their way up to the portico, where Caroline Frisk was standing with her parents, the duke and duchess of Albany.

"Aunt Theresa!" Alice cried, kissing the duchess on both

cheeks. "Uncle Eddie. So lovely to see you. And Coco!" She squeezed her cousin tightly.

Having grown up with two brothers and no sisters, Alice had always sort of idolized Coco—and it was easy to see why. Caroline Frisk was one of the most glamorous socialites on the London scene. Her wavy blond hair, trimmed and styled especially for today, hung in layers around her razor-sharp cheekbones—the same severe cheekbones that Alice had inherited from her own mother. Coco's custom-designed dress was canary-yellow and adorned with diamonds—which was conservative for her, considering that once, in a tabloid scandal, she'd turned up at a ball wrapped entirely in cellophane and nothing else. In fact, Coco had had her share of scandal. While at university, she'd been nicknamed Cokeface Frisk because of her notorious drug habit. But now, a few years out of rehab, she'd founded her own trendy lingerie line, Coco-a-Gogo, modeled by all her It-girl friends. It was about to hit shops in time for Christmas, and Alice was planning to have her stocking stuffed with cute little bra-and-panties sets.

"Have you said hi to Renzo?" Coco asked.

"No."

"Oh, darling, you must. You know he adores you. Renzo! Lorenzo! Look who's here."

Suddenly, Alice was bundled into a hug by a tall, powerful man, who grinned with his fiercely white teeth. "Alice! I am delighted to see you. It makes my Coco so happy that you are here."

"Thanks." Alice stared at her cousin's fiancé. Lorenzo da Fonseca wasn't one of those stars who was famous for his boyish good looks—he was famous for exactly the opposite reason. He was dark, rugged, and strong. He played tough, troubled men: sons bent on revenge. Unavailable lovers. Tortured assassins. He'd been known to make women faint with his pure masculinity. Luckily, he was a little bit too rough-and-ready to be Alice's type, but she could definitely see the attraction.

"Excuse me," cut in a publicist from *Vogue*, barging Alice out the way. "I *hate* to interrupt, but it's time for Renzo and Coco to pose for pictures. Say good-bye now. Move along. Move along."

"Good luck, Coco!" Alice called as she was shunted away. "See you later." She looked round. Tally was nowhere to be seen, so she grabbed another glass of champagne from a passing waiter and stood there holding it, hovering.

Then, across the courtyard, Alice glimpsed Tally's white-blond head, next to Mimah's raven one. Sonia and Seb were perched on a low stone wall nearby, and Jasper was behind them, holding a drink, talking to someone. Tristan.

Alice stared for a minute, watching T from a distance. Just like last night in the bar, she felt the urge to run to him—but then the image of him and that older woman sprang into her head. Alice slumped against a pillar. It was time she faced it—T was obviously moving on. He was probably snogging and sleeping with tons of beautiful girls, while she was still a virgin. For fuck's sake, she couldn't even lose it to a guy who seemed to be running some kind of brothel out of his hotel room! Alice shut her eyes. No, last night had been lucky. She'd found out about Boy before it was too late. She could still save her first time for someone special—whenever he might decide to come along.

With a sigh, Alice brushed a hand over her dress and headed down toward her friends.

"Sebby, Sebby," Sonia's voice was whining as she drew up. "I need a cigarette. Want to come smoke with me outside?"

Seb looked at her. "But we are outside."

"That's not what I meant," Sonia pouted. "I meant, do you want to come outside the *party* with me. You know, for some . . . quiet time?"

"Oh." Seb swirled his drink. "Uh, not really. Thanks. I'm fine in here."

Tally and Mimah snickered. Sonia looked like she was about to stamp her foot.

"*I'll* go outside with you, Sone," George Demetrios leered, rocking up with a fresh glass of whiskey.

Sonia sniffed. "In your dreams."

The sun sank lower, the light turned golden, and the shadows grew. Waiters descended with Italian nibbles: mini-mozzarellas, Parma ham, olives, bruschetta, fried calamari. The musicians changed. George Demetrios put his arms round Tally's waist, and the two of them danced drunkenly on the paving stones. Tally looked like a ballerina in her short white dress and gladiator-style heels that laced up to her knees. Jasper gave an exaggerated bow and asked Mimah to dance. Sonia grabbed Seb's arm and forced him to sway with her.

Alice bit her lip. The only other person without a partner was Tristan, standing a few feet away. Studiedly, she fixed her gaze straight ahead.

"Hey," said a voice right behind her. "How are you doing?"

Alice turned round. Rando was there, holding out a glass of champagne.

"Oh, thanks. I'm fine. It's just—" She glanced sidelong at T. "Isn't it funny, being surrounded by so many people but still having no one to talk to? It's like, sometimes I feel more lonely at parties than when I'm by myself." Alice didn't know why she was saying this to Rando. She'd never said it to anyone before, but something about his face just made her trust him.

Rando laid his hand on her bare shoulder. "Sounds like you need a break. Jas and I bought some weed last night. I've got some on me, if you feel like a joint?"

"Sure," Alice said. "That'd be great."

"This way," Rando said, and led her up the steps toward the entrance to the palazzo.

A pair of eyes followed their movements as they peeled off from the group.

"Hey, Jas." Tristan grabbed his friend's arm as Jasper danced past. "Where's Rando going?"

"Dunno. Probably to smoke with Alice. He and I found a good secret spot before."

Tristan's fingers tightened. "Where?"

"Chill, man. I'll take you if you want."

T shoved his hands in his pockets. He didn't particularly feel like getting stoned, and he hated being suspicious of a good mate like Rando. But still.

"Definitely," he said. "Just let me finish this drink."

CHAPTER FORTY-FIVE

Statues of wolves and naked ancient Romans decorated the palazzo's entrance hall. Rando and Alice pushed through swarms of guests, over the old wooden floorboards, toward a corridor leading out the side of the room.

"Where does this lead?" Alice giggled, as they slipped down the narrow passage.

"Kitchen," Rando said. "Shhh. Don't think we're meant to be here. Shit!" He stopped short. Right in front of them stood Lorenzo da Fonseca, mulling over a wine list with a sommelier.

Lorenzo glanced up and grinned. "Alice! What a surprise. Hello. Are you lost?"

"Renzo! Um, hi. No. We just wanted . . . I mean, we were looking . . ."

"Ohhh." Lorenzo glanced from Alice to Rando and back again, and winked luridly. "I understand . . ." Moving aside, he pointed to a narrow doorway. "You two can have some privacy out there."

Alice blinked. "No, no, that's not—"

"Thanks, mate," interrupted Rando, grabbing her hand. "We owe you one."

"No problem. I know how it is." Lorenzo made what was apparently meant to be a sexy clicking sound with his tongue.

"Hey," Alice hissed, as soon as she and Rando had emerged into the alleyway outside. "Didn't you realize what he thought? He thought we were . . . you know."

Rando laughed. "Yeah. I know. But we couldn't exactly tell him the real reason we were coming out here, could we? *Ciao, Lorenzo, we're just going to get high at your engagement bash. Hope you don't mind.* I mean, come on. Have you seen the size of that bloke? I wouldn't want to get into a fight with him."

"First of all," Alice retorted, "he's an actor. Do you think he'd care about us doing recreational drugs? And second of all, he's a total sweetie at heart."

Rando pulled a joint from his pocket. "Yeah, he really looks it." He lit up and drew in a breath, then handed the joint to Alice. "Here. You go first. You need it."

"Thanks," Alice said. Rando was such a considerate guy. Or maybe . . . maybe he had ulterior motives? No. Rando liked *Tally.* Didn't he?

"Hey, look." He nudged her. "See those two people up there?"

Alice squinted. In the shadows, where Rando was pointing,

a man and woman were standing very close together. The man was hiding his hands behind his back, and the woman was trying to grab whatever he was holding.

"Yeah." She raised her right eyebrow. "Maybe they're spies. Or party crashers."

"Totally."

"Let's investigate." As Alice tiptoed closer, the glint of diamonds and rubies caught her eye. The man seemed to have had jewelry behind his back, and was now fastening it round his girlfriend's neck. The woman grabbed hold of the necklace, then fell on her boyfriend, kissing him.

"*Grazie, grazie*, my darling," she sobbed. "I thought I had lost these. They are so precious."

Alice halted. Wait . . . That charming Italian accent . . . That lustrous brown hair . . . Those sparkling jewels . . .

"You're welcome, Sexy," said the man. "Kiss me again."

Just then a light in a window came on, throwing the man and woman into relief.

In a flash, Alice recognized their faces. "Oh my god!"

"Whoa!" Rando jumped a foot in the air. "What's wrong?"

"Adrianna? Boy?" Alice shrieked, throwing down the joint. "What the hell are you doing? You scum!"

Boy started toward her. "Alice? Rochester? No! It's not what it looks like, I swear."

"*Che è successo?*" cried a voice behind them. "Did someone scream?"

Lorenzo. Ignoring him, Alice spat toward Boy. "You bastard.

I know you're having an affair with Adrianna da Fonseca, so don't even try lying. That's *her* jewelry I saw in your room last night. She left it there. Didn't she?"

"No," Boy protested, starting to shake his head.

But Adrianna interrupted. "Yes," she cried, clinging to Boy's arm. "And what's it to you?"

"What's it to *me*, you mean!" Lorenzo boomed. "You're married to my father. How dare you embarrass our family like this?" He launched himself headfirst at Boy.

At that moment, Tristan and Jasper came strolling out the back door.

"What the—," T yelled. He, Jas, and Rando ran toward the fray to pull Boy and Renzo apart. "Al, hold my jacket," Tristan shouted as he passed, tossing it to her.

Alice caught the blazer just as a scrap of paper slipped from one of its pockets to the pavement. It looked like the page T had been holding last night. Distractedly, she unfolded it and read the title. "Not Watching You."

> *I didn't watch you at the pub—*
> *Your eyes so dark, your dress so white.*
> *I didn't watch how your hair shimmered*
> *Under the soft light.*

Alice's heart sped up. The noise in the background faded from her ears. Pub. Dark hair. White dress. Could this . . . Could this poem be about *her*?

I ignored you when you sat and
Sipped your drink, next to my friend.
I ignored you, but I watched you from
The start to the end.

The words on the paper blurred.

"Move, move!" Someone knocked Alice against the wall as a crowd of uniformed men burst out the back door into the alley.

Suddenly, Tristan was at her side, grabbing her arm. "Come on," he gasped. "It's security, they're here to break up the fight. We don't want to get caught in the crossfire. Follow me." He pulled her off down the street.

CHAPTER FORTY-SIX

Side by side, Tristan and Alice hurtled through the narrow passages of old Rome. The echoes of the fight in the alleyway soon died out, but the two of them kept running. And running. Then they started laughing. Alice felt like she never wanted to stop—but what was going through Tristan's mind? She glanced at him from the corner of her eye, her hair falling loose from its crystal clip and flowing like silk behind her.

"Wait." Suddenly, T's face turned serious and his footsteps slowed. "Do you hear that?" He touched her arm.

Alice paused, holding her breath. A low roar reached her ears—a roar that sounded like an earthquake. Or the sea at high tide. Or some kind of distant storm. "Weird." She cocked her head. "Is it a waterfall?"

T knitted his eyebrows together. Then a smile broke across his face. "Yes, brilliant! You're right."

"What, that there's a waterfall in the middle of Rome? Suuure. Of course."

"No, dimwit." T punched Alice playfully. She felt a spark of something at his touch, but he probably hadn't noticed. "I think I know where we are! This way." Jerking his head, T darted round a corner, through a shady alleyway, and into an open piazza. "Look," he told Alice as she emerged behind him. "There."

Alice gasped. Right in front of her, a gigantic marble sculpture rose from the paving stones, water cascading down its surface into a semicircular pool. The Trevi Fountain. In its center, the sea god Neptune towered in his shell-shaped chariot, drawn by two winged horses, frozen in time. The fountain's floodlights had just been lit for the evening. They cast a glow over the marble, and over the pool, where hundreds of coins, tossed in by visitors hoping for their wishes to come true, gleamed silver and bronze in the light.

"Beautiful," Alice murmured.

"I know." Tristan paused. "Rome's so like that, isn't it? You think you're just wandering the back streets, and then, all of a sudden, you stumble across something like this."

They stood there for a while in silence. Alice shivered a little in the evening air. She'd hardly eaten anything all day, she realized, and she was feeling kind of hungry after their mad dash to escape. She opened her mouth to speak.

bouncing up and down as she forced blonde, cherubic Flossy Norstrup-Fitzwilliam to listen to some boring story. Gabby's flab was wobbling so much that she looked like a giant jelly bowl. Ugh. This was the problem with coming back to school after ten days break: how quickly you started to feel like you'd never been away.

Alice heaved a long-suffering sigh and turned back to the letter in her hand. "Hoare?" she sneered.

"Now, now," Tally snickered, "I told you not to call Sonia that anymore."

"Oi," Sonia grumbled.

Alice giggled. "Shut up, Sone. No, really, can you believe this—our new housemistress's name is Mrs. *Hoare*!"

"Come on," Tally snorted with laughter. "Of course it's not."

"It is! Look, it says so in this letter Daddy got."

"Oh. My. God." Tally grabbed the paper. "How the hell are we meant to call her that without cracking up? We'll obviously have to ignore the woman for the rest of the year."

Alice shook her head. "It's just so weird that Miss Sharkreve's gone. Daddy says he's simply shocked that she left. He says he hopes our new housemistress is up to par, otherwise it might jeopardize our academic careers."

Tally rolled her eyes. Of course Alice's father would say something like that. Richard Rochester owned one of London's most eminent trading firms, was notoriously strict, and put a ton of pressure on Alice and her two brothers to do well. Everyone knew that the reason Alice worked so hard was because her father insisted she get into Oxford next year. He was counting on her to carry on the family tradition—especially since Alice's older brother, Dominic, had been too busy getting stoned at school to even think about Oxford. The fact that Dom was currently one of the coolest undergrads at Edinburgh didn't appease Richard Rochester in the slightest.

"Girlies, oh no," Sonia burst out. She was twisting a strand of her shiny, black hair around her manicured finger. "I've just thought of something bad. Miss Sharkreve was our house-mistress for an entire half term and she never once caught us breaking rules. Like, we never got punished for smoking, or for drinking in our rooms, or for sneaking out to town. What if this Mrs Hoare woman is the opposite?"

"She'd better not be," Alice frowned, "or we're fucked for the Hasted House Halloween social tomorrow night. How are we gonna survive a school party if we can't sneak in extra booze? The whole point of being a junior is that you're supposed to be able to get away with shit."

"Guys, chill," Tally yawned, sinking back into the couch. "We'll find a way to have fun, whatever she's like. Anyway, Mimah can just shove a couple of bottles down her top tomorrow. Smuggle the booze between her boobs." Tally giggled. "You can do that, right, Mimah? Give yourself a *booze* job?" Grinning, she stuck out her foot and nudged Jemimah Calthorpe de Vyle-Hanswicke, who was sitting scrunched up on the floor. Mimah had always been the bustiest member of their clique. "Mimah? Hello? Earth to Mime . . ."

"*Stop* that. What the fuck do you want?"

Tally recoiled at Mimah's harsh tone. Biting her lip, she scrutinized her friend. Mimah's face was pinched and pale. This couldn't be good. Mimah had had a million family problems over the past few months—surely no more had surfaced over fall break?

"Shhh!" a whisper rustled through the room. Footsteps echoed in the marble foyer and the junior class rose to their feet. Two women swept through the door. One of them was St. Cecilia's headmistress, Mrs. Traphorn. Sonia craned her neck, but only Alice was tall enough to see the other woman over the crowd.

"What does she look like, Al? Ali!"

"Stop poking me!"

Mrs. Traphorn strode to the front of the room and positioned herself near the large flat-screen TV. Her companion hung back in a shadowy corner, obscured by a large floor lamp.

"Good afternoon, girrrls," Mrs. Traphorn droned poshly rolling her *r*'s. "You may sit down."

As usual, the Trap had pinned her gray hair into a bun. She was sporting a sleeveless cardigan, a plaid skirt, and clumpy shoes. Tally shook her head. Teacher fashion overload.

"Welcome back to school," the Trap went on. "I hope you've all had a verrry prrroductive break. I have an important person to intrrroduce to you today." She paused and patted her bun.

"For fuck's sake," Tally hissed in Alice's ear, "can't the old bat get on with it?"

"As you all know," the Trap droned on, "Miss Sharkreve left St. Cecilia's at the end of last half term, to teach at a school in Scotland. We were extrrremely sorry to lose her."

Sonia snorted.

"But with me here today is Miss Sharkreve's replacement as junior housemistress, Mrs. Edwina Hoare." The Trap clasped her hands. "Mrs. Hoare joins St. Cecilia's from Pembroke Ladies' School, where she was a beloved housemistress for seventeen years."

"Seventeen years?" Tally sputtered. "If I had to stay at school that long, I'd kill myself."

"Shhh," Alice hissed. She was squinting at the house-mistress's obscured figure, but still couldn't make out her face. This was excruciating. If they ended up with a bitch or a weirdo, their whole junior year could go wrong. Fast.

"I'm sure I don't have to remind you," the Trap continued, "that at the end of last year, St. Cecilia's saw the sudden departure of its A-level English teacher, Mr. Logan."

Alice felt a set of nails dig into her arm. At the words "Mr. Logan," Tally had tensed up and turned very, very pale.

"The good news is, in addition to her housemistress duties, Mrs. Hoare will be taking over Mr. Logan's vacant post."

Alice gave her friend a sympathetic look. Tally had been trying for the past couple of weeks to get over her infatuation with the hot young English teacher who'd broken her heart. Since the second he'd arrived at St. Cecilia's in September, Mr. Logan had flirted outrageously with Tally, tricking her (and everyone else) into thinking they were in love. The two of them had even shared a secret, passionate kiss on a school trip to Dublin. Then it had turned out that Mr. Logan was secretly dating Miss Sharkreve, and the two teachers had quit their jobs and left the school. Tally felt sick at the memory.

"That's all I'm going to say, girls," Mrs. Traphorn intoned from the front of the room, snapping her back to reality. "I'm sure you're very keen to get to know Mrs. Hoare on your own, so I'll leave you to it."

"Finally," Alice breathed. She leaned forward as the new junior housemistress emerged into the light. The next instant, her face contorted in alarm.

KATE KINGSLEY has lived on both sides of the Atlantic, spending time in New York, London, Paris, and Rome—so she's more than qualified to chronicle the jet-set lives of the Young, Loaded, and Fabulous girls.

Kate also writes for magazines such as *GQ* in New York, where she's had the enviable task of interviewing fashion designers like Paul Smith and celebrities like James McAvoy. Kate is currently hard at work on her next book about the YL&F crew.